CURE FOR THE COMMON UNIVERSE

CHRISTIAN McKAY HEIDICKER

SIMON & SCHUSTER BFYR

NEW YORK LONDON TORONTO SYDNEY NEW DELHI

SIMON & SCHUSTER BFYR
An imprint of Simon & Schuster Children's Publishing Division
1230 Avenue of the Americas, New York, New York 10020

Also available in a SIMON & SCHUSTER BFYR hardcover edition
Interior design by Hilary Zarycky
Cover design by Greg Stadnyk
The text for this book was set in Electra.
Manufactured in the United States of America
First SIMON & SCHUSTER BFYR paperback edition June 2017
2 4 6 8 10 9 7 5 3 1

The Library of Congress has cataloged the hardcover edition as follows:
Names: Heidicker, Christian McKay, author.
Title: Cure for the common universe / Christian McKay Heidicker.
Description: First edition. | New York : Simon & Schuster Books for Young Readers, [2016]. | Summary: "Jaxon meets the girl of his dreams on the same day that his father ships him off to video game rehab. Now he must earn 1 million therapy points in a week, if he wants to be released from rehab in time for his date"— Provided by publisher.
Identifiers: LCCN 2015032260 | ISBN 9781481450270 (hardback) | ISBN 9781481450294 (eBook)
Subjects: | CYAC: Interpersonal relations—Fiction. | Self-Actualization (Psychology)—Fiction. | Rehabilitation—Fiction. | Video games—Fiction. | Dating (Social customs)—Fiction. | BISAC: JUVENILE FICTION / Social Issues / Friendship. | JUVENILE FICTION / Social Issues / Self-Esteem & Self-Reliance. | JUVENILE FICTION / Social Issues / Emotions & Feelings.
Classification: LCC PZ7.1.H444 Cur 2016 | DDC [Fic]—dc23
LC record available at http://lccn.loc.gov/2015032260
ISBN 9781481450287 (pbk)

for Broccoli

You know, in some human sports,
the winner is the one who scores the fewest possible points.
—GLaDOS, *Portal 2*

Enter Player Name

I was sixteen the first time I made a girl laugh.

It was an accident.

About twenty minutes before it happened, I had only one thing on my mind: protect the *Mona Lisa* from a horde of chipmunks.

“Squeeze a man boob for good luck,” one of the Wight Knights said through my headset.

“Squeezed,” I said.

Lightning carved across the computer screen. Thunder rumbled through my earpiece. Music swelled with horns, war coconuts, chanting chipmunks . . . and sneakers marching down the hall outside my door.

My shoulders tensed as the door opened, hall light making a glare across the battleground.

“Thought you were gonna get some exercise this morning.”

In the doorframe my stepmom Casey’s silhouette marched in place.

"I will this afternoon," I said. Then, into my headset: "Protect that alleyway, fellas."

"It's three o'clock," Casey said.

"Is it?"

I squinted at the soft glow around the edges of my blanket-covered window. My eyes went right back to the screen. I tried to ignore the *squeak, squeak, squeak* of Casey's sneakers and focus on the start of the battle.

"I got D," I said.

My warrior hacked through some scaffolding so that my penguins would have materials to build a barricade.

"I need you to wash the Xterra," Casey said. "It rained last night and now it's all speckly."

"'Need' is a funny word," I said. "I *need* to destroy this army of chipmunks."

Casey stopped marching and leaned against the doorframe in that pissed pose I assumed she'd had since high school. It was a safe bet, considering she had graduated four years before.

"Guys," I said into my headset, "if their mecha-manatee makes it down the pass, we're screwed."

"Do you ever wonder why you don't get girls?" Casey asked.

"Actually," I said, swinging my axe, "a girl just texted me last night."

"Can I read it?" Casey asked.

"No, you cannot."

"What did she say?" Casey asked.

"Pop her!"

This was to the Wight Knights about the Mama Sumo bearing down on my barricade.

"You know, Jaxon, you wouldn't get turned down so much if you just got some exercise," Casey said.

"Dammit. Chips are breaking through, guys."

I furiously clicked my mouse, executing whirlwinds to keep the wave of chipmunks at bay. I wasn't about to take advice from someone who just four years ago would have rejected a guy like me.

"You just gotta get out there," Casey said.

"Oh yeah? Is that all it takes?"

"That's all it takes."

I kept clicking my mouse. "Should I strap on a Fitbit and march around the house like an idiot, painting my nails and complaining about a few speckles on my—*Dammit*." My warrior was obliterated in a juicy splatter across the asphalt. "You're killing me, Casey. Guys, I'm in regen. Hold them back."

My warrior's spirit soared over the streets of Arcadia to the nearest graveyard.

Casey's silence made me spin around in my chair.

She glared at me.

"Oh God," I said. "Are you gonna cry again?"

She whirled and squeaked down the hallway.

"Don't worry!" I called after her, rolling across the floor in my desk chair. "I'll get the door!"

I slammed it and then rolled back to my computer. My warrior was still regenerating in the graveyard, tendrils of muscle wrapping around his bones.

I took out my phone and reread the text from that girl:

ewwwww jaxon just asked me out

Pretty sure she had meant to send it to someone else.

"Taste my axe!" my warrior said.

Raised from the dead, I trucked out of the graveyard back toward Plinky Plaza as heavier steps came down the hallway. Again my shoulders tensed as the door opened. The Xterra's keys plopped onto my desk.

"Clean the SUV, or I'm canceling your game account," my dad said.

"You can't," I said, eyes on the screen. While guiding my warrior back into the fray, I opened my drawer and pulled out my school transcript. "Four-point-oh. Remember?"

The battle was swallowed in black.

"Wha—" I spun around and found my dad holding my computer cord, unplugged.

"We're renegotiating," he said.

"Dad, I'm in the middle of a *tournament*!"

"And?" he said.

"Rrg!" I threw off my headset, snagged the keys, and flew out the door, hoping to return home before the Wight Knights lost the battle. I hopped in the Xterra, tore out of the driveway, and sped through the streets of Salt Lake City, shading my eyes from the bright July sky. For me, summer did not mean picnics, hikes, or tossing balls of any kind. It meant I could adventure through Arcadia for twelve hours a day without my dad hassling me. . . .

Until now, for some stupid reason.

I got to Sparkle Chrome, parked in the last garage to avoid a jock from my high school who was washing his Mustang, and then spent three whole minutes trying to get the token dispenser to accept my crinkled five.

reeeeeeen

reeeeoooooon

reeeeeeen

reeeeoooooon

I hit the dispenser. "Come *on*."

If the Wight Knights won this game, we would be only four wins away from being in the top 1 percent of the top 1 percent of *Arcadia* players in the world. And that was halfway to becoming professional.

I unfolded the five's corner, smoothed it against the dispenser's edge, and tried again.

reeeeeeen

reeeeoooooon

"I will end your life," I told the dispenser.

reeeeeeen

reeeeoooooon

"Rrg!"

I was my guild's tank. Without my warrior's muscle and cotton candy axe, the Wight Knights' guts were going to be strewn across the Plaza. If I could just make it back in the next ten minutes . . .

reeeeeeen

reeeeoooooon

I kept hitting the dispenser until some saint in a yellow hat wandered over and traded my shitty five for a crisp one.

reeeeeeen

. . .

plink-plink-plink-plink-plink!

I slammed the tokens into the slot, and big red numbers began the countdown.

10:00 . . . 9:59 . . . 9:58 . . .

I unholstered the spray nozzle, punched the high-pressure button, and started hosing down the Xterra. I whipped out my phone and group-texted the Knights:

AFK! DAD STUFF. HOLD OFF THOSE CHIPMUNKS OR I WILL SMOTHER YOU WITH MY MAN B—

That was when she screamed.

I looked up and found that my aim had wandered from the Xterra onto a girl near the token dispenser. I let off the spray gun's trigger, but it was too late. She was drenched.

The girl's mouth hung open. Her arms dripped at her sides. She stared at me in shock.

"I—I—" I had no words.

I stood there like an idiot for a full ten seconds. The girl finally rolled her eyes and shook droplets from her fingers. As she squeezed water from her hair and pinched the wetness from her earlobes, I began to realize how beautiful she was—smooth pale skin, glossy black braids, lips like bouncy castles that I just wanted to *leap* onto.

I stared at this dripping beauty who needed my help—never mind that I was the one who had soaked her in the first place.

"Uh," I said, looking around the car wash, "I'd offer you my shirt, but I haven't been outside for a while, and my skin might give you snow blindness."

The girl looked at me, and for half a second I thought she was going to chew me out. But then . . . she laughed. She *laughed*.

"Nah, I'm good," she said. She wrung out her T-shirt.

Normally I'd try to make myself look cool in front of girls. Chivalrous, at the very least. But right then I felt relaxed, relaxed enough to use humor I'd use with the Wight Knights.

Because no way was a girl I'd just hosed with water going to keep talking to me.

No way.

Right?

The girl nodded toward the Xterra. "That's a pretty big target to miss, dude."

"I wasn't aiming at the Xterra." I looked at the spray gun. "I thought this is what girls did at car washes. Wore white T-shirts and giggled while they got sprayed with hoses."

The girl laughed again. *Twice* she laughed.

"Wet T-shirt contest isn't till five o'clock," she said, waving out her shirt, giving me little glimpses of her stomach.

I held out the sprayer. "You want revenge? I don't look too good in a wet shirt, but . . ."

The girl snorted. "Tempting."

She didn't leave.

Instead she closed her eyes, tilted back her head, and pulled her shirt taut toward the sun. Her boobs were very apparent under her wet shirt. Looking at them made me self-conscious about my own boobs, which were big for a guy's, but not, like, Chun-Li-size or anything. I glanced down and remembered I was wearing a *Super Mario* mushroom T-shirt that read *I don't wanna grow up*. Ugh. Why did I even own that stupid thing?

I crossed my arms over my chest, trying to conceal the *Super Mario* mushroom and my man boobs as best I could. Having the Wight Knights joke about my chest was a lot different from a girl seeing them in real life.

"So, uh, what's your name?" I said.

The girl kept her closed eyes toward the sun. "Serena."

"I'm Jaxon."

"Pleasure, Jaxon," she said, because apparently that's what beautiful, interesting girls say when they meet someone—*Pleasure*.

There were a few moments of uncomfortable silence while some guy vacuumed out his truck in the background. My lack of experience caught up to me.

"Uh, nice to meet you, Serena," I said. "Sorry about the . . . yeah."

I turned away before uncrossing my arms, and then continued to spray the Xterra.

6:34 . . . 6:33 . . . 6:32 . . .

I had completely forgotten about the battle of Plinky Plaza. One hundred percent of my focus was on Serena—beautiful, dripping Serena—in my periphery.

She was back at the token dispenser.

reeeeeeen

reeeeoooooon

reeeeeeen

reeeeoooooon

"Good luck with that thing," I called over the spraying. "It hates awesome people."

"How did you get it to work?" she asked.

Oh God. We were still talking. I could keep this conversation going. I glanced at the dude in the yellow hat with unwrinkled bills. If he gave her a new bill, she would get her tokens and leave. I looked around for Serena's car.

"Um, what are you washing?" I asked.

She pointed. Leaning against the brick wall of the car wash was an old purple Schwinn bicycle, all muddy and scratched up.

"Just bought it for twenty bucks," she said, walking over to the bike and wiggling the handlebars. "Guy told me the wax here does wonders."

Did people still ride bikes? I hadn't since I was nine. Hence, man boobs.

"Bring it in," I said, nodding to the garage.

"You sure?" she asked.

I nodded at her soaked T-shirt. "I owe you."

She grabbed the bike's handles and rolled it in. I aimed the sprayer, but she held out her hand, quirking her lips in this adorable way. "You mind? I don't want you getting distracted again."

She hosed mud off the Schwinn while I leaned against the wall, arms folded firmly over my chest. My phone vibrated in my pocket. I ignored it.

"So do you, um, hate me forever?" I asked.

She shrugged. "I like things that knock me out of my usual routine. Like bumping a record player. Might make life land on a better track."

And that was when I knew I would fall in love with her.

While she sprayed, and my phone vibrated, I did a quick search of my brain for cool things to talk about. All I did was play video games and study for school. That didn't leave me with many options.

"So, uh, did you know that the guy who wrote *The War of the Worlds* came up with the idea for the atomic bomb thirty years before it was invented, and that he even named it?"

"Really?" Serena said. "Huh." She wasn't looking at me, but she didn't sound bored.

"Yep. Um. Yeah. There are a lot of sci-fi authors who made really interesting discoveries. Like, Jules Verne came up with the idea for the submarine, and— " My phone would not stop vibrating. "Uh, excuse me."

I had seven texts from the Wight Knights:

Dude where r u?

Dude.

Dude!

Location?

DUDE WHERE ARE YOU?

We are getting fucked.

You are fucking us.

I'd been away from the battle for more than fifteen minutes. If I left immediately, I could still make it back . . .

I put my phone on silent.

"Where was I?" I said.

"Jules Verne?" Serena said.

I smiled. She'd listened.

Once I'd wrung my brain of every cool, non-video-game fact I could think of and the Schwinn was clean and shiny and looked like it cost more than twenty dollars, Serena rolled the bike into the sun to dry.

"Welp," she said. "Thanks for the cleaning. For the bike *and* me."

She gave the bottom of her shirt a final squeeze. No more drips.

My heart started to stammer. She was going to leave. I didn't want her to leave; I wanted her to stay. I wanted her to remain in my sight until we went on a date and had our first kiss and she realized what a stellar guy I was and that she should probably be my girlfriend. And while I was sure there was absolutely positively no way I would ever get a date with this girl, what if actually there was a way and the only way that it would happen was if I opened my stupid mouth and did something about it right that second?

"So, um," I said, "I still feel bad about spraying you before. . . . In fact, I—I don't feel like we're even."

She held out her hand for the water gun, like this was an invitation to spray me. I didn't hand it to her. We both smiled.

"Did you have something different in mind?" she said.

"Uh, yeah, actually. Would you maybe, like . . ."

Serena raised her eyebrows, like, *Get to the point, dude*.

"Uh, you know, like, want to—"

RRRRNNNT!

The car wash's timer buzzed, making me jump.

The big red numbers flashed 0:00.

"Little jumpy, are we?" she said.

"Ha, yeah." I scratched the back of my neck and looked at the ground. I could feel my man boobs pressing against my shirt.

"You were saying?" Serena said.

I hesitated.

I had somehow, impossibly, briefly, momentarily been charming with this girl when I'd thought there was no chance whatsoever that I would see her again. And this had made me just relaxed enough to make her laugh not once, not twice, but *three* times.

Well, two laughs and a snort, technically.

"What-about-dinner?" I said, and then didn't breathe.

She took a moment to consider the question, like the token dispenser thinking about whether to accept my crinkled five.

Had I screwed it up?

I had.

I was sure I had.

Shit.

"When?" she asked.

"Tonight?"

"I can't tonight."

"Tomorrow?"

"Busy tomorrow. I'm busy till Thursday."

"Thursday?" I suggested.

"Um . . ." She clicked the Schwinn's gears. I could have sworn she glanced at the mushroom on my shirt. "Sounds good," she said. She mounted her bike, one foot on the pedal, one on the asphalt. "I'd hug you good-bye, but, y'know." She frowned at her damp shirt.

"Ha. Right," I said. "Maybe we could hug on Thursday."

That was the stupidest thing I could have possibly said. Serena still giggled.

Oh God, what if she changed her mind between now and Thursday?

"Can I call you?" I asked.

"Nope," she said. My heart nose-dived. But then she patted her pocket. "No phone. I'm not on Facebook either."

A Luddite! Of course! This girl was anti-technology! That

was why the bicycle. And the record-player reference. That was why she didn't recognize my *Super Mario* shirt. I made a quick mental list of things to never talk about as long as she and I were dating. To be honest, it included most of my life.

Serena pushed off the pavement and pedaled in small circles around the car wash parking lot, moving far away, then close, then far again. "Meet me at Mandrake's on Broadway," she said. "Know it?"

"Uh, no."

"It's real good. And they never ID. I'll be there at seven."

She straightened the handlebars and pedaled down the sidewalk.

"Great!" I waved good-bye with the sprayer. "See you at Mandrake's on Thursday at seven!"

She disappeared around the corner.

I had a date. A real-life date. Suddenly the future didn't seem so war torn. The bright July sky looked almost pretty.

My phone vibrated again.

Ur dead to us.

I smiled. For the first time in years, I didn't give a damn about the Wight Knights. Or *Arcadia*. I had just performed a miracle.

Then again, maybe I could get in one last game before I started preparing for my date.

The Xterra was still pretty dirty. I had only managed to clean the front half, and I was out of tokens. Screw it. Casey could stand to have the ass-end of her vehicle speckly for a few days.

On the drive home I couldn't stop smiling. I imagined making Serena laugh over and over again while we dined at Mandrake's. I'd have to find something nice to wear. That was for sure. Should I get my crack waxed? Did people actually do that? If so, where? And was there something the waxer could sign that declared that if they ever saw me in public, like on a date at Mandrake's, they'd have to pretend not to recognize me? The back and shoulder wax was a must. Serena was worth it, I just knew. But what if during the date I bent over to pick up her dropped fork or something and my shirt came up and she saw that I was basically an overfed Hobbit? Could I lose about thirty pounds by Thursday? Probably not. But she didn't seem to care about my weight.

Did she?

Would she have said yes if she did?

Probably not.

Would she?

I took a deep breath and smiled. I thought I had four whole days to think about these things.

Turned out I had about four minutes.

Loading . . .

When I got home, two tanklike Tongan men were standing in the driveway.

My dad stood between them.

He was holding a suitcase. My suitcase.

I parked in the street, and was about to get out when Casey walked out of the garage, pushing my computer chair. She left it at the curb and then headed back inside without making eye contact.

All thoughts of getting my crack waxed vanished when I saw one of the tanks point at me and ask, "That him?"

My dad nodded.

I shut off the engine. My heart started to pound, and not in a pleasant, Serena way. I didn't get out of the Xterra. I didn't unlock the doors. I didn't know what was happening, but whatever it was couldn't be good. The sun started to bake the air-conditioning away.

My dad walked up and rapped on the passenger window. "Come on out here, Jaxon. So we can talk."

Before my dad retired, they called him the Mountain. Not because of his stature but because he would plant himself in people's living rooms and refuse to budge until he'd made a sale.

I glanced at the tanks, who cast ominous shadows on the driveway. I didn't move. My dad tried the handle.

"Tell me what's happening through the window," I said, my voice wavering, "and I'll decide if I'm going to get out or drive away."

My dad signaled to the tanks, who stepped in front of and behind the Xterra, blocking me in. I pressed into my seat.

"Okay," I said. "Tell me through the window, and I'll decide if I'm going to commit vehicular manslaughter."

"You're going to rehab," my dad said.

"I'm *what*?"

"You're going to re—"

"I heard what you said." I rolled down the passenger window, just a crack so that my dad's hand couldn't get through. "What am I supposedly addicted to?"

"Video games."

I was too stunned to speak for a second.

"Video game rehab? That can't be a real thing."

"It's real," my dad said in his maddeningly calm voice. "And you're going."

I gripped the steering wheel and tried to gather my thoughts.

Did I play a lot of video games? Yes. Did I love them and believe they were the fastest-growing medium that was quickly approaching a golden age that would transform the world for the better forever? Yes.

Was I addicted to them?

No. No, I was not.

"You can't be addicted to video games," I said. "It's a *compulsion*."

Casey came out of the garage holding two handfuls of wires. Even in the heat of the sun, my skin ran cold. The wires were from my computer. My window to adventure . . . to my friends. Casey was dismantling it.

She dumped the wires into her Jetta's open trunk, next to my monitor. Then she finally looked at me. "We're selling your computer and buying a treadmill," she called.

"Can you hold off on that for a minute, sweetie?" my dad said.

She made a show of brushing her hands clean and went and leaned against the porch. At least she'd stopped marching in place.

"An addiction *is* a compulsion," my dad said.

"No," I said, trying to keep the tremors from my voice. "It isn't." My dad and I had had the video game argument dozens of times. I'd done my research. "You stop doing a compulsion if something good comes into your life." I thought of Serena's laugh. "With an addiction, you can't stop, no matter how much you want to. Like alcohol." I looked at

Casey and yelled, "Or organic cottage cheese!"

She glared. My dad ignored that comment.

"I've been timing how long you spend in that room of yours. Every time I hear things start to blow up and die—"

"I don't *just* play violent video games," I interrupted.

"You know what I mean," my dad said. "Every time your stepmother or I hear anything that sounds like a game, we start a timer. You have clocked—" He took a little piece of graph paper out of his back pocket. "You've clocked more than two hundred and fifty hours in the last month alone. That's more than a full-time job."

I tried to hide my own shock at that number and attempted another approach.

"*Dad.*" I looked him dead in the eye. "I *can't* go to rehab right now."

"You absolutely can and will."

"You don't understand. I just met a girl."

My dad narrowed his eyes. "Where?"

"At the car wash," I said. "That's why the Xterra's still dirty. I used the money to clean her bike."

He glanced at the spotty back end of the Xterra, then back at me. "What's her name?"

"Serena. She had a Schwinn. Purple."

The Mountain didn't budge. "Show me her number on your phone."

Shit. Why did my new girlfriend have to be a Luddite?

My hands didn't leave the steering wheel.

"Facebook?" my dad said.

I shook my head, and he gave a smile that seemed a touch more satisfied than disappointed.

A fear took me then. What if Serena had just pretended not to have a phone or Facebook?

No. No. I'd made her laugh.

Still, this conversation was spinning dangerously into unbelievable territory. I hadn't had a date since I'd started living under my dad's roof. Or . . . ever. Serena was the first good thing to come into my life in a long while. She was the great hope, the light at the end of the tunnel, the end game, my *Call of Duty*. . . . Only, I wasn't going to shoot her.

"You always want to discuss things like adults," I said. "Let's discuss this."

The tank in front of me heard this and rested his foot on the bumper. The Xterra dipped under his weight.

"Don't let him talk you out of anything!" Casey called from the porch. "Dr. Phil said *do not let them negotiate*! You just have to get him down there!"

My dad glanced back at her, then at me. He may have been a tough old bastard, but he could be reasonable sometimes.

"All right," he said to me. "I don't know how adult you are, hiding in the car, but all right. Let's discuss this."

I gripped the steering wheel, quickly trying to formulate my talking points. We may have had this argument dozens of times before, but this time was different. This time he had two guards the size of refrigerators, and I . . . I had a date on Thursday. My suitcase sat in the driveway. Clearly rehab wouldn't be an overnight stay.

My dad stood tall, feet firmly planted. "You gonna tell me you don't play too many video games?"

"No," I said. He had me beat there. He even had a piece of graph paper. "I'm going to ask you what's *wrong* with video games."

"Well," my dad said, leaning against the Xterra, "you're not getting any exercise, for one. You never do anything your stepmother or I ask you to. You— "

"Dad. *Dad.* I asked you what's wrong with *video games.*"

He sighed. "Violence," he said, like it was obvious. "World's a lot more violent than when I was younger. Now that kids can simulate killing each other, they want to try it in real life."

"Riiiiiiight," I said. "'Cause they didn't have *any* violence when you were a kid. Except, y'know, Vietnam. Or how about Korea, before that? We can keep going back if you'd like. Hitler never played video games."

My dad nodded. "You can't ignore that kid who ran his dad down with the car."

The incident had made national news. But instead of the media focusing on a number of other factors that could have caused the kid's violent outburst—bad living environment, bullying, depression—they focused on the fact that his dad had just taken away his copy of *Halo*.

"I was joking about the vehicular manslaughter," I said, gesturing to the tank in front of the Xterra.

My dad rubbed the back of his neck. "You might not go out and hurt anyone. But what *good* are those games doing you?"

"Hand-eye coordination," I said.

"You seem to have missed the whole back half of the Xterra here."

"They're good for learning how to code."

"I haven't seen any Java manuals in your room."

"They're better for the environment than a lot of hobbies."

"So is running."

"I could make millions as an Esports player."

"Where's the check?"

"Online games help break down international borders."

"By fighting?"

"They help people from different countries understand each other."

"By calling each other 'bitch'?"

"That's a term of endearment!"

I collapsed onto the steering wheel. I had never imagined my romantic future would hang on a single video game debate.

I sat upright and snapped. "Games can help kids overcome dyslexia, *and* they help old people become better drivers."

My dad smiled. "It's a good thing I'm not raising an elderly person who can't read."

My head fell back onto the steering wheel. My jaw trembled at the thought that I was going to lose the first shot I'd ever had with a real girl. The ironic thing was that I was only having this argument so I could go on a date and have a good excuse to *not* play so many video games.

"Son," my dad said, his Mountain voice crumbling a bit. "You're just not living up to your potential. I'd rather see you go out and fail in the real world than succeed in a world that doesn't exist. I'm not seeing any skills in you that you didn't have before your mom bought you that machine."

It was a Nintendo Wii. She had bought it for me the first Christmas after my parents divorced. In the card, she'd written:

Your dad is going to hate this.
But I hope you love it.
XO,
Mom

"Dad . . . it's not like I can play so many video games that I throw up on the carpet and lose consciousness for two days."

He sighed. "This is not a conversation about your mother."

"I'm not the one who brought her up."

We stared into each other's eyes, trying to reach something deeper. I broke contact and clicked the turn signal left, then right, and then left again.

"I've tried reasoning with you," my dad said. "I've tried getting you out in the world. So has your stepmother. I don't have any other options."

"And if I really did meet a girl, Dad? Wouldn't you want me to go out with her and start something healthy in my life? Something that could get me away from games?"

My dad hesitated for a second. His eyebrows relaxed. My heart gave a little leap of hope.

Casey shouted from the porch. "What are you letting him tell you? Do not listen. It is *time to go*!"

I scowled at her. "You know she plays *Candy Crush*, right?"

My dad refurrowed his eyebrows and took up his Mountain stance again.

Dammit.

"Do you remember that time you promised me you'd stopped playing *Warcraft* and gave me the copy of your game?"

I rubbed my forehead. "Yeah."

I'd let him take the disc because he hadn't known the game was already downloaded to my computer. He caught me playing five minutes later.

"Guess I don't have much reason to trust you, then."

"Dad, this is *different*. This girl is *real*. And she thinks I'm great for some reason."

"Think how impressed she'll be with your new skills when you come home."

The driver door popped open, and a hand seized my elbow. The tank from behind the Xterra gently but firmly pulled me out of the Xterra and into the sun.

I looked at my dad. "He had the spare key the whole time?"

"I didn't want you to think I don't respect your opinion," he said.

"No," I said. "You just wanted me to think my opinion mattered to you before you had me dragged away."

The other tank retrieved my suitcase from the driveway while the first led me to a copper-colored Oldsmobile on the other side of the street. He spread my arms and then gave me a thorough pat-down and emptied my pockets, handing my wallet, iPhone, and fingernail clippers over to my dad.

"Have fun!" Casey called, waving from the porch.

She went inside and slammed the door.

That was it. I was cast out of Arcadia. No more Caligari District. No more goblin carnival. No more pastel spaceships soaring us to other universes to enlist anthropomorphic fighters. No more adventures with the Wight Knights.

That was when I realized . . . when I thought of Serena, I didn't care about video games.

One of the tanks opened the back door of the Oldsmobile.

My dad held out his hand to me. I didn't take it.

"What?" I said. "You think I'm going to go off and learn some valuable life lesson and then come back and be the perfect son who treats your child bride better?"

"Actually," my dad said, still holding out his hand, "I'm hoping you come back and treat yourself better."

"You're an asshole, Dad," I said. "And I don't mean that as a term of endearment."

"Okay, Jaxon." He gave me a flat smile and put his hand in his pocket. "Good luck."

The tank lowered my head into the Oldsmobile and shut the door.

Tutorial

Two rules," the tank in the driver's seat said. "Don't swear and don't say nothing about the music." He tossed a granola bar into my lap. "Tell me if you need to use the bathroom."

He started the engine and the car filled with gospel music. *Elvis* gospel music.

"You saw me crying in the chaaaaaaaapellllllll . . ."

The other tank climbed into the passenger seat and sighed. Apparently he had to follow the rules too.

"They call me Command and him Conquer," the driver said. As if they weren't intimidating enough.

From the backseat I noticed that Command kept his poofy hair tied back in a neat bun, while Conquer let his roam free. Conquer also had a much bigger equator. They looked strong enough to tame a rabid ox, let alone my weak ass. I wouldn't be able to escape them if I tried. Besides, the backseat had no door handles.

"We got one more pickup," Command said, throwing the gear into drive.

The car rolled forward. My stomach took a moment to catch up.

My dad waved from the porch. I looked away.

While Elvis sang another song—*"With arms wide oooooooopeeeeeennnnnn"*—Command drove east to the rich side of Salt Lake. We pulled up to a three-story house with dozens of windows. Command climbed out of the Oldsmobile and knocked on the front door. A pretty woman with sad eyes answered, and they went inside.

The car cooled and made ticking noises. I surveyed the neighborhood. If I could leap over the front seat and out the driver's side door before Conquer clamped on to my ankle, maybe I could get a running head start and hide behind the shrubbery. After he and Command gave up the search, I'd walk downtown and camp at Mandrake's, sleeping in their alcove, washing up in the bathroom, and working on my charming conversation with the waitresses until my date on Thursday. Hopefully they'd have some after-dinner mints.

I had nothing to lose. I would bolt in three . . . two . . .

"You thinking about escaping?"

Conquer adjusted the rearview mirror to meet my eyes.

"Yes," I said.

"They all do." He chuckled and stretched. "This ain't no video game."

The tension uncoiled in my legs. "Thanks for clearing that up."

A minute later Command exited the house, leading a skinny kid with tattoo sleeves.

"The *hell*?" Conquer said under his breath.

I may have been suffering from gamer's squint, but this kid looked like he'd just been pulled out of an iron lung. It seemed the only thing preventing him from falling dead in the driveway was Command's supporting hand.

Command opened the backseat door, and the kid slumped in next to me. His head was shaved, his ears gauged, and his arms writhed with homemade tattoos—frayed wires spitting electricity. The kid looked like an electric warlock . . . with only one hit point left.

"Two rules."

Command repeated the business about swearing and music and then tossed another granola bar over his shoulder. It hit the kid in the chest, but he didn't even flinch. His dark eyes, slumped head, and drooping lip made me briefly reconsider my argument that it was impossible to be addicted to video games.

Briefly.

"So," I said. "What are *you* in for?"

The kid was already asleep.

Command pulled onto the freeway, and we headed west, across the tracks, and through the industrial side of town. Soon the city gave way to salt flats, and the pit in my stomach deepened. Just as an *Arcadia* character steps on an ill-rendered piece of ground, slips through the game's polygons, and hurtles into the black unknown, I was falling through the world. My beautiful fantasy world of trumpets, dancing buildings, and cotton candy skies was being replaced with the pant of air-conditioning, the slimy feeling of vinyl against the back of my neck, and—"Hrr . . . *Hrrmph* . . ."—the smell of vomit every time we stopped to let the electric tattoo kid throw up.

Three Elvis-Sings-Gospel songs later, we came to a small casino town, cruising under a large sign of a mechanical cowgirl kicking her giant neon leg. We didn't stop there. We continued on through the desert until even the out-of-service gas stations disappeared, and then pulled off the main road and kept on driving.

Dunes rose up around the car in dull waves.

"You're not going to make me dig holes, are you?" I asked.

"Nope." Command chuckled. "We're just going to make you have fun."

That sounded so much worse.

The sun dipped in the sky, and the electric warlock slumped into the middle of the seat. I remained wide awake, mentally mapping every turn, road sign, and the size and slope of every dune. I was determined to know exactly where I was imprisoned and how to find my way back.

But as the desert stretched on, I realized it would be impossible to walk back. Not unless I wanted Thursday's date to be a crow feasting on my belly meat. After that unpleasant realization, I just kept an eye on the electric warlock's drool, slowly creeping toward my leg.

Finally, as Elvis sang of coming to the garden, we arrived. The rehab facility was a windowless, cream-gray box of a building, nestled among dunes that stretched to the horizon.

It looked as lonely as a LEGO lost in an infinite sandbox.

Command parked in a dusty lot, pulled my suitcase out of the trunk, and opened my door. He escorted me to a white entrance, which opened without a key. Clearly, everyone here knew the walk back to Salt Lake would be impossible. Command gestured inside. I took one last glance toward the east. The desert would have stretched on forever, were the sky not there to stop it.

I went inside.

Like a stage right out of *BioShock*, two concrete hallways stretched left and right along the building's outer walls—one long, one short, both flickering fluorescent. The place smelled like rusty pipes and hummed like dead static.

Welcome to Rapture, I thought, and a darkness opened inside me.

Conquer practically carried the electric warlock in after us.

"Kid's not doing so hot," Conquer said, lightly slapping the warlock's cheek.

"Take him to the Fairy Fountain," Command said. "We'll get him guilded later."

Conquer hefted the kid's body down the short hallway, and Command put his nose three inches from mine. "Do I need to give you a cavity search?"

My butt clenched. "Um, huh?"

"Games are pretty small these days," he said, walking closer and pressing me against the wall. "Tamagotchi, iPod Touches."

I swallowed. "I might have a big butt, but I don't use it for storage."

He smiled. "Just messin'."

He knelt down, unlaced my shoelaces, and took them. In case I tried to play cat's cradle with them, I guess.

He led me down the long hallway. "Time to meet G-man," he said.

"The bad guy from *Half-Life*?" I said, laceless shoes flapping off my feet.

Command chuckled. "That's what the players call the clinical director. Don't tell him why. Game talk is forbidden here, but the guy's never played a video game in his life."

We passed doors stenciled with different symbols: a candle, a music note, a cauldron, a computer chip. At the end of the hall, Command stopped and pointed up a staircase to a metallic door.

"Good luck," he said.

I swallowed and scaled the stairs.

How the hell did I get here?

How the hell did I get out?

I had to convince them I did not belong.

If this was the meeting where the clinical director decided whether or not someone who'd been committed was truly addicted, whether there had been some kind of mistake and this kid should be immediately released so he could go on his date with the cute girl from the car wash, then I was ready to be the most well-adjusted gamer he had ever met.

This would require me to be a charming person . . . which I was not.

I smoothed my *Super Mario Bros.* shirt and opened the metal door.

"Juuuust a moment," a slim man in a gray suit said. He was sitting at a small desk, pressing a row of stamps onto an inkpad, one by one.

The office looked like it had been built for epileptics. No loud colors. No sharp corners. No decoration of any kind. Not even accreditations. There was a desk and two chairs, and that was about it.

"Done!" The director stood from his desk, lightly punching at his hip to get all the way upright. His bright green eyes fixed on me. "Jaxon," he said, in a voice that was warm but all business. He came around the desk and offered his hand. "Welcome to Video Horizons, the first video game rehabilitation center in the West."

I shook his hand.

And even though I was exhausted . . .

Even though I felt stripped and humiliated and out of my element . . .

Even though I was terrified about not making it to my date . . .

I smiled.

"Thanks for having me. It's *great* to be here."

"Really?" The director took a step back and gave a pleased frown. "No one's ever said that before."

His teeth looked like they'd never been flossed, and I could smell moss when he spoke.

I smiled again and shrugged. "How often do I get a free desert vacation? Ha-ha."

The director shook his finger at me. "I like your attitude. Have a seat."

He gestured to the chair opposite his desk while easing his stiff hip into his. I sat. The fluorescent lights fizzed.

Over the years I'd picked up a couple of sales tactics from my dad:

1. Be passionate about the client's interests.
2. Mimic their actions to make them feel you're relatable.
3. Use humor as a lubricant.
4. Act like a normal human being for once in your life.

That last one was personal advice for me.

"I'm the clinical director here at Video Horizons," the man in the suit said. "My name is John Borno, but everyone here calls me G-man because I'm the master of games."

"*Pleasure*, G-man," I said.

He smiled. "I like to personally greet each of our players when they first arrive." He made a circular motion with his hand. "Give a rundown on how this place works."

Players? Hadn't I been committed there to *stop* being a player?

"Lay it on me," I said.

"First of all, Jaxon, we encourage players not to use their real names while here. This allows you to retain patient confidentiality when you return to the real world and maintain a *healthy* online presence." G-man dropped the business voice. "But it also means you get to come up with your very own player name. It can be anything you want. Anything."

"Ooh!" I said, trying to sound enthused. "Um, gosh, this is exciting. How about . . ." I drew a total blank. That is, until a three-tailed fox helicoptered through my head. "Miles Prower?"

"Love it!" G-man said. He clicked a pen and wrote it on a chart with about a dozen other names. Then he stared at the name. "Oh! I get it. Clever wordplay."

"Thought you might like that."

"Well, *Miles* . . ." He leaned back into his chair. "Video Horizons opened about two months ago. We don't even have a logo yet, but our population has practically *doubled* every week due to the ever-climbing number of kids who are afflicted with an electronics addiction. You might be asking yourself, is it really that many?"

"I *was* asking myself that," I said.

Actually, I was wondering what Serena would think if she could see me right then. She'd probably throw her Schwinn at me and run.

"Up to *thirty percent* of youths are addicted to video games," G-man continued. "It's a growing concern in our society. That's how we were able to earn enough grants to acquire this old military training center." He smiled at the fluorescent lights as if we were in some pleasure palace. Then he grew serious. "Humans spend more than three billion hours a *week* in the gaming world. If you were to add up all the time players have spent in *World of Warcraft*, do you know how much it would amount to?"

Six million years, I thought.

"No," I said.

"Six *million* years," he said.

"That's crazy," I said.

My dad had fed me the same statistic. I'd probably contributed a couple of years myself.

"Video Horizons is focused on slowing that number's growth," G-man said.

"An admirable mission," I said.

"I'm glad you think so," he said.

"I do think so," I said.

I didn't. G-man didn't understand gamers. And he certainly didn't understand me. When the real world rejects your efforts for sixteen years, when you're mocked at school, when you can't get a date, when you don't get picked for sports, when your knowledge of Japanese gods is worthless, even *frowned* upon, it's hard not to turn to a community where your talents are appreciated.

Also, you get to kill dragons.

"You'll find that we're a bit different from a regular rehab,"

G-man said. "Video game addiction isn't as serious as a drug or alcohol addiction, but that doesn't mean it's not a major concern. Especially if you've been playing some of those games that have no end. I think you know the ones I'm talking about."

I exaggeratedly rolled my eyes. "I do, unfortunately."

The Wight Knights were probably so pissed at me right then, trying to battle through Skyscrape Arena without their trusty tank who had been torn away from the world and hurtling to . . . whatever the hell this place was.

"But don't mistake us for strict disciplinarians," G-man continued. "We're not trying to re-create the video game recovery facilities they have in China. You know, with the militaristic drills, and flashing colorful lights into your pupils at six a.m."

"Thank goodness for *that*!" I said, faking a chuckle.

"No, we actually try to have some fun here at Video Horizons. We operate on a revolutionary system that appeals to a gamer's sense of success. We are going to try to reprogram your behavior by breaking your game habit with—get this—another game. Think of it as the PlayStation 5 of addiction therapy."

"Wow," I said. "You are really speaking my language."

He narrowed his eyes and leaned over his desk.

I leaned in too.

"We've devised a system where players such as yourself earn experience points."

"That sounds like a video game," I said, coloring my voice with intrigue.

"It *is* like a video game. But it's the video game of *life*. Instead of leveling up pixels and polygons, ones and zeros, you are going to level up"—he swiveled his finger in my direction—"*you*."

"Me?" I said, touching my chest.

"You got it."

So Video Horizons had gamified addiction therapy. It wasn't a terrible idea . . . so long as *I didn't have to do it*.

G-man reached into a drawer and took out a scrolled-up piece of paper printed and cut to look like ancient parchment. He quickly scribbled something at the top and then slid it across the desk. Below "*Miles Prower*" written in shitty cursive were five columns labeled with pictures of a brain, a ball, a paintbrush, a sandwich, and a smiley face.

"We have all kinds of classes and activities here at Video Horizons," he said. "Music, racing, martial arts, cooking, and many, many more that I don't want to spoil for you. . . . Spoiler alert!"

"Ha!" I said, even though he had somehow, impossibly, misused that phrase.

"For every real-life skill you pick up within these walls, your teachers or guild leader will stamp your scroll with a certain number of experience points." He pointed to the stamps on his desk, each with a different number on its handle. "A thousand points for eating a healthy meal, two thousand points for painting a picture of a pretty sunset, *ten thousand* points for playing a whole song on a guitar. You'll also receive points for laundry, food prep, doing the dishes, stuff like that."

"I actually do all my own cooking and cleaning at home," I said.

"Excellent," G-man said.

I didn't tell him it strictly involved Hot Pockets and paper towels.

"You may think it's strange that we're substituting one game for another," he continued, "but if our point system gets you addicted to running and cleaning dishes instead of playing games, so be it. Once you've earned enough points to sufficiently 'level up'"—he actually did air finger quotes—"you're free to go home. Any questions?"

I dreaded the answer to my first question. But I had to know. What was my Bowser? What was my Deathwing? What Video Horizons final boss did I have to defeat to get back to my date?

"How many experience points do I need to . . . level up?"

G-man gave a sly smile. "One million, of course."

My shoulders must have deflated, because he put up his hands defensively. "I know that sounds like a lot. But think of all the skills you'll pick up. Think of all the people you'll impress back home. We believe the life lessons you learn here at Video Horizons will give you a much richer life in the real world. I mean, how many dates will the highest *Pac-Man* score get you, right?"

I tried to smile but felt my eye twitch. This was too much. I'd already scored a date without this place and its stupid experience points.

"And, uh," I said, dreading another answer, "how long does it take the average player to earn a million points?"

"Let's see . . ." G-man tapped his desk and considered the ceiling. "The fastest player did it in just two weeks. But she was a former Olympic athlete, so she *killed* in our tournaments."

My skin went cold at the word. I was certain these were not the kind of tournaments I'd be good at.

G-man teetered his open hand in the air. "But I'd say it takes your average player about four weeks."

Four *weeks*? I imagined all the suitors Serena would charm between now and then. Suitors better suited than me.

This was it. It was time to close the sale. I had to convince G-man that I was so well adjusted he should let me go right then. There had to be a series of things I could say, a specific path through our dialogue tree that would get me out of this.

"Have you ever locked up someone who didn't belong here?" I said. "Someone who had a dad who just wanted to get rid of his kid so he could hang out with his new child bride . . . or something?"

G-man considered me for a moment. "If we did take in a patient—sorry, *player*—who shouldn't have been committed . . . I believe it would become quickly apparent that the individual was well-balanced physically, mentally, and emotionally." I swear his eyes flashed to my man boobs for a second. "After the first week's assessment, we could have a conversation with his or her parents to find out what the real trouble was."

Dammit. I didn't *have* a whole week. This meant I'd have

to compete. Not only compete but destroy this Olympic athlete's record by earning a million real-life experience points in four days. I could do it though, right? This couldn't be that hard. What did an Olympic athlete have that I didn't, anyway?

G-man showed his mossy teeth. "The important thing is that you have *fun*."

No. It wasn't.

"What if I win in four days?" I asked.

He gave a flat smile. "You won't."

"What if I do?"

"The game is built so that players who are ahead—your jocks, your geniuses—will be given a handicap, and those kids who might be lagging behind a bit will be given bonuses. We want everyone at Video Horizons to feel like a hero."

Great. Like *Mario Party*. The most unfair game ever created.

"You got somewhere to be?" G-man asked.

I put on the biggest grin I could muster. "Nowhere but here."

"Tell you what," he said, "if you win in four days, I'll drive you out of here myself. Deal?"

I nodded. "Deal."

"So, player Miles Prower," G-man said in a nauseatingly enthusiastic voice, "are you a bad enough dude to earn a million points here at Video Horizons?"

He'd said the facility had opened just two months before. That meant the game was brand-new. It was still in beta. It had to be broken in places. All I had to do was find those broken areas and exploit them.

I smiled. "How many points if I polish your desk *right now*?"

We both laughed.

"Oh!" G-man reached back into his drawer. "We don't want to forget these." He handed me a map and a class schedule. "This is how to find your way around, as well as a breakdown of points. Aaaaaand here's your adventure pouch."

He really meant faux-leather fanny pack.

"Cool," I said. I stretched the adventure pouch's strap to its limit, clicked it on, and then got up to leave.

"Oh, Miles. One last thing." G-man pulled the cap off one of the stamps. "Every day, I'll give you a thousand points if you high-five me with a positive attitude."

He held up his hand.

I hated high fives. But I needed any points I could get.

I smiled big and swung my hand . . . but it whooshed through open air. At first I thought I'd missed, but then I saw that G-man had dropped his hand at the last second.

"But with so many slaps a day, my hand can only take so much." He put the cap back on the stamp. "I think I'll save my high fives for players who are a little less sarcastic."

Guilds

"Time for your guilding," Command said, escorting me back down G-man's staircase.

I stopped walking. "Guilding?"

He chuckled and took my arm. "Don't worry. You'll keep your balls."

We continued down the hallway, passing a cafeteria, a laundry room, and, oh God, a community shower room. At the end of the hall was a black door with "The Hub" painted in the white, mad-slash handwriting of a serial killer.

Behind it, whispers hummed like electricity:

"Talk to the cat. She'll tame the Darkroot hunters."

"Just cracking the warthog will make it blow."

"You can't stop the bleedout! It's the bleedout!"

Normally I'd be stoked to join a guild. But I had the sinking feeling this was going to be very different from *Arcadia*.

What waited behind that door? A stripping and whipping?

A chair, an injection, eye clamps, and a game controller? A single pull-up?

As Command led me toward the Hub, I gazed back toward the green light of the exit. Beyond that door, beyond an impossible stretch of desert, beyond sand and road and dead gas stations, Serena was bending space and time to tug at my heartstrings. . . .

Command pushed open the door, and the whispers stopped.

The Hub was shadowy and cavernous. It smelled like gasoline. Light from three tall, frosted windows shined on dust and brick and a small wooden stage. The space looked industrial, like it had once been used to manufacture robot soldiers or something. But now it felt uncomfortably empty, like an MMO no one wanted to play. Everything was colorless except a bunch of beanbag chairs in front of the stage, where about a dozen teens sat . . . and stared at me.

Command marched me toward the stage. The teens watched. Without phones or 3DSs to distract them, these gamers were creepily attentive. The longer they stared, the more I felt my self-conscious parts bloat, becoming paler and hairier. I tried to avoid eye contact. I never did do well with people in person. Not even gamers. That was why the car wash had felt like a miracle to me.

"Afternoon, everyone!" G-man jogged onto the stage and set down a folding chair. "We've got a new player starting today! Come on up, Miles!"

I felt everyone's eyes on me. I felt my face turn red. I felt my feet turn to concrete. Somewhere the building's plumbing gurgled.

Why would my dad do this to me?

Why couldn't I go have a normal week before I went on a normal date?

Why had I played so many stupid video games?

"Miles?" G-man tapped the chair.

Command gave my back a little push, making me trip up onto the stage. I sat in the chair.

I should be getting my back waxed right now.

G-man clapped me on the shoulder. "I want you all to give a big Video Horizons welcome to . . . Miles Prower!"

"Hi, Miles," the gamers said.

They sounded as pleased as a cow in a cement mixer.

Somehow I worked up the guts to look at the crowd looking at me.

Gamers, especially hard-core gamers, especially hard-core gamers who play enough to be sent to a video game *rehab*, fill every possible moment with beating the next level, getting the high score, or leveling their character. Exercise, showering, and overall hygiene tend to go out the window. But these kids looked . . . clean. Their greasy complexions had been scrubbed away, their pale skin tanned, their colorful gamer tees tossed out. It was as if they were slowly transforming into versions of their gaming characters. And no one looked happy about it.

"*Guilding time,*" G-man whispered with excitement. He

didn't seem to be looking into the same sea of dead eyes I was. "Miles, we want you to think of Video Horizons as a place of magic." He put his mouth too close to my ear and cast his hand out over the audience. "A place where classes are filled with wonder, activities are filled with surprises, and side quests await around every corner."

I stared at my hands and wondered what Serena was up to. Probably feeding Ethiopian children or something.

G-man squeezed my shoulder. "Which of the three guilds will help you achieve your greatest potential?"

I glanced up and noticed that the Hub's beanbag chairs were arranged into three columns of red, green, and purple. At the front of each, an adult held a sign with a different mis-spelled video game reference.

"Will it be . . ." G-man pointed to the red group. "The Master Cheefs?"

The guild stood and gave a grunt salute that would have made the *Skyrim* theme song blush. They were led by a muscly coach who had a tan like a burned carrot. These looked like the action gamers, the type who shoot every red thing in sight before teabagging your character's corpse.

"Will it be . . . the Sefiroths?"

The green guild stood and hissed at me. Then one broke into a coughing fit. Their guild leader, a slight woman with silver hair, helped the coughing kid sit down.

"Or will it be the Fury Burds?"

The final guild—just two girls and a prepubescent kid—

stood from their purple beanbags and half-assedly flapped their hands like little wings while trying to whistle. Their guild leader was HUGE. His hands looked big enough to scoop up Command and Conquer and make them fight each other like action figures.

"So, player Miles," G-man said, squeezing my shoulders. "Who's it going to be?"

I frowned at the gamers. I remembered when guilds had been fun—that morning. What did G-man know about fun or magic? Had he ever joined a raiding party to defeat a wad of bubble gum that was attacking downtown Arcadia, sticking its citizens to the streets and collapsing buildings with popped bubbles? No. No, he hadn't.

Still. I had to play this Video Horizons game. For Serena.

Which guild would help me get out of there and to my date the fastest? The sickly Sefiroths? The futile Fury Burds? Part of me wanted to be in what was clearly the strongest of the guilds—the warriors of *Halo*—the Master Cheefs. But their almost-athletic builds intimidated the *hell* out of me.

Also, one of the Cheefs kept grinning at me. He was as skinny as a wire, wearing a big white gangster tee, and sitting in his beanbag like a breeze had slumped him over. His hair hung like black straw around an expression that was boredom and chaos both.

He gave me a venomous smile and shook his head as if to say, *Not my guild.* The nerves came alive in my teeth.

"Um . . ." I swallowed. "I choose—"

"Not so fast," G-man said. He reached behind the stage and brought out a black shoebox with an oval cut out of the lid. "Let's let the Box of Fate decide."

He shook the box at me. I stared into the dark oval. This was it. I'd randomly choose a powerful guild that would humiliate me, or a shitty guild that would make me lose. I reached inside. There was only one piece of paper in the shoebox. I looked at G-man, who smiled with his fuzzy teeth. Had he taken the others out because I'd been a smart-ass in our first meeting? Was he trying to prove that it was impossible for me to win in four days?

I pulled out the paper and read it. My stomach dropped.

"What does it say?" G-man asked.

When I didn't answer, he snatched it out of my hand.

"Master Cheefs!"

The Cheefs gave an audible groan of disappointment.

"Really, Cheefs?" G-man said, hand on hip. "Is that how we treat a new player? Scarecrow?"

The kid with the slanted grin shrugged. "What'd I do?"

The other Cheefs snickered.

What would Serena think if she knew that even a bunch of gaming addicts didn't want me in their guild?

Still, I didn't blame the Cheefs. They didn't need bloated Miles Prower slowing down their escape from rehab.

"Well, shucks," G-man said. "I was hoping we could introduce a little *diversity* into some of the guilds." I looked at the athletic Cheefs and knew exactly what kind of diversity he meant. "But I suppose it won't work out that way." He crumpled up the piece of paper.

The Cheefs cheered.

G-man pointed at them. "Minus a thousand points for every player on the Cheefs for poor sportsmanship."

The Cheefs moaned. Oh God. Didn't G-man know they would take this out on me?

"Miles," G-man said, touching my shoulder again, "we'll stick you in the Fury Burds, I guess."

The Burds didn't react, except for their giant leader, who gave an enthusiastic series of deafening claps.

"Go find a seat," G-man said, patting my back so hard, it stung.

I slouched toward the Fury Burds. My guild.

The giant guild leader shook my hand, which practically disappeared inside his.

"Good tidings, Miles!" he said, grinning. He drew me close and whispered, "*When you're in the guilding chair, these meetings can feel longer than a* Final Fantasy *cut scene. Heh-heh.*"

I managed half a smile.

A bird tweeted through the overhead speakers.

"All right, everyone!" G-man called from the stage. "Before you head off to guild therapy, say it with me now! One, two, *three*!"

The players chanted in their unenthusiastic voices: "I am not a gamer; I am a player of life."

And just like that, I was.

NPCs

"To the Nest, adventurers!" the giant guild leader said.

I followed the Fury Burds out of the Hub and along the eastern corridor. The prepubescent kid kept glancing over his shoulder at me. He couldn't seem to keep his tongue in his mouth.

We climbed another staircase to a purple door painted with a picture of a bird's nest. Inside, the two girls combed through an activity chest while the smaller kid started unfolding chairs with the effort of a squirrel trying to pry open bear traps.

"Thank you, Fury Burds mayor!" the giant guild leader said. He took the kid's scroll and stamped it.

I stood there like an idiot.

The Nest was a small, gray brick room that smelled like dead grass. A half wall divided the far wall in two, with four bunks on each side. On the right side of the wall was a punching bag and a crafts table. On the left was a workstation and the activity chest. Above the half wall was a small, barred window that looked over desert dunes and a pale sky. A bird-themed clock above the door said it was a quarter after canary—5:13.

Four days to earn a million points.

The guild leader's hand thunked down onto my shoulder. "Let's start guild therapy, shall we?"

I nodded, like what he'd said was perfectly normal, and joined the circle of chairs. The small kid immediately sat next to me. The two girls also sat, holding circles of wood that framed perforated pieces of cloth. The fluorescents flickered on the dead-fish gray of the walls. I needed a Red Bull.

"Greetings, players!" the guild leader said. His voice was so big and warm that for a moment it felt like we were gathered around a crackling hearth in Azeroth. Y'know, as opposed to being in a gray-brick jail cell. "We have a new player joining us today. Greetings, Miles!"

I gave the guild a flat smile and a small wave.

Earlier I had failed to convince G-man that I was a healthy or good person. I needed a new tactic. When you find yourself in a dungeon that's too high-level, you remain stealthy. You memorize the layout of the passages and study the enemies' movements from the shadows while searching for a way to get the hell out.

"Normally," the guild leader said, "we would have guild therapy during this block, but because it's Sunday, we're a little more relaxed, and I can give you a proper welcome." He gestured around the circle. "I want you to get to know your guildmates. You'll be pretty close with these guys for the next few weeks."

Not if I could help it.

Going clockwise from my chair were the two girls—a larger Asian with short shiny black hair, and a girl with dark skin, her hair bleached white. Then there was the giant guild leader, and finally, the small kid and me. The kid was sitting so close, I could feel him breathing.

"I'll begin," the guild leader said. "They call me Fezzik. I'm a very nice man, but I'm also a giant. Heh. Guess I don't have to tell you that part."

The bigger girl raised her hand. "Do we have to listen to this again?"

"You can stitch for points if you'd like," Fezzik said.

The girls started to sew. The small kid kept his attention fixed on me.

"Miles, they say the best kind of sponsor is one who has experienced the same addiction," Fezzik continued, "or as I like to say, has gone on the same dangerous quests. I'm no different from you. I've experienced gamer regret. I've come out of a gaming haze and discovered the world had left me behind without any real connections or appreciable skills."

My dad had used similar words when trying to discipline me. But I knew I had enough "appreciable skills" to get by in life. I could build a computer from scratch. I could order underwear online. I could microwave Hot Pockets.

Fezzik rested his elbows on his knees so that his eyes were

more level with mine. "No one loves a giant. Just like in fairy tales. I don't know if people are worried I'm going to break them or what, but when you're my size, no one invites you to things. No parties. No football games. No dates."

Something squeezed inside me. I may have complained about my looks and my luck with girls, but it would be nearly impossible to find love with a giant's stats.

"So one day I gave up on it all," he said. "I went to Costco with my savings and bought three shopping carts full of food. Then I shut myself up in my apartment with an *Arcadia* subscription."

My eye twitched. I hoped he didn't notice.

"I stayed there for six straight weeks, ordering an extra large supreme pizza every night, and spending every possible moment in Arcadia. I would've stayed longer, but then my sobering moment came. The thing that smoked me out of my cave. I'd been fighting the Click Clack God for four straight days—waiting for him to respawn again and again so I could get him to drop a pair of epic titanium cuff links—when I ran out of food. The fridge was empty. The cupboard was bare. I couldn't afford pizza three times a day, so I needed another Costco run. But . . ." Fezzik gave a giant-size sigh. "When I tried to leave my apartment, I couldn't fit out the front door."

My eyebrows leapt to the top of my forehead. *Don't laugh, don't laugh, don't laugh.*

Fezzik pinched up his shoulders like he was still trying to find a way out of that door. "I squeezed and squeezed until

I was afraid I might get stuck in the frame." His shoulders released. "Finally I had to just . . . give up. I went and sat on my couch." He shook his giant head, ashamed. "That moment hit me like a bucket of ice water. I didn't want to be one of those people who had to be lifted through a hole in the ceiling by a crane after I died. So I sat there in my apartment for days, eating nothing, playing nothing, just staring at the wall until I lost enough weight to fit out my door again."

It was so quiet, I could hear the girls' needles threading through cloth.

"BUT—" Fezzik lifted his giant hands and let them fall with a big *SLAP* onto his lap. "That was another life. The Emperor is long behind me."

"Wait," I said. "You're the *Emperor*?"

Fezzik blushed and tried to contain a smile.

I nearly dropped to my knees before the most famous player ever to grace *Arcadia*. I looked around the circle.

"You guys are sitting in front of a god," I said.

"I doubt that," the Asian girl said.

The white-haired girl stared admiringly at Fezzik, but then quickly dropped her gaze when the Asian girl looked her way.

"Tell them!" I said to Fezzik. "Tell them what you did!"

Fezzik waved his hands. "No, no. I left that life behind long ago."

The small kid next to me bounced in his chair. "Tell us, tell us, tell us, tell us, tell us!"

"Yes. God. Please," the Asian girl said. "We're *dying*."

"Well," Fezzik said, cheeks red from the attention, "my guild was the first to complete the Jack and Lop quest. I obtained Eeqwuan's blade and fed it to Gurglaxe, the lava amphibian, in order to acquire the Toasty Scythe, which I took into the Temple of the Horn and used to decapitate the Mallow King, earning me the Jackalopesus mount. I used it to build the Pyramid of Atmo . . . which earned me the title of Emperor."

I caught the girl with white hair secretly smiling as she stitched.

"I didn't sleep for ninety hours," Fezzik said. "I'm not proud of it."

He clearly was.

I wanted to invite the giant guild leader to join the Wight Knights guild, but that seemed inappropriate in a video game rehab. So I just said, "It's a pleasure to meet you, Emperor."

"No, no," Fezzik said. "Don't call me that. Like I said, that was another life." He took a deep breath and exhaled. "The point is, I know what it's like to get lost in a digital world and watch the real world leave you behind. More than most, probably. Heh. Think of me as your healer, Miles. The white mage of the guild."

"A-*hem*," the Asian girl said. "White?"

"Excuse me," Fezzik said. "I'm your *healer*. I'm here to give you a phoenix down in life."

He gave an infectious chuckle, and I smiled. For real this time.

Fezzik gestured around the circle. "Let's go around and

have everyone give a brief introduction: name, tier, and why you're here."

"What's a tier?" I asked.

"It's just which quarter of a million points the player has. You're a first tier." He gestured to the big girl, who kept her eyes on her cross-stitch. She looked annoyed enough to crumple the chair she sat in. "Meeki?"

She kept stitching. "I'm Meeki. I'm a first tier. I'm *not* addicted to video games. I'm here because a controller *accidentally* slipped out of my hand during a Wii tennis match against my brother, and it *accidentally* gave him a concussion."

"Meeki," Fezzik said. "Did the controller accidentally break the television too?"

She dropped her needle and made an annoyed sound. "I already *told* you. The Wiimote *bounced off my brother's head* and *then* hit the TV. I'm *not* a violent person."

"Meeki," Fezzik said, "your avatar's name was 'mekillyoulongtime.'"

Meeki rolled her eyes and then pointed in my face. "I'm gay. So *don't* flirt with me."

"Uh . . ." I scowled. "Don't worry."

The Nest door opened, and Command led the electric warlock into the room. He didn't look dead anymore, but he didn't look *not* dead either. No way could he look that terrible because of a gamer hangover.

The small kid next to me leapt up, creaked open another chair, and set it down to my left. The electric warlock slumped into it. Meeki and the other girl scooted over to give him and his sunken eyes some space.

"Greetings, new player!" Fezzik said. "What are we going to call you on this adventure?"

The kid held his head up from his legs and gurgled something that sounded like "Zxzord."

"Heh. Okay." Fezzik gestured to the dark-skinned girl with the bright white hair. "Next, meet our mystic elf."

The girl set down her cross-stitch and shook her white hair so it partially covered her face. Then she quickly tucked it back behind her ear again, like hiding her face was a thing she was trying not to do anymore. She was one of those eternally gloomy-looking people, like someone had left her out in the rain and all her happy had seeped away.

"My name is Aurora. I'm a third tier. . . . I don't want to talk about video games today."

"Sounds good to me," Fezzik said. "What would you like to talk about?"

Aurora tucked the other side of her hair behind an ear. "It's pleasant not to stare at a computer screen anymore. I . . . *see* things. Like, flies are adorable. Have you noticed? They clean themselves like kittens." She mimicked the action. "They lick their legs and then wipe off their big spotty eyes. It's amazing. Their proboscises are like tiny little gummy straws . . ."

Her voice was so floaty, it went straight in one ear and out the other. I studied the Nest's half wall, which had been tagged with video game references, some of which had been painted over. Through the paint, I could still see the silhouette of a *Super Mario* question mark block and the Triforce from *Zelda*, but "the cake is a lie" and "praise the sun" hadn't been painted over at all. I wondered if G-man eliminated obvious references but thought the last two were about healthy eating and outdoor fitness.

"I could watch flies for hours," Aurora said.

Meeki pointed at me again. "She has a boyfriend."

Again I scowled. Why was this girl such an asshole?

"Soup?" Fezzik said.

The squirrely kid fidgeted in the chair next to me, eager to tell his story. He seemed so genuinely wholesome, I was surprised he didn't have a flower bud growing out of the top of his head.

"I'm Soup, and I'm a first tier," he said, way too close to my face. "My stepbrother got me into video games. He liked scary stuff like *The Last of Us* and *Dark Souls*, except I didn't, 'cause they're too scary, but I like all video games, so it didn't really matter. I used to have to do things for him so that he'd let me watch him play, like get him drinks or take off his shoes and stuff, but then he died, and then I could play as much video games as I wanted."

Before my heart even had a chance to flutter, Soup continued. "*I* like the 3DS. I like *Harvest Moon* and *Animal Crossing*, but my favorite is *Nintendogs* 'cause my parents won't let me have a real puppy." Soup's eyes shifted from happy to a sad glisten. "But then they said I didn't play outside enough and they took my 3DS away . . . and they let my poodle, Minus, starve to death. You kinda look like my stepbrother."

Soup stared at me like I was supposed to say something to that. I opened my mouth, but then he perked up and jumped onto his knees.

"My favorite part of Video Horizons is all of it. It's like one big *Animal Crossing*. That's why even though I've been here for a month and a week, I'm still only a first tier. I don't even *want* any points. I wish it was my first day. No, first minute! First *second*!"

"Heel, Soup," Fezzik said, chuckling.

He hooked Soup's shirt collar and pulled him back into his seat. I squinted away a headache. I'd been listening to the kid for two minutes and already felt like I'd had too many energy drinks.

"Miles," Fezzik said, "remember these faces. Your guild-mates will help you earn points so you can return to the out-side world where your real adventure will begin."

I did look at their faces: Meeki, Aurora, Soup, and the electric warlock, whose head still hadn't left his hands. Hell, my dad thought *I* had a problem? I never ate so much that I couldn't leave the house, or cracked a family member in the skull with a Wiimote, or bemoaned the death of a digital dog more than a real human being. The only thing I was guilty of was being turned down by girls too many times and not wanting to spend time with my shitty stepmom or controlling father.

I might have played more video games than most, but at

least I'd had a good reason. Unfortunately, that was probably what everyone in that circle thought about themselves.

"Miles," Fezzik said, "do you want to tell us the tale of how you came to Video Horizons?"

Aurora and Soup turned to me.

"My name is, um . . . Miles Prower. I've been a gamer my entire life, but I've been playing *Arcadia* for about two years." Fezzik gave a grunt of acknowledgment. "Sometimes as much as, uh, five hours a day. But I'm done with that now. Because . . . well . . ."

I studied my guildmates. The non-player characters who would help me escape. If I could make it out of there in time for my date, then I could show G-man, my dad, and all of the girls at my school that I wasn't like these weirdo gamer inmates. That I actually did deserve to go out with someone as lovely as Serena.

"I need to get out of here as soon as possible," I said. "See, I made a girl laugh for the first time today. My stepmom asked me to wash her Xterra, so I went to the car wash, and I met this cute girl there. Apparently some dickhead had sprayed her with one of the, um, sprayers, so . . . "

I told them the story. Or, at least, a version of the story.

When I finished, Meeki looked up from her cross-stitch and gave me a poisonous look. "So, what, your princess is in another castle, and you gotta go save her?"

What the hell? Did Meeki have to eat someone's heart every day in order to survive or something?

“It wasn’t like that,” I said. “She was interesting . . . and interested. And she wasn’t wearing a pink dress.”

Soup laughed. A little too hard.

Meeki crossed her arms tight and narrowed her eyes.

“And what was this fair maiden’s name?” Fezzik asked.

Meeki cleared her throat. “We don’t know if she’s fair *or* a maiden.”

Fezzik chuckled uncomfortably.

“Uh . . .” I thought about patient confidentiality. I thought about my exaggerated story of how she and I had met. I thought about how she had drawn me in. . . .

“Her name was Gravity,” I said.

Meeki snorted.

“Gravity,” Fezzik said. “Excellent. Thanks for sharing, Miles.”

He didn’t say anything about trying to get me out of there as quickly as possible so that I could get to my date. Instead he tried to nudge some life into the electric warlock. “Greetings, Zxzord! I think that’s what you said your name was. Heh-heh. Would you like to share the tale of what brought you to Video Horizons?”

Zxzord rubbed his face like he was just waking up. He wiped his nose, cleared his throat, and spoke for the first time. “Heroin.”

Meeki laughed so hard, it made Soup jump. The sound made Zxzord cradle his head again. Meeki’s laughter trailed off. In the ensuing silence Zxzord dropped his hands and took in our shocked expressions with raw eyes. He spoke in his undead warlock voice. "Every time I went into my room to shoot up, I told my parents I was playing video games." He sniffed. "So they sent me here."

Everyone in the circle shifted their limbs, as if one of his frayed wire tattoos could lash out and electrocute us. Holy shit. While we'd all chased digital dragons, Zxzord had actually been *chasing the dragon*.

"Maybe *Mario* mushrooms are a gateway drug," Meeki said, and snorted.

Zxzord pressed his palms into his eyes. "I don't know why more people don't just kill themselves."

Fezzik grew red and made a sound like a Wookiee. "Heh-heh. Sounds like someone needs a health potion! Um, uh, let's get you to G-man's office, shall we?"

He helped Zxzord to his feet while the Fury Burds dispersed around the Nest. Meeki worked the punching bag, Aurora continued cross-stitching what looked like a dog with leprosy, and Soup whipped sheets off two of the bunks.

Again, I stood there like an idiot.

"Hey, Miles," Meeki said. "You want me to grab you some cross-stitching materials so you can start earning points?"

"Oh, um, that would be great," I said.

"Too bad. I'm not your slave." She hit the punching bag again.

Fezzik poked his head back into the room. "Fury Burds mayor?"

"Yeah?" Soup said.

"Would you give Miles the tour?"

Before I could protest, a smile burst across Soup's face, and he ran up to me.

"Welcome to V-hab!" he said, throwing wide his arms.

"Thanks," I said.

"Get it?" he said, poking my stomach fat. "V-hab. Like, rehab for video games?"

"I get it," I said, brushing his hand away.

Soup cracked up, sucking in laughter like he was having a seizure.

"If you need anything, anything at all, just say, 'Soup, I need . . .' and then fill in whatever you need."

I need a million points, I thought.

Soup patted my arm. "Don't worry. Everyone's a grouchy cow on their first day." He squeezed my hand. "I'll make sure nothing bad happens to you while you're here."

Save Point

After Soup's exhaustive tour of the Nest ("And this is the thread drawer, where we keep different colors of thread, like yellow and purple and black and . . ."), a woodpecker rattled through the Nest's speakers, and we all headed to the Feed, a toasty little cafeteria filled with sizzles and good food smells.

"This is where you can eat," Soup said.

"Yeah," I said. "Got it."

Meeki pushed past us and stepped behind the steaming food troughs, slipping on a hairnet and cellophane gloves. The Feed had just about everything, from reheated pizza and Coke to veggie stir-fry and green tea. Hanging above the troughs were two pictures—one of a smiling salad with "1,000" written beneath, the other of a frowning candy bar with a big "0."

All I wanted was a chocolate doughnut with sprinkles. Okay, that isn't all I wanted. I wanted a chocolate doughnut with sprinkles and a Red Bull. I wanted the Wight Knights in my headset screaming inappropriate shit about motorboating my man boobs. I wanted to block out all of Video Horizons and its players and focus on a screen where I could decapitate cowbots, so my brain could just relax a bit.

"I'll take the veggie stir-fry."

Meeki held out the spoon to me. "You can serve yourself."

I didn't take the spoon. "Aren't you getting points for doing this?"

She scowled and slopped veggies onto my plate.

I took my food to the cook, a squat, hairy man with a stylish apron that made him look like a bearded Fabergé egg. He wore a name tag that read COOKING MAMA. He scratched his beard and stamped my scroll.

+1,000

My first points. At this rate I'd be released from V-hab in just under three years.

While Soup ordered food, I tried to slip away, but someone blocked my path. Scarecrow. The skinny Master Cheef with greasy straw hair.

"In case it wasn't clear," he said, "I think you're a pile of shit, and I'm going to make you lose at everything you try."

I searched his eyes. "Why?"

He gave a crooked grin. "If I told you, it would spoil the surprise."

He patted my cheek and walked away.

I stayed frozen with my tray, until Soup hooked my arm—

"Come on!"—and led me to a table by a window that overlooked the shadowy side of a giant dune.

"This is the Fury Burds table," he said.

"Clearly."

We sat, and Soup sort of let his knee fall against mine. I sorta knocked it back. Behind us one of the Sefiroths whispered, "*Who would win in a fight? Snake from* Metal Gear *or a million* Pikmin*?*"

Aurora sat across from me and Soup with exactly one half of a piece of white toast and a small cup of horchata, which she nibbled and sipped delicately. She must have caught me staring because she said, "I get points for eating anything at all."

I glanced at her too-thin arms, then quickly took a bite of Feed food.

I immediately spit it out.

"*Blech*. What the hell is this?"

Aurora looked toward the kitchen. "The Sefs were on dinner duty. They microwave everything. Even eggs."

"Ugh." Maybe I *would* lose thirty pounds by Thursday.

"WIZARD NEEDS FOOD!"

Fezzik joined our table with a modest amount of food for a guy his size.

"How's Zxzord?" Aurora asked.

"Healing at the Fairy Fountain." Fezzik nudged me. "That's what we call the sick bay. They're going to do some tests to see if he's faking or not."

"Faking a heroin addiction?" I said.

Fezzik shrugged.

"I'll sew him a get-better spell," Aurora said.

"That would be nice," Fezzik said.

Zxzord had his journey. I had mine.

"How can I start earning experience points?" I asked.

Fezzik chuckled. "No need to start grinding yet, adventurer. If this were a video game, you'd still be in the first *town*. But that reminds me. You do get five thousand experience points just for showing up to guild therapy. Let me just get out my Buster Sword. . . ." He took my scroll and unholstered a stamp from his belt. "FIVE THOUSAND XP!" His voice thundered through the Feed, and he stamped my smiley face column.

"Great," I said, tallying the wet numbers on my scroll—6,000 points.

I felt a swipe across my jeans and looked down to find Soup laying a napkin on my lap.

"In case you get messy," he said.

I did not murder him.

"Tomorrow is Monday," Fezzik said, "so you can earn *lots* of XP playing sports in the Coliseum."

And I thought my butt had clenched when Command had wanted to give me a cavity search. Never in the history of words has there been a more terrifying phrase than "sports in the Coliseum."

"I know how ya feel," Fezzik said, chuckling at what must have been my horrified expression. "Most exercise I ever got as a gamer was when I accidentally dropped my remote under the couch. Heh-heh."

Aurora's horchata cup echoed a giggle.

"Sports?" I said. "Do I have to?"

"Depends on how fast you want out of here." Fezzik held his spork aloft and bellowed, "Any player willing to brave sweat and sulfur must simply pluck up a sword . . ."

He explained that every day, players could test their non-gaming prowess in different types of tournaments. Mondays were dedicated to sports: baseball, basketball, tennis, and other words that made my manhood shrink. Tuesdays were team-based puzzle solving. Wednesday was a kart race. Thursday would be devoted to a big paintball tournament. And Friday was a sand-castle-building competition.

"We're gonna build a castle right up to the freaking sky!" Soup said, throwing his hands toward the ceiling.

I would not be there for sand castle Friday.

I would *not* be there for sand castle Friday.

Fezzik continued, "In each of the competitions, players can earn two hundred and fifty thousand points for first place, two hundred thousand for second, and a hundred and fifty thousand for third."

So yes. In order to be out of there by Thursday, I would have to sports. And not just sports. Even while earning points from classes and extracurricular activities, I'd still have to medal in all the tournaments.

I dropped my spork onto my unfinished stir-fry and rubbed my face. Soup rubbed my back.

"Don't do that," I said.

His rubbing turned into small pats.

Aurora stamped up toast crumbs with her pinky finger and ate them one by one.

"Is everyone here pretty bad at sports?" I asked, scanning the scrawny and round faces in the cafeteria. "I mean, they'd have to be, right?"

"Not the Master Cheefs," Fezzik said, scooping up peas. "Some of those kids got hooked on video games only after they got a sports-related injury or broke up with someone."

I scowled and choked down my veggies and wondered why I had never taken Casey's advice and exercised at home: push-ups, jumping jacks, *jog* every once in a while? Hell, why not at least do a few curls with the game controller while playing *The Binding of Isaac*? Because I'd never thought I'd find myself in a position where going on a date with a beautiful girl would hinge on performing well in a sporting event. That's why.

I thought about running and throwing and catching and all the things I despised. I thought about burning lungs and burning desires. I thought about Gravity.

"Guess I'm playing sports tomorrow," I said.

"Quest accepted!" Fezzik said.

My heart started to beat no, *no*, NO, *NO*.

"I'm gonna go before I throw up all over the table," I said.

Before I could stand, Soup grabbed my food tray. "I got it! No problem. It's no problem. I used to do chores for a town of little animals *all* the time. It's no problem."

While Soup cleared my tray, I snuck out of the Feed and

took the long way around the rectangular hallway so I wouldn't have to see him again. The eastern half of the building was dark, the only light the green glow of the exit. As the hum of the Feed faded behind me, I heard tinkering.

I followed the echo to a slimy mop trail, which led to the backside of a janitor hunched in the far corner. His mop was propped against an open grate, and he was peering inside a wall vent, which was large enough for him to fit inside. Vapor from an e-cigarette coiled around his ponytail and ass crack as he mumbled. "They get points for doing a crap job cleaning up this place. Do I get a raise for cleaning up after them? No, I do not. Come on, you piece of . . ."

He pulled out what looked like a computer chip, slid it into a zip case, and then replaced it with another. He glanced up, saw me, quickly replaced the grate, and pushed his mop around the corner.

I walked up to the corner and squinted through the vent. Tiny green lights winked in the darkness.

What the hell? This was some serious *Myst* shit. . . .

Whatever. I wasn't there to solve mysteries. I was there to *win*.

Ugh. I was starting to sound like I was on a reality game show.

Back in the Nest, Fezzik placed a finger to his lips and pointed to a lump in one of the bunks. Zxzord was snoring.

"So is he on heroin, or not?" Meeki asked.

"G-man thinks he's exaggerating," Fezzik said. "But that is none of our business. Tonight let's try to make the Dust Fairy's job a bit easier."

The rest of us quietly cleaned the Nest for a few thousand points each, until an owl hooted for lights-out. Meeki disappeared behind the half wall, and Aurora slipped out of the Nest. I tossed my pouch onto the top bunk diagonal from Zxzord's so I wouldn't have to listen to his snoring. I climbed the little ladder and slipped under the covers while Fezzik hummed the sleep song from *Final Fantasy*.

"Rest well, adventurers," he said. "Tomorrow your quest continues."

He switched off the light, and green star stickers glowed to life on the ceiling.

I looked at the bird clock, lit by the Nest's green exit light—10:02. Owl o'clock. Less than four days until my date. Less than four days to earn a million points. Usually I loved challenges like this. The odds stacked against me. A boss no one had defeated. A record no one had beaten. But that was when I could do everything with my ass in my desk chair, controlling a warrior avatar who wields an axe the size of a bison. Without those, how was I supposed to win at "sports in the Coliseum"?

Something pressed into my back through the mattress below. Two small feet.

"Psst! Miles!"

I closed my eyes.

"*Miles? . . . Miles? . . . Miles? . . . Miles?*"

"I'm asleep."

"You want me to cross-stitch for you? I'll give you all the points."

"Wait . . ." I stuck my head over the edge of the bed. "Seriously?"

Press Start

I was woken by an electronic rooster, a warbled *grok-a-drrdle-gdoo* blaring through the blown-out speaker above my head. I rubbed my eyes and tried to figure out why I wasn't looking at the glowing gray breasts of the Kerrigan poster above my computer. Instead I was looking at a shitty watercolor portrait of what might have been Felicia Day.

A freckled nose peeked over the edge of my bed.

"Mooooorning," Soup crooned.

Outside the window the sun made blinding sparkles on the dunes. It was only then that I remembered that, not unlike Harry Potter, I had been escorted (kidnapped) by a giant (two Tongan men) and whisked (driven) to a magical land (desert) where I was sorted (humiliated) into a new house (guild) to learn new skills that would result in points (against my will).

I covered my face with my pillow.

Soup snorted. "You're funny."

The rooster choked out another call. The speaker didn't have a snooze button. Neither did Soup. I couldn't sink back into bed until my dad came in and stole my blanket. I had to be a warrior. For Gravity.

I uncovered my head and took a deep breath.

"Want me to get your pants for you?" Soup asked.

"Yes."

I sat up and tried to blink life back into my brain. It was seven a.m. First time I'd woken up before noon all summer.

"Rise, adventurers!" Fezzik said, jostling my bunk. "Prepare for the day's quests!"

Aurora was already dressed and cross-stitching. Zxzord snored below me. Behind the half wall, Meeki groaned. I slid out of bed.

"Pants!" Soup said, presenting them.

I slid them on.

"Cross-stitch!"

He held up a white piece of cloth poorly stitched with the words *Miles n Gra*. "I haven't done the 'vity' or the '4 ever' yet."

"Shh," I said, blocking the cross-stitch from Fezzik's sight.

"Oh, right," Soup whispered. *"But do you like it?"*

"Uh, sure."

It was the most hideous thing I'd ever seen, but I needed Soup to keep farming points for me.

"Will you give it to Gravity?" Soup asked.

"Absolutely," I said, as I fantasized tossing the cross-stitch out the window as G-man drove me home on Thursday.

"Yesss!" Soup took the cross-stitch and skipped to Aurora. *"He loved it!"*

A huge hand clapped me on the shoulder. "Strap on your armor, adventurer!" Fezzik said.

I unzipped my suitcase. My dad hadn't packed any of my favorite shirts, of course. No "Still Alive," no Cardboard Tube Samurai, no Finn and Jake. Instead he'd bought a pack of Hanes large V-neck shirts that were too small, a pack of tighty blackies, a pack of plain white socks, a pair of white pants that could unzip into shorts, and a pair of laceless tennis shoes. He'd also thrown in his orange Home Depot hat.

Worst. Armor. Ever.

I squeezed into a T-shirt, clicked on my adventure pouch, and slipped on my shoes, leaving the Home Depot hat behind.

I took one last look out the window, across the endless dunes. Could I fill my pockets with enough bottled water from the Feed to survive the walk across the desert? Doctors said I retained a lot of water weight, and I would have a hell of a tan for my date . . . or I'd just get lost and die.

Let the game begin, I guess.

After brushing my teeth with a toothbrush carefully prepared by Soup, and turning down his offer to apply my deodorant, I followed the shuffle of feet down the dead, fluorescent hallway to the Hub for Monday assembly. I kept my eyes on the floor the whole way, hoping to avoid any chance encounter with Scarecrow. I was anxious enough without seeing his crooked smile.

In the Hub I quickly snagged a beanbag chair between Fezzik and Aurora so that Soup couldn't sit next to me. While G-man took the stage and discussed personal accountability, I unzipped my adventure pouch and tried to make sense of my picture-based schedule through the fog of less than twelve hours of sleep.

The week was packed with activities, each less appealing than the last. Still, I needed to speed-run this game, executing every class and chore perfectly, without ever having played it. Of course, if I could just win four golds in the tournaments . . . That wasn't going to happen.

Every day there were three class blocks—sports, life skills, and arts and music—but players could choose the kind of class within those categories that most appealed to them. The options for first block were jogging, aerobics, and the class obviously designed for lazy kids, tai chi. Jogging was worth the most points, so I circled it grudgingly. I continued to circle the most challenging classes throughout the week, until a shadow fell across my schedule.

"You're my eggy daddy," Meeki said.

I looked up. The assembly had ended. The players were lined up at the stage, collecting eggs from G-man.

"Were you not listening?" Meeki asked, then rolled her eyes before I could answer. "You're already a terrible father." She stuck an egg into my face. "You and I take care of this together. For every day that it doesn't break, we get ten thousand points."

I narrowed my eyes at the egg, then at Meeki. I didn't trust this. This was the girl who'd spent my first guild therapy session ridiculing absolutely everything I'd said.

"Why don't you ask Aurora?" I said. "Y'know, because . . . y'know."

"First of all, she's not my type. Second of all . . ." Meeki huffed. "Look, dude, do you want the points or not?"

I looked at my schedule. Ten thousand points a day would really help me out.

"Okay."

Meeki bit the lid off a marker and drew on the shell. "We trade off every day. I'll take him first." She showed me the egg. It had a face now. One eye was narrow like hers, one wide like mine. My half of the egg was smiling. Hers was in a scowl.

"Looks just like us," I said.

"What are we going to name him?" she asked, annoyed.

"Do we have to for points?"

Meeki shook her head. "Terrible father," she said, and left.

Someone tapped me on the shoulder. I let my head flop back onto the beanbag chair and found Aurora cradling her own egg, decorated with constellations. She had wrapped a scarf around her head and spoke in a fragile voice. "You wouldn't want to help a poor widowed mother out, would you?"

"Um . . ."

Aurora's lip quivered.

I hesitated, wondering if I could cheat by raising two eggs

to earn double points. But then I remembered G-man deducting points from the Master Cheefs for bad sportsmanship. I couldn't risk losing any points in the next four days.

"I already told Meeki I would," I said.

Aurora nuzzled her egg. "Maybe we can get child support points. C'mon, Megg White."

She exited the Hub, leaving me feeling pretty studly that two girls wanted to raise eggs with me . . . until I remembered that their other options were Soup and Zxzord.

Two small hands rubbed my arms from behind. "You hungry?" Soup said. "I could hear your stomach growling all meeting!"

I shrugged him away. "I'm starving."

For breakfast, Cooking Mama laid out ingredients in the Feed's kitchen and told us to make whatever we wanted, reminding us that healthy food would earn us points. One of the Sefiroths made open-mouthed Pac-Man pancakes that looked like they were chasing raspberries. I wanted those pancakes. I was hungry enough to lay waste to the entire stack. Instead I made a runny, over-spiced tofu scramble for my guild.

"Thanks, Miles!" Soup said.

"I did it for the points," I said.

+6,000

When the clock struck cardinal, Aurora asked, "Would you like to tai chi with us, Miles Prower?"

"Not enough points," I said, and headed out to the racetrack.

The sky was bright and hot. A powerful wind blew sand off the dunes in painful invisible lashes. It was the kind of day I'd usually spend locked in my room, battling marble cherubs that had escaped from the medina's fountain. But no. I had to run. And not just run. The schedule said each lap was worth 1,000 points. In order to reach my desired PPD (points per day), I'd have to run *ten laps* around the sandy track that wrapped around the building. I quickly did the math. . . . Yep. That was nine more laps than I'd ever run in my life.

I felt something next to me. I turned around and found Soup standing in my shadow.

"What are we doing?" he asked. "Running?"

I ignored him and walked up to the muscly coach with a carrot tan, the Master Cheefs' guild leader. Everything about him made me want to run, from his metallic Oakley sunglasses to his crossed arms to the veins in his neck. Even the nipples pressing through his sweat-resistant tank top looked angry.

"Uh, what do I do?" I asked.

The coach pointed down the track. "You run. It's not rocket science."

A little fan whirred at his feet, making his shoelaces flap. All I wanted was to lie down in front of it.

I walked to the starting line, where a couple of large Master Cheefs stretched themselves in positions impossible for my body.

I hate this, I hate this, I hate this.

"We got this!" Soup said, leaping and punching into the air.

His enthusiasm made my man boobs sag.

The coach blew his whistle. The Master Cheefs shot ahead while I set off one plodding foot at a time. A burning wind dried my eyes and filled my lungs with fire. My bones felt fragile. I wanted to be home. Home, where my warrior had infinite endurance and I got 100 percent more ass support.

Soup did not help. He had so much energy, he actually ran backward in front of me, so I had to look at his stupid smiling face the whole time.

"Don't crane your neck back and don't breathe out so hard and don't make your arms flop around," he said. "You're doing great."

After what felt like an eon of running, I heard the Master Cheefs' sneakers pounding down the track from behind, about to lap me. As they passed, I couldn't tell if they were huffing or laughing. This was what a rhinoceros with osteoporosis must feel like when being chased by a pack of hyenas.

After a lap and a half I nearly wobbled off the track.

"Gotcha!" Soup hooked my arm and pulled me back between the track lines. "You can quit anytime! But you don't want to!"

"I will throw up on you," I told him.

"That's okay!" Soup said.

I ran three laps.

I went blind, threw up my scramble, and Soup practically had to carry me back to the building . . . but I ran three laps.

+3,000 points

• • •

Between classes I tried to blink the purple spots from my vision while washing dishes in the Feed for a bonus 2,000 points. Then I dragged my bones to the hazy electric symbol room for a class with G-man, whom I high-fived with the least sarcastic smile I could muster. *+1,000*

"If you guys are going to live a life fueled by electronics, you might as well learn how the darned things work." He taught us about transistors as we soldered tiny bits of metal onto circuit boards.

"What game is this?" Meeki asked, waving one in the air.

"Actually, that's a calculator chip," G-man said.

After that, I watched her solder 80085 onto her board.

+2,000 points

When the chickadee chirped at noon, I dragged myself to the Feed. I was exhausted. I felt like dying. I did not die. Instead I filled my tray with zero-point foods and joined the Fury Burds table.

"Cheap highs, like shopping and sugar and epic loot, don't last," Fezzik said. "They're like a star in *Super Mario Bros.* You may feel invincible for a brief period, but after the comedown, you'll be just as vulnerable as before, if not more so."

I avoided the guild leader's eyes as I scarfed down mashed potatoes and chocolate milk. I realized I was doing exactly what he was warning us against, but I was starving and needed the energy for "sports in the Coliseum."

"How goes the adventure, Miles?" Fezzik asked.

"Fine," I said through a mouthful of mashed potatoes.

"Aurora, you're a third tier," he said. "Any advice for the new player?"

"Um," she said. "Don't burn yourself out trying to get home too soon."

She slid her fingers next to my lunch tray. Her knuckles were scabbed and swollen.

"Too much cross-stitching," she said.

"Don't have to worry about that," I said, taking another bite.

"Nope!" Soup said, and winked at me.

I subtly shook my head at him.

". . . and that's why *Last of Us* sucks," a voice said. "Except when the chicks make out, of course."

Scarecrow passed our table, his arm around a girl who giggled and playfully pushed him away.

"He's such a douche bag," Meeki said.

Aurora nodded.

"Language, Meeki," Fezzik said.

"Sorry," Meeki said. "He's a device that cleans out vaginas."

Fezzik didn't argue with that.

The tension in my chest uncoiled a bit. It's not so bad when the person who mysteriously hates you is widely considered a douche bag.

"I don't know what Dorothy sees in him," Aurora said, looking after Scarecrow and the girl.

"Their player names are Scarecrow and *Dorothy*?" I asked.

"The other two Cheefs call themselves Lion and Tin Man,"

Fezzik said, pointing toward the bigger guys, who'd lapped me on the racetrack—twice. "They changed their player names together last week."

Great. My mysterious archnemesis was the leader of a Yellow Brick Road gang.

Someone sat and collapsed onto the table next to me.

"How's the dream world, Zxzord?" Fezzik asked.

Zxzord kept his head hidden in his arms. "I've been shitting the La Brea Tar Pits all morning."

Fezzik made his uncomfortable Wookiee sound.

Aurora reached under her tongue and inexplicably offered Zxzord a pearl.

"Paint what inspires you in the real world," the Sefiroths' silver-haired guild leader said in the paintbrush room. The walls were covered with hideous watercolors.

Meeki painted armor. Aurora painted stars. Soup sat too close, as usual, and painted what looked like a chubby kid trapped in a Pokéball.

"That better not be me," I told him.

He slowly slid it off the table and crumpled it.

By the end of class, there was a hideous watercolor portrait on the wall—a dripping, smiling, black-haired stick figure, standing at what might have been a car wash.

25,000 POINTS **3 DAYS, 4 HOURS UNTIL GRAVITY**

Ragdoll Physics

I have been a hero.

I have hefted my axe and climbed the jagged mountaintop. A blizzard lashed my armor as I approached a behemoth that vomited venomous lava onto any who tried to steal its treasure. I have stared that demon in its eyes of chaos as it howled for my death. And I was not half so terrified as when I went to play some casual sports with a few video game addicts.

My heart was practically hammering out my brains as the Fury Burds trudged the sandy path to the Coliseum. It was the kind of terror I'd felt a thousand times at my high school. Like my body was about to be assaulted—by health.

In the high desert sky, clouds drifted across the sun, making the sand dull gray one moment, flashing gold the next. *Oh God, please let me win that gold.*

"Okay, Miles," Soup said as we walked. "Remember,

breathe in harder than you breathe out, solid arms, and keep your chin down."

I ignored him and just focused on not throwing up again. Then he tapped me on the shoulder.

Soup pointed. "The Coliseum."

A chain-link fence wrapped around a flat stretch of compact sand holding a few courts and an Astroturf field. It was like a tornado had swept up my least favorite things in the world and dumped them into the middle of the desert.

God I needed a Red Bull.

"Go warm up, Fury Burds!" Fezzik called.

Meeki, Aurora, and Soup went off while I tried to get a sense of my surroundings. The Sefiroths were on one half of the basketball court, looking awkward. They slapped at balls, tripped over absolutely nothing, or tried to touch their toes and fell short by a foot or two.

The Master Cheefs were on the other half of the court, looking valiant. Scarecrow dodged and shimmied around Dorothy with her big shoulders, and around Lion with his swaying mane. He dribbled the ball between Tin Man's tall legs before performing a perfect layup, as easy as pushing a button.

In order not to aggro any of the Cheefs, I took the long way around the courts and found the muscly coach and his nipples.

"Excuse me?" I said.

"Yeah?" he said, not looking at me.

"Um, could we play something easy today?"

Now he turned. He glanced at me over the top of his sunglasses, like even in a video game recovery center, this was the most pathetic question I could ask.

"I, uh, need to get a lot of points."

He turned his back to me. "Basketball tournament today."

Shit. Scarecrow was going to wipe the concrete with me.

I searched the courts, feeling helpless. Lots of video games have hint systems. Right then I needed a little Navi fairy floating around my head like in *Zelda*. A winged bouncy orb of light that could flutter to objects and give me clues about what I needed to do next.

Didiling-ding-ding-ding-ding!

I imagined my own Navi painting the Coliseum with shiny fairy dust. Which sport would ensure my blistering success? The fairy lit the peeling white paint of a square cross-sectioned with two lines.

Four Square.

I may not have been able to throw a ball, but I was pretty confident I could block one with my body.

"Can I play Four Square instead?" I asked the coach.

"No, you cannot. That's for players with health troubles."

Navi sailed back and twinkled above my shoulder.

Didiling-ding-ding-ding-ding! Feign an illness, Miles!

"Oh, um, I have asthma."

"That so?" the coach said, pinching some snot out of his nose.

I made my breath ragged, so that it had a slight whistle to it. "Yeah. My dad thinks there's something seriously wrong with me, but he's a Christian Scientist so he doesn't believe in medicine. That's why I couldn't get a doctor's note for G-man."

The coach stared me down. I could feel his nipples burrowing into my soul. "That true?"

Half true. I nodded.

"This facility isn't about winning, y'know," the coach said.

Didiling-ding-ding-ding-ding! Try threatening him!

"I know it isn't about winning," I said. "I just don't want to have an attack all of a sudden and flop around on the court and then for Video Horizons to have a lawsuit on its hands."

The coach glared at me. He pinched more snot from his nose, shrugged, and pointed to the Four Square court. "Go fill a square."

I nodded like that was exactly what I'd expected would happen. I went to the ball rack, and grabbed what I hoped was a Four Square ball. It was raspberry-red, pocked with little star-shaped indents, and had a peeling logo of a place called Happy Sun Summer Camp.

I bounced it a few times. It felt . . . unnatural. Video games, for all of their hand-eye coordination, do not prepare you for sports. Pushing a button on a controller is a far cry from hurling a weighted sphere through the atmosphere while accounting for gravity, distance, and my damned fingers that never seemed to want to let go of the ball at the right moment.

My recovery might have been set up like a video game, but

I did not have the luxury of reloading so I could try it over and over again. I had to do this perfectly the first time.

I brought the ball close to my lips and smelled the sweet rubber. "*Okay, ball,*" I whispered. "*I need you to listen to me very carefully. My entire romantic life hangs on this game. So when you come at me, I want you to be as light and easy to predict as a bit of dandelion fluff. But when I hit you, I want you to leave my fist like a meteorite.*"

"Who you talking to?"

I turned and found Soup, right in my shadow again.

"Okay, new rule," I said. "If I can feel you breathing, then you're standing too cl—" Something dawned on me. "Do you have any undeclared health issues?"

"Huh?"

"Never mind. Wanna play Four Square?"

"If you're playing!"

"*Great.*" I squeezed his little shoulder. "Listen, buddy, pal, friend, ace. I need you to throw this game for me."

His nose crinkled. "Like, don't win but let you win instead?"

"Yep."

"Okay!" He leapt onto the Four Square court.

"Thank you so mu— Okay, *oops*. Stay behind your line. You don't have to stand so close."

"We need two more," Soup said, looking at the empty squares.

I searched the Coliseum.

"Go ask that kid," I said, pointing to a Sefiroth who walked without swinging his arms. "And *that* one." I pointed to another, lying on the asphalt, belly hanging out of the bottom of his shirt.

Soup fetched them.

"Miles," I said to the new players, trying to sound intimidating.

"Devastator," the kid with the stuck arms said in a pinched voice.

"Sir Arturius," the chubby one said, nervously squeezing his hands together. "Even *Final Fantasy* has its blitzball, right?"

They were perfect.

"Can I be commentator?" Soup asked.

"If you do it under your breath," I said.

I got *real* low, filling my square. I was a wall. I was a *Halo* shield. I was the little rocket ship in *Galaga*. I could stop an asteroid field.

The game began.

Every time Devastator or Sir Arturius sent the ball in my direction, I hammered it at Soup, who let it pass.

"Point!" I called.

Soup didn't even have to help much. Devastator kept missing the ball with his awkward arms, while Sir Arturius tried to hit the ball back with so much force that it threw him forward in his square, leaving the back wide open for me to fill with rocketing raspberry red.

"Point!"

On my date I'd be able to tell Gravity how I had heroically won a sporting competition since we'd last met. I'd just be vague about the circumstances.

"Point!"

Devastator fumbled. Sir Arturius sweated. Soup didn't try. And I kept winning.

Until the whistle blared.

"All players to the Four Square court!" the coach called.

I froze as the Cheefs, Sefs, and Burds gathered around us like an impending storm.

Keeping one foot in my square, I leaned in to the coach. "Uh, I thought you said this was just for kids with health troubles."

The coach shrugged. "Maybe they all have asthma too."

I looked at the Cheefs, sweaty from the basketball court. Dorothy spit, Tin Man cracked his knuckles, Lion tied his locks into a ponytail, and Scarecrow blew me a kiss. My confidence evaporated into the summer sky.

The coach patted my back and whispered, "*You think I'm gonna give you points without you working for it?*" His whistle screeched into my ear. "We're changing today's tournament because one of our players has asthma."

"*Lame,*" Lion said.

Soup touched my love handle. "Miles? Do you have asthma? Do you need me to get you water?"

"No."

"Okay, if you pass out, I can do mouth-to—"

"Do not finish that sentence, Soup."

"Okay."

Scarecrow stepped up to Sir Arturius. "Get out of there for a second."

The kid happily obeyed, and Scarecrow moved into his square.

"Mind if I step in?" Dorothy asked Devastator, squeezing his arm.

"Okay," he said, and exited, arms fixed to his sides.

Tin Man slapped the back of my arm. "Move."

I gazed up at all six foot three of him. "No."

Tin Man seemed confused. Like no one had ever said no to him before. He looked at the coach, then back at me, huffed, and then rejoined the line.

"*My* square," Lion growled at Soup.

Soup hugged the ball to his chest. He looked at me, then back at Lion's red face. "No," he said.

I smiled and decided to let Soup sit next to me during the next assembly.

The coach put his whistle to his lips. "The tournament will begin—"

"Actually?" I put my hand into the air. "We already started. I have eleven points."

He snorted. "There are no points in Four Square." And he blew the whistle.

"What we playing?" Scarecrow asked, punching the ball

out of Soup's hands and spinning it between his own. "Bus Stop? Tea Party? Around the World? Shark Attack? I say Shark Attack."

Shark Attack implied blood. Tea Party didn't sound too bad. I was about to say so when Scarecrow lifted the ball into the air, his other fist behind it. "No fake-outs. No cherry bombs. We good?"

My stomach nose-dived right to my feet. No, we weren't good. I needed sports experience. I needed to have joined the basketball team instead of the AV club. I needed a Red Bull. I needed to *win*.

Soup raised his hand. "How do you play?"

Scarecrow sighed and dropped the ball to his side. "Four squares." He pointed to the roman numeral in the corner of each of our respective spaces. "If someone's eliminated, everyone else cycles toward the one square. Winner is whoever spends the most time in this square. Don't know why you guys didn't take it, but too late now."

Damn. Scarecrow was in square one. I was in square three. Scarecrow had to be eliminated and I had to survive two rounds to even have a *chance* at scoring.

Scarecrow spun the ball. "The ball can only bounce into your square once, and then you have to hit it into another square. We keep going like that till someone screws up. Like this." Scarecrow dropped the ball, let it bounce once, and then punched it into my square. My knees pinched together a second too late as the ball flew right between my legs. The crowd giggled as someone tossed the ball back to Scarecrow.

"Filthy casual!" Lion secretly called into his hand.

Why do you hate me? I wanted to ask Scarecrow. I stood there like an idiot instead.

"We cool?" Scarecrow asked.

"Cool!" Soup said.

"Cheefs get a handicap," the coach said. "Minus fifteen seconds for every minute spent in the serve square. Sefs get plus fifteen."

At least I wasn't in the Cheefs.

"Forty-five minutes," the coach called, and held up a stop-watch.

"I'm taking you out first," Scarecrow said, pointing at me.

"More like . . . No," I said. "You aren't."

His neck was covered in hickeys, as dark as blackberries. *He* didn't have to worry about getting to a date on Thursday. A breeze kicked up from the east, blowing sand across the court. I closed my eyes. If I could experience a miracle at a car wash, I could experience one on a Four Square court. That ball would bend according to my Gravitational pull.

Again I got low, dangling my arms between my legs like Donkey Kong.

It happened in a matter of seconds. Scarecrow gave the ball a little lift and gently bumped it into Dorothy's square. Dorothy clasped her hands and smashed it as hard as she could into Soup's. Soup lunged and was *just* able to tap it into my square. This gave me plenty of time to . . . awkwardly slap the ball back to Dorothy.

She must have been the one who'd given Scarecrow those hickeys, because she politely tapped it to him. And Scarecrow, well, he did exactly what he'd said he was going to do. He waited until the ball was an inch off the ground and then nailed it into my square.

My body dove. My arm swung. My fingers skimmed the rubber.

I missed.

The whistle screeched and the coach pointed his thumb over his shoulder.

"P'wnd!" Lion cried.

Dorothy high-fived Scarecrow.

Numb, I walked off the court. Meeki held up our egg child, which somehow looked disappointed in its father. That was it. Two hundred and fifty *thousand* points out the window. I didn't even get third place, which was the minimum I needed to be free by Thursday. Game over. No date for me.

I began the walk of shame back to Video Horizons.

The whistle screeched again. "Hey, dummy."

I turned around. The coach pointed to the corner of the number four square where a line of players wrapped around the court. "You're not out. You just get back in line."

"Oh!" I said, hustling back to the court. "Okay, sorry. I don't know how to . . . Okay."

Soup moved up a square into my spot, while Meeki handed the egg abomination over to Aurora and cycled into the number four square.

"Too pretty to game!" Lion called sarcastically.

Tin Man chuckled into his hand.

Fezzik frowned at the coach to see if he was going to do anything about it. He didn't.

There were six players ahead of me in line. Usually I'd relish this spot. Not this time. It would take forever to get back into the game. My fate could be decided long before then.

Aurora stood outside the line, cradling her egg like it was a real baby.

"Why aren't you playing?" I asked.

"Fingers," she said, showing me her hand sores again.

"Right. Yeah."

That was too bad. I thought I could probably beat her at Four Square.

On the court Soup looked at me like he'd just dropped my goldfish down the disposal, because he hadn't kept me from getting out.

I'm sorry, he mouthed.

I mouthed, *Stay in.*

He looked confused.

Stay!

I had to hand it to him. Soup sure knew how to obey. I'd never seen a kid so stressed. Every time he hit the ball, he bared his teeth like he was receiving electroshock therapy. I'm pretty sure he didn't blink for seven whole minutes.

Meeki, meanwhile, was unstoppable. She seemed almost bored, swatting the ball into the other squares like it was a cartoon bird that wanted to sing to her. She got Dorothy out, and she and Soup moved into the three and two squares. While I rocked from foot to foot in line, every other player who stepped into the four square—including Tin Man and Lion—wilted under the awesome power of mekillyoulongtime.

"Meeki the Destroyer!" Fezzik called, then grinned at the Sefiroths' silver-haired guild leader.

The coach checked his stopwatch. "Scarecrow in the lead with eleven minutes. That's with the handicap."

I was up again. It was Scarecrow, Soup, Meeki, and me—squares one through four. I needed to take Scarecrow's place in the first square and then remain there until the *end* of the tournament. It was time to get aggressive. It didn't matter how low the ball came into my square. It didn't matter how fast. I hit it back with every ounce of me that had to see Gravity again.

The game raged on. My fate bounced between the four of us like a raspberry-colored lightning bolt. I was Ryu, heroically punching back everything that came at me. Soup was stretchy-limbed Dhalsim. Meeki was blurrily fast E. Honda. And Scarecrow used the same move over and over again, like Blanka's cheap-ass electric attack. It was frustrating, but now I'd figured out his trick. Low and to the left. Every time.

Finally Soup fell. He couldn't have been happier, though, because it meant I stepped into the three square.

The coach blew the whistle. "Twenty-four minutes left! Crow in the lead with twenty-one!"

Only two minutes before Scarecrow took the gold. Every fiber of my being was electric with terror. I was going to lose. I knew I was going to lose.

The whistle screeched, Scarecrow lifted the ball, and we began again. In the crowd Soup started up a lively commentary. "Scarecrow hits it to Meeki! Meeki nails it back! Scarecrow powerhouses it to Miles, and Miles *devastates it* to . . . some kid I don't know. The kid misses! Boom goes the dynamite!"

The whistle blared.

"Shut up, kid," the coach said to Soup. "No one wants to hear that."

Soup swallowed his lips and stared at the concrete.

Fezzik patted his sad little shoulder. "Um, Coach?" Fezzik said. "May I speak to you privately for a second?"

The two stepped away from the court to the edge of the Coliseum so that the players couldn't hear their conversation. *Get 'im, Fezzik,* I thought. Also, it was nice to catch my breath for a minute. My heart was going crazy.

While Scarecrow spun the ball on his finger, Soup cupped his hands around his mouth. "*Psst. Meeki,*" he whispered *way* too loudly. "*Let. Miles. Win.*"

Scarecrow dropped the ball. "The fuck is this?"

I gave a little shake of my head and tried to communicate death to Soup with my eyes.

Scarecrow pointed at Meeki and stared at me. "You make an alliance with the Great Wall of China here?"

Meeki's mouth fell open. Lion stifled a laugh with his fist.

"Her grandparents are from Vietnam," Soup said.

"I don't give a shit," Scarecrow said. "You guys are cheating."

"We're not," I said.

Meeki's mouth still hung open.

"Whatever," Scarecrow said. "I'll beat your asses anyway."

The smirk on his face twisted my insides. He couldn't say something like that and still be allowed to win. *I* should win. This kid was getting in the way of my date and looked like he knew it. Like he could taste my heart breaking.

I didn't want my anger to throw the game, so I channeled it into my hands. I picked up the ball. I'd get my revenge by beating Scarecrow in Four Square. . . .

But then I threw the ball at his face instead. I was expecting him to flinch and block it. I was expecting to maybe throw him off a little, make him regret messing with me. I was *not* expecting the ball to crunch his nose, making blood explode all over his white gangster tee.

Scarecrow covered his face and doubled forward. "Fuck!"

"Oh my God," I said, reaching out to help. "I'm *so* sorry. I am *so* sorry."

"Got him!" Soup said, and held up his hand.

I did not high-five him.

"Yo, Coach!" Lion called across the Coliseum.

Oh God. What had I just done? I'd just lost the game and thrown away every point I'd earned so far.

Lion kept trying to get the coach's attention, lifting his hand high and pointing at me, but Scarecrow caught his arm and pulled it down. He pinched his nose and gave Lion a look. Then he spit blood onto the concrete.

"Hey! Miles!" Soup said, hand still raised for a high five. "You avenged Meeki's honor!"

I still didn't high-five him. "Scarecrow, I didn't mean—"

Meeki shoved me. *Hard.* She pointed in my face and yelled, "Nobody puts princess in a castle!"

"Huh?" I said.

She grabbed Scarecrow by his collar and socked him in the mouth. He dropped to the ground like a rag doll. The whistle blared from afar as the coach and Fezzik came running. I quickly stepped behind Soup as Fezzik grabbed Meeki's arm and the coach helped Scarecrow to his feet.

Fezzik shook his head. "Come with me, guys."

"He called me Great Wall of China!" Meeki yelled.

He escorted her and Scarecrow to Video Horizons . . . leaving me on the Four Square court.

The coach blew his whistle. "Double disqualification. Meeki and Scarecrow." He looked at me and pointed into the serving square. "Game on."

I stepped up, took the ball, and awkwardly tried to spin it between my hands as three new players stepped into the two, three, and four squares.

My odds of winning had just *dramatically* increased.

The two best players had been disqualified.

Soup would cycle in, ready to throw the game.

The Master Cheefs times would be halved.

I lifted the ball, and . . .

TOOK BRONZE!

In a sporting competition!

The coach snorted and grudgingly stamped my scroll.

+150,000

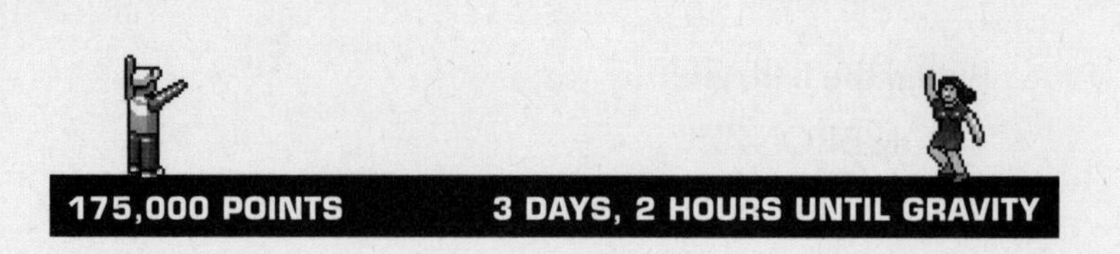

Hit Points

At five o'clock a loon gave a mournful cry, and Soup and I triumphantly returned to Video Horizons for guild therapy.

When we arrived, the Nest was dark. The lights were out, the blinds shut.

I paused in the doorway. Soup peeked under my arm.

"Welcome," Fezzik's voice said from the darkness. "Join the circle."

I took careful steps forward, blindly feeling in front of me. Soup followed, touching my back. I was too exhausted to push him away. My knee cracked into a chair. I sucked in through my teeth, carefully felt my way around the chair, and sat down.

Soup sat next to me and put his mouth to my ear. "Miles, why did you crunch Scarecrow's nose for Meeki?"

"Shh!" I said, glancing at Fezzik's giant form. In the darkness I couldn't tell where the guild leader was looking.

"*Do you* like *her?*" Soup whispered.

"She's *gay*."

I didn't tell him I hadn't even been thinking about Meeki when I'd thrown the ball at Scarecrow. I'd only been thinking about winning at Four Square. It had felt heroic, smashing the nose of an asswipe who'd clearly deserved it. That feeling had only lasted a second, though—after Soup had pointed out that I'd stood up for Meeki and before she'd decided to take the moment for herself.

Aurora's blurry white hair floated through the darkness and joined the circle. Zxzord snoozed in the bunks. My eyes adjusted, and I saw that Meeki was already sitting across from me, arms folded tightly around her chest. I swallowed.

What had happened in G-man's office? Had she told him what I'd done? If being unsportsmanlike lost a player 1,000 points, how many would I lose for possibly breaking someone's nose?

"Are we ready to begin?" Fezzik asked.

No one answered.

All I knew was that if the blame for Scarecrow's bloody nose fell solely on Meeki, then I would get to keep the points I'd earned in Four Square. That would mean I'd only need two golds and a silver in the remaining tournaments.

Pff. *Only*.

There was a click, and a flashlight illuminated Fezzik's giant pale face. His mouth hung slack. He spoke in a haunted voice.

"A gamer in China cuts off his own hand so he'll stop

playing games. A gamer in America runs down his father with a car because his dad took his copy of *Halo* away. A gamer in Sweden calls in a terrorist threat on a *StarCraft* opponent's house, and then watches over the webcam as a SWAT team shoots the opponent's little sister through the chest." Fezzik's floating face looked left, then right. "It's time . . . for video game tales . . . from the grave!"

I could practically hear Meeki's eyes roll. For once, I agreed with her.

"Fury Burds," Fezzik said. "Do video games cause violence?"

Silence.

Everyone in the circle except Fezzik had seen me throw the ball at Scarecrow's face. But no one was saying anything. Soup's silence made sense. He was unreasonably dedicated to me because I looked like his deceased, abusive stepbrother. I'd somehow earned Stockholm syndrome by proxy. But what about Aurora? And why did Meeki want to take all the blame?

"I don't think so," Aurora said.

"Great," Fezzik said.

I tensed as he handed her the flashlight. *Please don't give me away, Aurora.*

She held up the light, throwing shadows across her face. "My boyfriend gets real mad sometimes. But I don't think games make him that way. He says they help him let off steam."

"And what do you say?" Fezzik said.

"Nothing, usually," Aurora said.

"I mean, how do you feel about violence in video games?"

"Well," she said, "he's never hit me or anything."

"Have you ever thought he was going to hit you?"

Aurora looked at her fingers and shrugged.

"Is not hitting enough to make a good boyfriend?" Fezzik asked.

She shrugged again and passed back the flashlight.

"Thanks for sharing, Aurora," Fezzik said. "Scroll?"

She passed him her scroll and he stamped it.

Wait, we get points just for saying obvious shit?

"Video games definitely don't cause violence," I said.

"Miles!" Fezzik said. "Excellent. Why not?"

He passed the flashlight to me. I'd had this argument with my dad a thousand times. Now I could finally earn points for it.

"Well, correl—"

"Put it up to your face," Fezzik said, pointing at the flashlight.

I tried not to look annoyed as I angled the light toward my chin. "Correlation does not imply causation. If video games made people violent, then Japan would be the most violent country in the world. It's not, so . . ."

I tried to hand the flashlight back so I could get my points, but Fezzik said, "You don't think there are any instances where video games make someone violent?"

I froze. Did he know what had happened on the Four Square court? Had he seen? Was he sneakily trying to get me to confess? I knew video games didn't make me violent. Douche bags like Scarecrow just made me want to throw balls at them. Still, I needed to shift the focus away from me.

"Uh, violence is just human," I said. "It comes from feeling threatened." I looked at Meeki. "Like, if someone calls you a bad name . . ."

"Or something really racist," Aurora said.

"Right," I said. "Or something really racist. Then you just want to lash out. That has nothing to do with video games."

I passed the flashlight and my scroll to Fezzik. While he stamped it, I looked at Meeki. She kept her eyes down. I kept staring until she finally looked. I smiled. She scowled.

I could not win with her.

"Anybody else?" Fezzik asked.

Soup raised his hand and took the flashlight. "Once, in *Super Mario 64* on DS I took an . . . an innocent penguin . . . and I . . . I threw him off the side of a sky island." His eyes gleamed like gold in the light. "Sometimes I can see him in my dreams . . . falling forever."

"Thanks for sharing, Soup," Fezzik said, taking back the flashlight. "Who here has heard of the *Tetris* Effect?"

Aurora raised her hand. "Is that where you play so much *Tetris*, you see blocks floating on the backs of your eyelids?"

"That's it," Fezzik said. "Those patterns can trickle into other parts of your life, like when you put groceries on the shelves. And the effect isn't limited to *Tetris*. If you play too many video games, you can start seeing pieces of it everywhere. And not only visually. But patterns for how to be successful in life."

It was dark, so I grimaced. I could see where he was going.

I had played plenty of violent video games, but I never felt like decapitating my stepmom when she counted my breakfast calories.

"You only have one choice in most games," Fezzik said. "That choice is violence. You push buttons to shoot, stab, punch, kick, or snipe people in the head. I want to ask you guys if you think this behavior translates into the real world."

Another silence.

"Yo, why do people get pissed at *Grand Theft Auto* but never at LEGOs?" a voice said from the bunks. "You ever stepped on one of those things? Fuuuuuuck."

"Hush, Zxzord," Fezzik said. "You're supposed to be healing."

Aurora raised her hand. "Not all games are violent. Like *LittleBigPlanet* or *Katamari Damacy* or—"

"*Animal Crossing!*" Soup said.

"Yeah," I said, "*Plants vs. Zombies* isn't going to make me go on a rose-cutting spree."

"Plants are violent enough as it is in the real world," Aurora said.

"Wait for the flashlight, Aurora," Fezzik said, passing it toward her.

When it came around to me, I had something important to slip in, so I held on to the flashlight.

"I mean, even violent video games can make you empathetic," I said. I looked at Meeki. "Maybe you use your violence for good."

"Ugh," Meeki said.

Fezzik finally turned his attention to her. "Meeki, would you like to talk about today's incident on the Four Square court?"

I held my breath. *Please don't turn me in.*

Fezzik tried to hand Meeki the flashlight, but she waved it away. "I don't want anyone seeing up my nostrils. I'm buying you all tweezers, by the way."

"Okay," Fezzik said, "do you want to talk about it without the flashlight?"

"No, thanks," Meeki said.

"You're going to lose a lot of points for that punch. A hundred thousand."

My stomach clenched.

"You're just lucky his nose wasn't broken," Fezzik said. "Otherwise, it might've been more."

Meeki looked bored by this.

He kept on. "You're here for a specific reason, Meeki. You hit your brother in the head with a Wiimote. I think it's good that you stood up for yourself with Scarecrow, but you should know better than to resort to physical violence." He gave her a long look.

Oh God, I had to stop this.

"If you talk to me about what happened," Fezzik said, "I may be able to talk G-man into reducing the number of experience points you'll lo—"

"I'm glad she did it," I said.

Fezzik nodded and handed me the flashlight.

"Scarecrow was being a jerk, and he deserved to be punched in the face. I don't think violence is good. But I don't think Meeki was wrong. She was standing up for herself . . . and I think that's really cool."

"Yeah!" Soup said.

Meeki gave me death eyes. Fortunately, Fezzik was taking the flashlight back, so he didn't see.

"Sometimes you need a healer," he said into the light. "And sometimes you need a warrior. Meeki is our warrior." He shined the light on her. "But the Four Square court isn't a battlefield."

I swallowed. "Exactly."

Fezzik held out his hand to me. "Scroll?"

"Oh!" I said. "Sure. Thanks."

I handed it over, and he stamped it. "Miles, I'm giving you an additional five thousand points for good teamwork and for being open about your feelings."

"Thank you!"

Meeki scoffed. "There are other ways of being violent besides punching people, y'know."

"Like what?" Fezzik asked, trying to hand her the flashlight.

She didn't take it. "Let's see . . . Like railroading over other people's turn to talk, or making someone take the fall for something terrible you did, or being creepy about a girl you just met."

I clenched my hand between my legs.

"What do you mean by that, Meeki?" Fezzik asked.

She didn't respond.

"All right," he said, flustered. "You need to go meet with G-man for your demerit."

Oh no, she hadn't gone yet. What if she was just waiting to tell G-man?

Fezzik stood and turned on the Nest's lights. We all squinted in the blinding fluorescents. "The rest of you can have some quiet contemplation time before the woodpecker rattles for dinner."

Soup stacked our chairs. Before Meeki could leave the Nest, I stopped her by touching her arm. I had to make sure she wasn't going to turn me in.

She glared at my hand. "Touch me again, and I'll spend the rest of my points laying your sorry ass across the floor."

I dropped my hand.

She slammed the door.

I felt Soup by my side.

"What is her deal?" I asked.

Soup scratched his hair. "I dunno."

"Is she pissed because she wanted to be her own hero?"

"Probably!"

"But she was just standing there, doing nothing," I said. "Someone had to stand up to that douche bag."

"Yeah. *You*." Soup smiled. "You can tell Gravity that awesome story of when you were like 'Bah!' and Scarecrow was like 'Graaaaaaah nooooooooo!' and then was like *Brrlluuuuhhhhhh*."

He dramatically fell to the ground.

I couldn't tell Gravity that story, not without telling her about V-hab. Unless maybe I told her that the incident happened on a random street corner somewhere. I heard someone say something racist to some girl and decided to step in . . .

I crawled into my bunk. "I'm going to take a nap. It's been a long day."

"Okay, Miles," Soup said. "I'll work on your cross-stitch."

"Perfect."

I stared at the star stickers and tried to feel good about the tournament. I had won a bronze medal in a sport, was 150,000 points closer to my date, and had avenged a girl's honor by crunching a douche bag's nose, even if I hadn't meant to.

I tried to rest, but couldn't.

Nobody puts princess in a castle.

What the hell did that mean anyway?

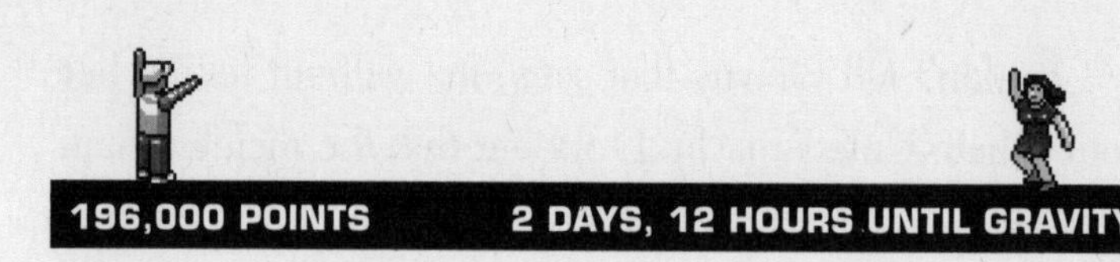

Cheats

The next morning I woke to the strange sensation of an egg being laid in my belly button.

Set. I mean *set* in my belly button.

Luckily, I didn't roll over. Otherwise my and Meeki's offspring would have become a yolky splat across my stomach.

"Take care of him today," Meeki said. "But do not talk to me or look at me, or else this will be *the last child you have*."

She stormed off.

"Mooooorning." Soup's nose peeked over the edge of my bed. "Time to get up! It's Tuesday. That means you only have two days to get back to Gravity!"

I pushed him away by the forehead.

I was sore from Four Square and running three laps, so it took me a while to get dressed. I slipped an ankle sock around the lopsided face of the egg abomination and then slid it into my pocket.

With Scarecrow and the rest of the Master Cheefs roaming the halls, most of Video Horizons now felt like enemy territory. I told Soup to steal me some zero-point food from the Feed, and I used the time to shower in the communal bathroom while no one else was in there. Still, just in case, I undressed in the shower, hung my clothes over the railing, and then kept the curtain firmly pressed to the tile with one hand while I tried to clean myself with the other.

I wanted to . . . *think* about Gravity, just to unwind a bit, but then Soup hopped into the shower next to mine and whistled a hollow imitation of the *Super Mario Bros.* theme. I carefully dressed in the shower, getting my white pants wet, and after having successfully cleaned myself without anyone seeing my man boobs, stepped out just in time to see Soup's penis.

"Breakfast!" he said, pointing to hash browns steaming on the sink.

That day's sports block included weightless workouts, water balloon dodgeball, and, again, tai chi. Most players ran outside to play with the water balloons, but I wanted to avoid the Master Cheefs. Also, I was wearing white pants with black underwear.

Tai chi was taught by Fezzik in the candle room, where light rose and fell like a dragon's snoozing. The only other players were Aurora and, because I was in there, Soup. You look stupid doing tai chi, but no stupider than wiggling around in front of a Wii. We followed Fezzik's movements, as if defending ourselves against an invisible horde of ninjas.

Aurora kept breaking free from Fezzik's instruction, moving like a sheet in a thunderstorm. I couldn't decide if I was annoyed or impressed.

+2,000 points

Music was taught by the Silver Lady, who handed out ukuleles and had players follow along while she plinked out "The Bear Went Over the Mountain."

I started to feel antsy. I wasn't making enough points in these classes to give me room to fail miserably in any of the remaining contests. I didn't like my odds of earning any medals in the remaining days, let alone two golds and a silver. The Four Square tournament had been a total fluke. And that had been *before* Scarecrow wanted to murder me.

The Silver Lady played "Hot Cross Buns" while I dreamed of playing the Spanish guitar at Mandrake's, melting Gravity's heart.

In the Feed I ordered the beet-and-spinach salad for 1,000 points, while keeping my eyes peeled for enemies. As I crossed to the Burds' table, I noticed Scarecrow slouched in the corner of the Master Cheefs' table. His lip was split, his nose a yellowish purple. There's a moment in games when you've leveled up so much that the enemies who once killed you with a single swipe now look harmless, adorable almost. I tried not to smile. Scarecrow was so skinny and pathetic. What had I been afraid of?

Just then Dorothy, Lion, and Tin Man sat down with

him and glared in my direction. I quickly headed to the Fury Burds' table.

Because of Soup's awesome performance in Four Square, I let him sit next to me. He petted the joint-custody egg he'd just received from Aurora.

"I will name him Muffin," Soup said.

"I thought it was Megg White," I said.

"It is Muffin now."

Behind us some Sefiroth with thick-rimmed glasses and all-black clothes started freestyle rapping.

> "Ain't no beatin' this sand, Ozy.
> No more feelin' nice 'n cozy.
> The cold hard fact is you need better data.
> So go right ahead,
> Stay ignorant, playa."

Ugh. Nerdcore. Hard-core rap about video games.

"Who is that?" I asked.

"Parappa," Meeki said, a little dreamily.

"If he doesn't shut up, I'm gonna throw my spork at him," I said.

Meeki gave me a look.

"What?" I said.

The look got worse.

"Fine," I said. "I'll throw something less sharp."

"I'm getting a doughnut," she said, and left.

What the hell was her problem?

Soup danced his egg along my lunch tray. "Muffin could use some companyyyyyy."

I groaned but then took the Abomination out of my pocket and set it on the table.

"They're on an eggy playdate," Soup said.

I ignored him and ate my dirt-flavored salad while an angry wind blew across the roof, flickering the Feed's lights.

A girl I recognized from the Sefiroths walked up to our table.

"Hello," she said.

Her flowing hair and flower-girl voice reminded me of a weeping willow. She was so close, I could see acne scars under her thick makeup.

"Um, hi?"

"I just wanted to come over and say thank you." She touched my shoulder, and I tensed up. "Scarecrow's *such* a jerkhole."

My shoulder relaxed a bit. "Yeah, he is."

Soup nodded.

My fear of the Master Cheefs started to thaw a bit. If I had some allies in the Sefiroths' guild, I could be protected. Even if they were a little sickly. I could walk the hallways in safety and be more relaxed in the tournaments. Even if they were warm bodies who couldn't fight.

"I'm Dryad," the girl said, tossing her hair over one shoulder. "You're Miles?"

Soup stuck his hand between us. "My name is Soup. I'm his partner. We're a team."

"Cool," Dryad said. "Aww, your egg is so cute."

"Mine's not the cute one," I said. "Mine's the lopsided one."

"That's the one I'm talking about," she said. "May I?"

"Sure." I handed her the Abomination.

"Aww," she said, patting its little egg head.

The egg slipped from her hands. My hand shot out to catch it, but my grabbing fingers tipped it away . . . and my and Meeki's little Abomination splatted across the Feed floor.

Dryad covered her mouth. "Oh *no*. I am *so* sorry."

"Uh . . ." I looked into the wide eye of the broken shell. Not getting 10,000 points a day would *seriously* set me back.

That wasn't my only concern. Meeki was buying a doughnut. What would she do to me?

I felt Dryad's breath on my ear. "You think it's cool to break people's noses?"

I jerked back. "Huh?"

She stared at me with so much intensity, it scared me.

I shook my head. "I'm not the one who broke it."

"Yeah," Soup said. "Scarecrow was the one who called Meeki the Great Wall of China."

Dryad's eye twitched uncertainly. "That's not what he said."

"Yeah huh!" Soup said.

BANG! Dryad slammed her fist down, shattering Muffin and

splatting Soup and me with yolk. She hurried out of the Feed.

Soup sat in gooey shock. On the other side of the Feed, Scarecrow gave me a crooked smile and then slipped out after her.

What a coward. Couldn't even execute his own egg assassinations. Was *Dryad* the one who'd given Scarecrow those hickeys? Or was it Dorothy? Both? How many women did he have? Was there some sort of Scarecrow Manson family?

Soup let out a little whimper. He sucked in his lips, trying not to cry while he collected the shattered, scattered, starry eggshell. I considered going and telling Fezzik, who was behind the food troughs, but then he might've asked why Dryad had done it, and that would have placed 100,000 of my points in jeopardy.

Aurora and Meeki arrived at the Burds' table and saw the splattered eggs. Meeki's mouth fell open just like it had on the Four Square court.

I put my hands up. "It wasn't my fault. That willowy Sefiroth chick came over here and smashed them."

Meeki said nothing, just kept that same dumb shocked expression on her face.

Soup sniffed.

"Oh, come on." I said. "It sucks to lose the points, but they're just eggs, dudes."

If anyone had a right to be upset, it was me. None of them had dates to go on.

Aurora picked up a bit of eggshell and stared at it with her satellite eyes. "They grow up so fast."

Puzzler

During life skills block I harvested the stupid spinach I'd be eating for dinner that night, while Soup swept around the garden like a *Harvest Moon* sprite, patting the tomatoes like they were tiny heads and saying things like "Plump up, my little honeys" and "You're so engorged today!"

Finally the canary sang and we returned to the Nest for Tuesday's team-based competition. As always, Zxzord was asleep in the bunks. I was kinda jealous . . . of the relaxing. Not the heroin withdrawals . . . if they were even real.

I joined the guild circle, sitting right next to Meeki, who immediately got up and sat on the opposite side. Fine. If she didn't want me to apologize, I wouldn't.

"Greetings, adventurers!" Fezzik said. "Today you'll be leveling up your spell-casting abilities."

Soup gave a few little claps. "Yesssss."

Fezzik held up a Ping-Pong ball that had been painted purple. "Fury Burds," he said, "your quest is to guide this magical orb from the Nest all the way down to the Hub and into the Box of Fate."

We stared at him.

He held out the ball on his open palm. "Aren't you guys going to say, 'Oh, that's easy' and try to carry it to the Hub?"

"We're guessing there's a catch," Meeki said.

"Heh. There *is* a catch." He tossed the ball and caught it. "You can't touch the orb. And the orb can't touch the floor. And no, you can't just grab a tissue and carry it. The orb cannot come into immediate contact with something you're touching. Any questions?"

Meeki raised her hand. "Why does it feel like V-hab was designed for four-year-olds?"

"I like it!" Soup said, hurt.

Meeki smiled. "I rest my case."

Fezzik dropped his adventure voice. "Video Horizons accepts players ages eleven to seventeen, so we have to strike a balance with challenges like this." He looked at our blank faces. "Fine. Use your engineering skills to get this Ping-Pong ball to the box in the Hub before the other guilds. Is that better?"

There was a general grunt of assent.

"Do we get points?" I asked.

"Same as the tournaments. First place is two-hundred and fifty thousand for each player."

I flipped my chair backward, straddled it, and focused on the orb.

Meeki was right. This did feel juvenile. But if I was going to get out of there in time, I had to treat this contest like it was my fucking job.

"You have until the loon cries," Fezzik said. He stood up, put a pillow on the bunk above Zxzord, and then placed the purple Ping-Pong ball on the pillow. "I think this is going to be tougher than you guys think."

Soup, Meeki, and Aurora stood around the orb.

"It can't touch the floor?" Aurora asked.

"Nope," Fezzik said.

"And it can't touch us?"

"No."

"Does telekinesis count?"

"Aurora," Fezzik said, "if you can make that ball float with your mind, I'll give you a million points right now."

I kept my focus on the ball. Could we somehow hit the ball so it glided all the way down the stairs, down the hall, and perfectly into the Box of Fate?

No. This wasn't *Super Monkey Ball*.

"Hurry, adventurers!" Fezzik said. "The other guilds are probably hard at work!"

"Yeah, probably not," Meeki said. "What happens if we drop it?"

"You lose five thousand points off the reward, and you have to return here and start over."

"We could build a train!" Soup shouted. "A little train that carries the ball in its caboose." He shook his own caboose.

"Let me get this straight," Meeki said in a cutting voice. "You want to construct a fully operational miniature engine and then lay small rails that perfectly run out of the room down the staircase and up into the box?"

Soup bit his bottom lip. "I guess that's dumb, huh?"

I focused on the orb. Could we somehow tilt the floor so . . . No. This wasn't *Marble Madness*. Besides, the floor was lava. The floor was death. The floor was an infinite fall into failure.

Meeki snapped her fingers. "We could build a bridge. We could use straws and spaghetti to make rails that lead all the way down—"

"That was my idea!" Soup said.

"Yeah, but mine actually works."

"I'll go see if there's enough straws and spaghetti in the Feed," Aurora said, leaving the Nest.

"A thousand points to all three of you!" Fezzik said.

"Wait, we get points just for coming up with random ideas?" I asked.

"Of course," Fezzik said. "This is so you guys can work on team-building. I can't give you points for just sitting there. Zxzord, I'm looking in your direction."

In the bunk Zxzord rubbed his face. "Don't drop the ball, dudes."

"Thanks for that," Meeki said.

I kept my eyes on the orb.

Before the Wight Knights had come along, I'd gone on plenty of *Arcadia* raids where the other players had been nothing more than dead weight for me to drag around. This was no different. The Fury Burds were competing against gamers who all thought just like they did.

We needed something new. We needed innovation.

Aurora returned to the Nest, arms full of things from the Feed. "I also got plastic cups so we can make a tunnel for the stairs."

"Brilliant," Meeki said. "The ball will build up momentum to get down the hallway."

"Nice!" Fezzik said. "Another thousand for Aurora."

I ignored them. I wasn't in this for a measly thousand. I was going to win the whole quarter mill.

Aurora dumped the straws and spaghetti onto the floor while Meeki got glue and string from the crafts chest. Using a pair of safety scissors, Meeki punched out the bottoms of the cups.

I focused back on the orb. What if the rails ran out the window and around the building to . . .

No. That was stupider than Soup's train idea.

Soup danced around Meeki and Aurora. "What can I do? What can I do? What can I do?"

"You can crawl into the activity chest and stop giving me a headache," Meeki said.

Aurora handed him a handful of spaghetti. "You can start laying these out to the door."

"Okay!" Soup said.

After laying just three noodles, he leapt to his feet and shouted, "We need a *Portal* gun! I'd aim at the ball and be like *pthoo*—blue portal!—and then aim at the ceiling over the Box of Fate and be like *pthoo*—orange portal! And then drop, *plunk*!"

"Have your parents ever had you tested for anything?" Meeki asked.

I *really* focused on the orb. I was determined to find a better solution than Meeki's.

What if it wobbled off the thin spaghetti rails? What if it didn't gain enough momentum in the cup tunnel to get all the way down the hallway? Aurora and Soup were right. We needed telekinesis. We needed a *Portal* gun. The orb needed little wings just like my Navi sprite—

Didilingdingdingdingding! Soar, stupid.

"Stop what you're doing!" I said, jumping to my feet.

Meeki and Aurora looked up at me, pinching straws, dripping glue.

"We need every extension cord we can find," I said.

"Um," Fezzik said. "I think your guild is onto a pretty good idea here. Do you think you could incorporate—"

"It's not gonna work," I said, rushing to the door. "Straws are flimsy and spaghetti will snap. My way will be faster and more dependable. Trust me."

"Well . . . ," Fezzik began.

"If it works then we all earn points and we get out of here faster, right?" I said to my guildmates.

Aurora and Meeki went back to gluing. No wonder they'd been stuck here longer than a week.

"Fine," I said. "Keep building your rickety spaghetti bridge. I'm doing this idea."

"Take Soup with you," Meeki said. "Please."

Fezzik did not look happy.

"Soup?" I sighed. "You wanna help?"

He jumped and punched the air. "Yes!"

As we descended the staircase, I said, "Okay, I need you to go grab all of the extension cords you can find."

"Okay! Where are they?"

"I don't know. The Feed? The Hub? Ask the Dust Fairy. I can't tell you everything to do."

"Okay, right, yeah, thanks."

He scampered away, like a *StarCraft* SCV, off to collect energy. I was only slightly worried. The difference between Soup and SCVs was that the bots were programmed not to screw up.

I ran outside and searched the horizon. The coach was spray-painting parallel lines along a compact stretch of sand.

Just a simple fetch-quest, I told myself.

"Hey, uh, Coach. Mind if I borrow your little electric fan?"

The coach kept spraying. "Yes, I do. What do you want it for?"

Didilingdingdingdingding! Don't tell him about the contest! He'll think you're cheating like before!

"G-man asked me to grab it," I said.

"It's in the supply closet, and I've got the only key. I'm not taking time away from—"

"I think Zxzord has a fever?" I interrupted. "You know"—I cleared my throat—"the kid with the *heroin addiction*?"

The coach glowered at me.

Back in the Nest, I held the fan above my head.

"*Dun-un-un-un!*" I tried singing the *Zelda* treasure song.

Aurora glanced in my direction. She and Meeki were still busy gluing. They had put together, like, three feet of stable rails. Three out of around fifteen we needed just to get to the stairs.

"Where's Soup?" I said.

"He's not back yet," Aurora said.

"Peons," I mumbled under my breath. I patted Meeki and Aurora on their backs. "Don't worry! We're gonna win!"

Meeki continued gluing, only now with more ferocity. Finally Soup ran into the Nest, his little shoulders wound with extension cords. He looked and sounded like he'd just competed in the Ironman marathon. "*Hoof!*" he said, throwing down the cords and rubbing his sore little muscles. "I gotta lie down."

"Nope!" I said. "You need to start plugging those together!" I jostled his shoulders. "C'mon, buddy! Let's do this! I need you!"

His arms drooped as if they were made of cooked spaghetti. He dropped to his knees and started connecting the cords.

"Whoops," I said. "Unravel them first. Otherwise you might be plugging them into knots."

He nodded and started to unravel them.

"Soup," Fezzik said, "you can come up with your own ideas."

"It's okay," Soup said, unraveling. "I like it this way."

I carried the fan to Aurora and Meeki. "I'm going to need both of my hands, so someone needs to be my uncoiler."

They kept gluing.

"Guys, this is gonna work. Seriously."

Nothing.

"Okay, uh, Zxzord? Can you help?"

A light snooze came from the bunk.

"*Zxzord has died,*" Fezzik whispered, "*of dysentery.*"

"Fine," I said. "Soup? You think you can uncoil too?"

He looked up at me with a slack-mouthed face . . . and nodded.

"Yes! Okay. We got this. *We got this!*"

I hadn't felt a rush like this since the Wight Knights had saved Graham Cracker Plaza from the Milk Tide. I grabbed the first cord from Soup and plugged in the fan. It whirred cool air. I brought it over to Zxzord's bunk, and pointed it upward.

"Soup? Will you blow the orb off the pillow, please?"

Soup nervously crept up the ladder, as if Zxzord was going to spring to life and clamp on to his little ankle. He put his lips next to the ball and blew. The purple orb rolled off the pillow and onto the cushion of air, where it hovered about three inches above the fan in my hands.

"Oooooh," Aurora said.

Meeki snapped her fingers in Aurora's face and pointed downward. Aurora returned to gluing spaghetti.

I carried the fan and the ball toward the door.

"Eh?" I said to Fezzik.

"I guess that's not technically cheating," he said.

"Nope!" I said. "Ha!"

"What do I do?" Soup asked.

"I already explained it. You just uncoil the extension cords as I go and make sure I've got plenty of line."

"You're smart, Miles," Soup said.

"Thanks," I said.

"Don't you need your guildmates?" Fezzik asked.

"Do you guys want to see us win?" I asked the glue crew.

They didn't respond.

"Guess not," I said to Fezzik.

I stepped carefully out of the Nest, balancing the ball in midair, while Soup unraveled the extension cord behind me.

"Don't pull too hard," I said, "or it will unplug."

"'Kay," he said. I could hear his little teeth clacking together. "This is stressful."

"You're doing great."

We carefully walked down the staircase, Fezzik following behind to make sure we didn't touch the ball. At the base of the stairs, I looked left and right toward the two staircases at the far corners of the building. The Cheefs had made it out of their door and were quickly connecting toilet paper rolls from the recycling bin. It was a good idea, but it was taking them forever to tape them all together.

The Hub's door lay ahead.

"We're doing it!" Soup said.

"Of course we are," I said.

Halfway to the Hub, the door at the far end of the hallway swung open, revealing the silhouette of the coach. The fan wavered in my hand, and I quickly balanced the ball while searching for an escape. He couldn't catch me using his fan on anything other than the kid with the heroin addiction.

"Soup, fast, open that door."

He opened what turned out to be the music room, and he, Fezzik, and I went inside. The Dust Fairy whirled around, quickly shutting a vent.

"No class now," he said, waving away smoke from his e-cigarette.

"Yeah, I know," I said, peeking back down the hallway to see if the coach was gone. He was headed our way.

"Miles," Fezzik said. "What are we doing in here? The Hub is two doors down."

"No, yeah, I just . . ." I looked around frantically. "I left my schedule in here. Do you see it, Soup?"

Soup searched while the Dust Fairy held the vent's grate in place with one meaty hand. I stayed pressed against the wall, out of view of the door. The coach's sneakers squeaked closer. As he passed the door, he snorted, almost as if to say he could smell me.

"Not here," Soup said.

"Shucks," I said. "Well, let's keep going."

As Soup shut the door behind us, I got one last glance at the Dust Fairy's ass crack as he bent back over the grate and took another drag of his e-cigarette.

We continued down the hallway. I had taken a few steps through the Hub's door when Soup yelled, "Miles, stop! Stop, stop, stop!"

"What? *What?*"

The orange cord was taut, pointing a straight line down the hallway.

"God"—I glanced at Fezzik—"*dangit*, Soup. Did you get all the extension cords?"

"Every single one!"

"Ugh." I stood in the hallway with the purple Ping-Pong ball floating only a few feet from the Box of Fate. "Maybe we could go set this down in the Nest and search for more cords."

"Why are you fighting using your guild's help?" Fezzik asked.

"I'm not," I said. I guessed I could use some teamwork points. "Um, Soup, run back to the Nest and tell those guys we need their bridge. Tell them they don't have to build it all the way from there. Just have them bring it here."

"Aye, aye!" he said, saluted me, and ran down the hall.

"Unnecessary!" I called after him.

Fezzik had his arms folded. "So, it looks like you need your guild after all."

"I wouldn't if Soup had found more extension cords."

"That might be true—"

Little feet came padding back down the hallway.

Soup had to catch his little Soup breath. "They said . . . they're not . . . *coming*."

"What? Why? Did you tell them how freaking close we are?"

He nodded.

"Do they want to *win*?"

Soup shrugged.

"Well, go ask them!"

He ran back down the hallway.

"And don't come back without them!" I looked at Fezzik. "Why are you looking at me like that?"

"Every adventure party needs different kinds of skills—magic, stealth, brawn, healing."

The ball wobbled in the air, and I tried to keep the fan under it. My arms were getting tired.

"You're like the warrior," Fezzik said. "You go in swinging and try to do as much damage to the enemy as you can."

I had the ball in air equilibrium now.

"Meeki's our warrior," I reminded him. "I like to think of myself as more of a wizard who hangs back and figures out the problem and then swoops in to solve it."

Fezzik nodded. "If you are the wizard, how are you going to survive the heat of battle and get to your date with the princess if you don't have a healer? Or a tank to take all of the hits? Or Soup to run around grabbing things for you?"

Before I could answer, Soup came running back. "They wanna win. Just not this way."

"Seriously?" I held out the fan and the floating ball to him. "Hold this. Do not drop it."

Soup nodded, but it was a weary nod.

"Never mind," I said. "Stay here."

I headed back down the hallway with the fan and the ball, followed by Fezzik. I peeked down at the Cheefs, who were making unnerving progress down the hallway with their toilet rolls, and then took careful steps back up the staircase and into the Nest.

"Guys! I'm, like, three feet from the box with this thing."

"It's more like twelve," Fezzik said.

"Yeah, but we're *so close*."

Meeki and Aurora kept their heads down.

"Fine," I said. "The bridge is a great idea, okay? We need it to get the rest of the way. See? That's us working together. I brought it most of the way. Now you guys finish it off."

They didn't move.

"The Master Cheefs are getting close to winning! Come on!"

Aurora's eyes traveled from Meeki to me and back to Meeki again. "Levitation would help us win. And it is pretty."

"That's not the point," Meeki said.

"Well, then what is the point?" I asked. "Do you like being trapped in V-hab? Do you enjoy not playing video games and doing whatever BS activities G-man comes up with? I seem to remember that someone said that this place was for four-year-olds, like, twenty minutes ago. Now you're doing arts and crafts."

Meeki stood up.

"Yes!" I said. "*Thank* you."

She walked over to the wall and unplugged the extension cord. The purple ball bounced off the fan and onto the floor.

"What the fuck?" I said.

Fezzik sighed. "Minus five thousand from the final prize and minus one thousand to you, Miles, for cursed tongue. Give me your scroll."

"It's on my bunk," I said, swallowing my rage. I turned to Meeki. "I'm trying to help!"

"Help us lose five thousand points?" she asked.

"But you're the one who unplug—*grrgglfrxshsssrrrrrrgggg-ggg!*" I said, or something like that.

If I hadn't desperately needed all of the points that probably would have been taken away by the coach, I would have smashed the fan onto the floor right then.

Aurora dropped the spaghetti she was gluing, and stood up. "He's right."

"No," Meeki said.

"Yes," I said.

"We're just being stubborn," Aurora said. "The fan is faster. And I'm ready to not be here anymore. I'm setting aside my ego and working with Miles."

"A thousand points to Aurora for teamwork!" Fezzik said.

"Why don't I get any points?" I asked. "I set my ego aside,

like, five minutes ago and tried to work with these guys."

Fezzik chuckled uncomfortably. "I think you might need to think about why you finally decided to reach out to your guild."

I swallowed the thoughts that followed. My way would have worked if we had had enough extension cords. It wouldn't have just worked; it would have blown the other guilds out of the water.

Aurora collected the rails they'd built so far and carried them out the door.

Meeki followed, grudgingly.

"Don't come help," she said, pushing past me. "We'll let you know when we're ready."

I stood there holding the fan, feeling raw and mad and stupid.

Soup appeared in the doorway. "We can go make them snacks in the Feed while they build it!"

"Uh . . ." I looked at Fezzik, who had picked up the ball and was setting it back on the pillow. "Yeah, that sounds good."

Twenty minutes later Aurora and Meeki had built a plastic cup tunnel from the hallway to the Hub and directly over the Box of Fate. The Cheefs saw the partial tunnel and looked at us like we were crazy. Word got around to the Sefiroths, and everyone gathered to see what magic we were working.

Then I stepped through the doorway, heroically striding through slanted pillars of frosted light, cradling the purple orb on a cushion of air. I felt the Master Cheefs' glare as I tipped the fan so that the ball slid into the tunnel . . . and *zzzzzzzzzt* plunked into the shoebox.

"Fuuuuuuurrrrrryyyyyyyy Buuuuuuuuuuuuuuurds!" Fezzik called.

I high-fived Soup and Aurora. Meeki kept her arms folded.

"Oh, come on," I said. "Admit it was a good idea. We got there *way* before everyone else. And we got all the points!" I dropped my hand. "Or most of them. You know, because you unplugged our fan."

Meeki gave me a flat smile. "Maybe you should take all of my points, since you came up with the idea without us."

"What? No," I said. "No."

But I was kind of hoping that Fezzik would overhear and say that was okay.

The Burds returned to the Nest in silence, which was stupid because we had totally kicked everyone's ass. Fezzik was quiet because he didn't like the way I'd helped our guild win, Soup because he was exhausted, Meeki because she was an asshole, and Aurora because she was just a quiet person—I think. Whatever. I was used to people not liking me. I didn't need any of them. When I won, I'd have Gravity.

In the Nest, Fezzik called, "Plus two hundred and forty-five thousand to intelligence!"

It didn't quite have the same ring as two fifty. *Thanks a lot, Meeki.*

"Congratulations, Miles," Fezzik said, without that old crackling warmth. "You're a second tier."

He stamped my scroll, and I could practically feel golden fireworks streaming off me.

"Damn! Ass! Hell! Shit!"

It took a second for me to recognize Soup's voice.

"Uh, Soup?" I said.

"Bastard! Anus! Blow job!"

"Anytime he earns a lot of points," Aurora said, "he says every bad word he knows. It's sweet."

I stared at Soup in shock as he rattled off some pretty nasty phrases that he must have learned from his stepbrother. Fezzik sighed and wrote a tick mark for each one. "It would be hypocritical of me not to take the points away," he said.

Soon Soup's swearing slowed to a trickle. "Um . . . diarrhea . . . stupid . . . taint . . . dog diarrhea . . . dog taint . . ."

447,000 POINTS 2 DAYS, 2 HOURS UNTIL GRAVITY

Curaga

"Congratulations on a successful quest, adventurers!" Fezzik said in guild therapy.

The window blinds were open, and light off the dunes painted us all in gold.

"Of course, it isn't about winning the contest. It's about the fact that you found a way to work together as a guild. Although, heh, I think some of our heroes could use a balancing patch."

I knew he was talking about me. I didn't care. We'd won.

"I'm not going to award any additional points for guild therapy today," Fezzik said, "because I really want you guys to focus on how you're feeling and not on getting out of here."

Well, screw this then. I studied my fingernails. I'd definitely need to clip them before Thursday.

"Yesterday," Fezzik said, "adventurer Miles told us an exciting tale about the young lady Gravity."

Great. Now I had to pay attention.

"I was thinking about Miles's conundrum. We've all had our romances, our Aerises, only to watch her stabbed through the back by Sephiroth at the end of the first disc. I know you all know what I'm talking about."

Aurora nodded.

"It's pronounced 'Aerith,'" Meeki said.

"Apologies," Fezzik said. "There are new studies that claim that the cause of addiction is loneliness."

I glanced around the circle. No one was looking at the guild leader.

"Herodotus said that games were created so people wouldn't think about hunger. Perhaps video games were created to eliminate loneliness. They provide a reliable feeling you can return to again and again. They generate predictable relationships, dependable teams, and satisfying conclusions that are difficult to find in the real world. But these cozy digitally generated feelings can make us neglect our real relationships, isolating us even more. Today I want to ask you guys, what makes you feel lonely?"

Meeki's leg jittered. Aurora scratched her jeans. Soup's tongue kept escaping his mouth.

"Come on, Fury Burds," he said. "How am I supposed to cast Curaga if you don't show me where it hurts?"

The only response was Zxzord's snoozing.

Fezzik sighed. "Soup, let's start with you."

Soup kicked his feet under his chair. "I get lonely when I think about having to go home."

I glanced at the clock. It was a quarter after loon, Tuesday evening. I needed to be earning points, not listening to the problems of a kid with severe ADD.

While Soup opened up about home and his stepbrother, I did some more point juggling in my head. Now that I knew my average PPD, I redid my calculations. . . . Shit. Even with all of my classes and a gold medal in the kart race the next day and the paintball tournament on Thursday, I was going to fall about 8,000 short. That was a serious point gap. How could I make it up? G-man wouldn't let me go if I fell even a little bit short.

That was when I remembered Soup's cross-stitching. I started listening.

"You have a pretty vibrant community here, don't you?" Fezzik asked Soup. "That won't be easy to leave behind."

Soup exaggeratedly shook his head.

Fezzik patted his little shoulder. "Do you think the skills you learn here will make you feel more confident to get out in the world and meet more kids?"

"They all don't like me," Soup said. "They stay inside their houses when I come around."

For a split second I felt kinda bad for the kid. It was easy to forget that not everyone had a Gravity waiting for them once they got out of rehab. Some players would return to a friendless neighborhood. Others would return to slightly abusive boyfriends. Others would return to . . . heroin, I guessed.

"You've been an excellent guild member," Fezzik told

Soup. "I've seen you get better at painting and learn how to respect other people's boundaries."

Ugh. He used to be worse?

"I think when it's time for you to venture back into the real world, you'll be much better equipped at finding some buddies to play with." Fezzik turned to us. "Don't you guys agree?"

Meeki and I caught each other's eyes and for the first time didn't scowl at each other. We'd both said terrible things to Soup that day. We immediately looked away.

"You'll make lots and lots of friends," Aurora said, patting Soup's back.

"I don't want to," Soup said. "I just want you guys."

Meeki shuddered audibly. I suppressed mine.

Fezzik gave Meeki a look, then focused back on Soup. "Do you think you can keep point dodging and stay at Video Horizons forever?"

Soup pouted out his lip. "No."

"You spend a lot of energy helping out others instead of earning points for yourself. Do you think it's the only way to get them to like you?"

No. Shit. Let's not explore that. Why make him second-guess it?

Fortunately, Soup didn't respond.

"Okay," Fezzik said. "That's enough for now. Meeki! You've been here more than a week. We haven't heard enough from you. What makes you lonely?"

"I don't get lonely. I have Nutella. And a vibrator."

Blech. I did not want to picture Meeki as anything but clothed and far, far away from me.

Fezzik's face turned bright red, and he made his Wookiee sound. "Heh-heh. O . . . *kay*. Do you think sugar and—*hmm-mm*—physical stimulation are enough to lead a healthy, fulfilling life?"

"If you'd ever tried both at once, you'd know."

"Miles!" Fezzik said, unable to change the subject quickly enough. "What makes you feel lonely?"

Airports.

"Nothing."

"You want to see this girl on Thursday night," he continued. "Do you think she'll improve your life?"

"Um . . ." I had a flash of Gravity, sexily dripping at the car wash. "Yes."

"Why?"

"I don't know. I just . . . know."

I folded my arms. I suddenly felt very vulnerable, like Fezzik had a pickaxe and was mining straight to the center of my chest.

He did not let up.

"You've made a lot of progress over the last couple of days. You might be getting out of here sooner than any player ever has. Of course, you'll just be going home. Do you ever feel lonely there?"

I thought of the sound of Casey having a CrossFit in the living room. I thought of my dad's presence in all things, from the polished knives gleaming on the magnetic strip to the dustless blinds. I thought of my shoulders tensing every time my bedroom door opened. . . . And then I remembered my bedroom. My sanctuary. Stripped. For the first time, I realized that the Wight Knights wouldn't be waiting for me when I got home. Now that my computer was gone, they might not have a reason to talk to me ever again.

"Home's fine," I said, sniffing.

Meeki scoffed. "Yeah, 'cause you get to save imaginary princesses all day."

"You know," Fezzik said, stroking his chin, "you and Meeki remind me a lot of each other. It's like she's your Dark Link. Or, sorry, that's racist. You're each other's Dark Link. . . . Okay, okay, enough with the glares. You guys are going to set me on fire. Heh-heh."

Meeki and I were too appalled to even look at each other.

"Aurora!" Fezzik said. "You've opened up about many things these past few weeks. Your eating. The obsessions that hurt your fingers. But we haven't quite gotten to the root of it. And now you're almost a fourth tier."

Beneath her white hair, Aurora's eyes were closed, like she was astral projecting or something. "Can I talk about it in narwhal?"

"That sounds interesting," Fezzik said. "But no."

Aurora took a long moment, and then with a deep breath tucked her hair behind both ears in a single motion.

"I'm serving someone else's sentence," she said. "Max,

um, my boyfriend, loves playing *Arcadia*. He never wanted me to play with him because he didn't want his friends thinking he was a . . . pussy for playing with his girlfriend who sucks at games."

Fezzik didn't deduct points for her using the *p* word. He only listened.

I shifted in my seat. I'd said something similar to one of the Wight Knights about his girlfriend once.

Okay, I'd said the exact same thing.

"Max started ignoring me," Aurora said. "I'd come over to his house, and he wouldn't even look at me when I came into his room. Just say, 'Hey, babe.' Or 'In the middle of a game.' After a while he didn't even bother with those anymore." She picked at her fingers. "He was a lot different when we first went out. He bought me flowers and took me to dinner, and was happy with snuggling up with me all night, talking. I thought those days might come back. So I read fantasy books on his bed while he played games. And I waited."

For the first time in guild therapy, I was really paying attention. What the hell was Max's problem? Why would anyone want to play video games all day if they had a girlfriend? I would never do that.

"It got worse," Aurora said. Her hair slowly found its way back over her face. "One time I walked all the way to his house, but he didn't answer his door. I knew he could get distracted when he started playing, so I sat on his lawn and kept calling him and texting him."

Airports flashed through my head. I bent forward, holding my stomach.

"It was cold out," Aurora continued, "so I tried all his windows, and finally slipped in through the kitchen. I went into his room. . . . He didn't even look up. I asked if he'd gotten my calls, and he said no, even though his phone was sitting right next to his keyboard. He seemed really tense, so I went up to rub his shoulders, and his character just happened to die right then." Aurora pulled her right leg into her lap and held her foot. "He made a really mad sound and pushed back hard, and his chair rolled over my pinky toe. It hurt, but I tried not to show it. He said he was sorry and got me some ice and kissed my toe, but then said that it was kind of my fault for distracting him . . . and he went right back to playing."

She exhaled, making her hair briefly drift off her face. "So I got the game. I got on Max's server and made my own character. Anytime he didn't want to hang out with me in the real world, I played *Arcadia*. I just wanted to be with him. Even if it was only his avatar. Even if he didn't know it was me."

All eyes were fixed on Aurora. It dawned on me that everyone else in that circle had created an avatar to pretend they were someone different in a fantasy world, but Aurora had done it to pretend like she was a different person in the real world. What was she doing in V-hab?

"Max played a *lot* of *Arcadia*," she said. "So I played a lot of *Arcadia*. Hours and hours a day for months. My parents sent me here because they thought I was addicted to a game. But really, I was just addicted to Max."

We were all quiet for a bit. Then Fezzik started clapping. Meeki and Soup joined in, and I slowly followed. Aurora disappeared behind her hair.

"Thanks for sharing, Aurora," Fezzik said.

Aurora shook her head. "I feel bad about being here. Wasting my parents' money even though I'm not addicted to games."

"I don't think you're wasting it at all," Fezzik said.

He spent the next hour leading the group in a discussion about how women are misrepresented and mistreated in video games.

"I'll bet Scarecrow's a part of GamerGate," Meeki said.

I couldn't stop thinking about Aurora's story.

How could pretty girls feel lonely?

What was wrong with Max?

How could he be so stupid?

The woodpecker pecked for dinner.

"All right, adventurers," Fezzik said. "Thank you all for opening up"—he looked at Zxzord in the bunks—"or sleeping." We all laughed, as if Aurora's story had brought us together a little. "After dinner I want you all to take some personal time and think about what we've talked about until lights-out."

As we walked to the Feed, Soup let his head fall against my arm.

I waited a whole seven seconds before I knocked it back.

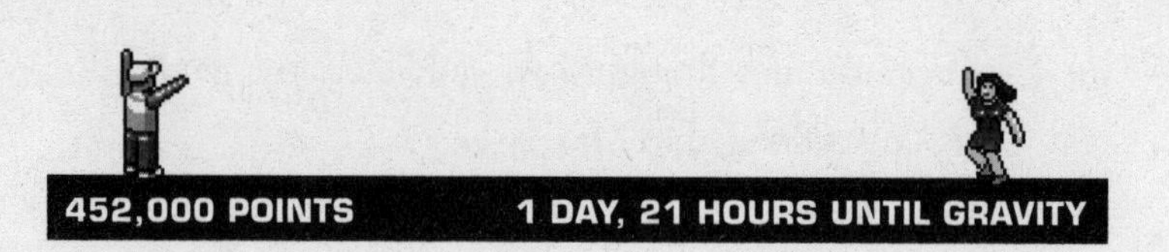

World Map

I was dreaming of rainbow racetracks looping through space, when someone shook my bed.

"Dammit, Soup," I said, eyes still closed.

"It's Fezzik."

I jerked upright. I expected the dunes in the window to blaze with morning light, but they reflected moonlight instead. It was ten p.m. I'd been asleep for thirty minutes.

"Congratulations, adventurer," Fezzik said. "You've unlocked star class."

"Really? Rad." I rubbed my eyes. "How many points is it worth?"

"Five thousand. But you should be more excited about what the Silver Lady has to teach you." He gave the bed another jostle. "C'mon. Aurora and Meeki already headed up."

Even though I felt exhausted right down to my bone marrow, I stumbled out of bed. Star class would bring my point gap down to three thousand.

In the corner of the Nest, Soup said, "*Hmph.*"

"Sorry, Soup," Fezzik said, opening the door. "This is the cost of purposefully losing points. You stay a first tier."

Soup grumped. Relieved, I waved good-bye and noticed he had a cross-stitch in his lap of what might have been a car wash. Sweet. It looked like the last 3,000 points might earn themselves.

Video Horizons was dark and green from the glowing exit lights. Our footsteps echoed down the corridor. Fezzik was not his usual jolly self. He was quiet. I assumed it was because of my performance with the Ping-Pong ball. If I was going to keep earning therapy points, I needed to get back in the guild leader's good graces.

I scuffed my feet along the concrete. "I've been thinking about what you said. About warriors and wizards and healers and all that stuff, and . . . you're right. I should work with my guild more."

"Everyone likes a well-balanced party," Fezzik said.

He seemed distracted, nervous even. He kept rubbing the back of his neck and clearing his throat. That was when I noticed he was clean shaven and wearing the most dapper attire one could find at a big 'n' tall store. I relaxed a little. Maybe his silence wasn't about me after all.

In the western corridor Fezzik took out a set of keys and opened a yellow door onto a staircase. As we climbed, I grew kinda excited. Not in a points way, but in an adventure sort of way. I'd completed the first level of a dungeon and was about to emerge onto . . . what? Something mysterious. Something new.

Fezzik's ass in my face kind of broke the spell.

At the top of the stairs, Fezzik opened another door, and a desert wind rushed over us. We stepped onto the roof.

As a gamer, I had gazed on breaktaking skies—*Skyrim* with its endless constellations, *WoW* with its smoldering horizons, *Halo* with its galactic ring. But I'd never seen the real sky look like this. Out in the desert, beyond the streetlamps, porch lights, headlights, and computer screens, the stars could throw their light all the way to Earth. Thousands glimmered in the crisp, dry air, and the sand dunes bowed before them, blue with reverence.

I realized that if I had someone to share the grandeur of the universe with, I could leave those video game skies behind.

A handful of players watched the stars through telescopes. I recognized a few Sefs and Meeki. And what night sky would be complete without the lunatic light of Aurora's white hair?

"No Master Cheefs?" I asked Fezzik.

"A couple of them tried jousting with the telescopes and were banned from the roof for a week."

"Perfect," I said.

The door creaked open, and the players hushed as the Silver Lady, the Sefiroths' guild leader, stepped onto the roof. She was so thin and her hair was so light, she resembled a ray of star shine herself.

Fezzik rushed over to hold open the door for her.

Ah. So that's how you keep the Emperor out of Arcadia.

The players sat on lawn chairs as the Silver Lady stepped onto a pedestal, the North Star shining above her.

"Good evening, stargazers," she said.

"Good evening," the players said.

It was so quiet, I could hear the wind carrying grains of sand across the desert.

"'Why does disorder increase in the same direction of time as that in which the universe expands?'"

I leaned forward in my lawn chair so I wouldn't miss a word. I imagined Gravity bathed in the warm glow of Mandrake's. She would set down her fork to stare and listen as I unraveled the mysteries of the universe.

"This is a quote from Stephen Hawking," the Silver Lady said. "It challenges us to wonder why as time moves forward, everything falls into chaos." She looked at the stars. "The objects of the universe are always moving away from each other. More and more quickly."

My excitement was overshadowed by a feeling of loneliness. But instead of the regular old loneliness I was used to, it was an expanding loneliness.

"Objects in space *must* move away from each other," the Silver Lady continued. "And they must do it more and more quickly. Otherwise, each object's gravitational pull would draw in the objects around it, and the universe would crunch back together in one big intergalactic crash."

I thought of the people who had moved away from me. My mom leaving when I was eight. Girls from my high school accidentally texting mean things as they fled. Being torn away from Gravity. Was this how the universe worked? Was

I doomed to sit in the middle of my existence and watch as everyone expanded away from me?

"Of course, there are objects in the night sky that try to reverse this process," the Silver Lady said. She turned her back to us and opened her hands to the sky. "Stars start their lives by expanding. They are an explosion, always pushing outward. But eventually, after billions of years, the star runs out of matter to burn, and it crunches up as easily as a soda can."

My head felt heavy so I rested my chin in my hands as I gazed up. I sympathized with the star. Being committed in a video game rehabilitation center due to uncontrollable forces didn't feel too different from being crushed by the nothingness of space.

The Silver Lady lifted her hands in a circle and began shrinking it. "The star's matter continues condensing and condensing, becoming heavier and heavier until the equivalent of *three hundred thousand Earths* fits into a space the size of this desert." She turned toward us, the circle between her hands no bigger than a pinprick. "The star becomes so heavy that it breaks through the fabric of the universe, falling out of time and space as we know it."

Falling through the world, I thought.

"Where does it go?" Parappa, the nerdcore kid, asked.

"Exactly," the Silver Lady said. "Where does it go?"

To video game rehab.

I felt so heavy and depressed, I thought I might break right through my lawn chair.

"All astronomers know is that the immense gravity of the

dead star begins greedily sucking in every object around it, trying to draw the universe back in." She looked at the sky again. "We know black holes are out there. But we can't see them. We can only hope to find their presence by the way light bends toward the blackness." She smiled at us. "Grab your telescopes, stargazers."

And so we spent the next fifteen minutes searching for nothing.

When I couldn't seem to find any black holes, just eyelashy blotches of light, I grew antsy and wondered if I was fighting hard enough against the crushing nothingness of Video Horizons. The surrounding desert seemed to grow vaster every day. What if I tried to walk back, but the dunes just kept popping up, endlessly rendering beyond the horizon?

I shifted my focus to the grounds nearer the facility. To the east was the Coliseum. Above it, I imagined a flag with an *M* for Miles: *Dungeon complete*.

But there were dungeons still to come.

To the north was an alien landscape of bizarre, blocky shapes, like a giant melting chess set. To the south was a stretch of compact sand with arching spray-painted lines and a lumpy blue tarp. And to the west was the parking lot with G-man's car, which, if I won, would drive me home, triumphant.

There was no possible way that the next two days could go as well as the first two.

"Stargazers?" the Silver Lady said. She passed out star charts and mini flashlights. "For each planet or star cluster you identify, I will award you five hundred points."

Yes, I thought, before remembering I never went outside and that every light in the sky looked the same to me.

"You may pair up with a partner," she said. "Four eyes are better than two."

The star chart looked like someone had sneezed white paint across a black piece of paper. If anyone wanted me to show them how to get the best ending in *Mass Effect*, I was their guy. But when it came to identifying stuff in the real sky, I needed help.

I scanned the faces in star class while Navi swirled to life around me, lighting my shoulders with fairy dust. *Didilingding-dingdingding*. She fluttered across the roof to . . . the spaciest person up there.

"Hey, Aurora."

"Hello, Miles Prower."

"You wanna be partners?"

"Partners in what?"

I pointed upward. "Finding stars."

"I like stars."

I smiled. "I thought you might."

I waved to Meeki, who narrowed her eyes at me and then teamed up with the nerdcore kid.

I laid the star map on the wide railing of the roof and squinted at it. "Okay, Aurora. You think you can spot everything on this chart?"

"Oh, I prefer stars' mythological names."

"What do you mean?"

"Do you want me to tell you your fortune?"

Oh God. I'd picked the wrong kind of spacey.

"I'm not bad at them," Aurora said, tucking her hair behind her ear.

"Listen," I said. "We need to work on this assignment. I need these points for—"

She ignored me and searched the stars. "I could tell you whether you'll get out of here in time for your date or not."

"Um, isn't astrology kind of"—I looked at the Silver Lady—"*anti*-astronomy?"

Aurora tilted her head toward the sky. "Objects on the edge of the solar system can influence Earth's orbit. The moon changes girls' periods. Isn't it possible that gigantic glittery objects in space can have *some* sort of effect? Even if it's in a billiard ball sort of way?"

"No," I said, remembering my physics class. "I have more gravitational pull on you than Saturn does."

Aurora bashfully pulled a strand of hair across her face. "You flatter yourself, Miles Prower."

"I wasn't trying to . . ." I sighed. "Fine." I crossed my arms. "Shock me."

Aurora bent over, lifted the hem of her long wool skirt, and pulled a smooshed dandelion puffball from her sock. I gave her a look like, *Where in the hell did you get a dandelion and how did it survive in your sock?* She didn't notice and held the puffball up against the night sky.

"The dandelion is the flower of the cosmos," she said.

"The yellow flower represents the sun, the white blossom the moon, and the scattered seeds the stars."

"Do they collapse and fall through the universe?" I asked sarcastically.

"Sorta." Aurora handed me the dandelion. "Hold this up so the blossom covers the moon. It works better if the moon's full, but this should do."

Why the hell not? I could use a good fortune right then. I closed one eye and lifted the dandelion so its sphere of white seeds nearly fit inside the moon's light.

"Blow," Aurora said.

I blew. The white seeds anticlimactically tumbled right over the roof's edge. Aurora looked upward, though, as if they were swirling among the stars. She stared into the sky so long, I swore I could see the Milky Way flow.

My knee started to jitter impatiently.

"Orion," she finally said.

I looked at the only constellation I knew—three stars in a glittery belt. "What does that mean?"

I wanted her to say, *You are going to get out of here Thursday night, right in the nick of time, having earned one million points by being a badass in all events—physical, mental, and emotional alike—proving to your dad and G-man and Casey and all the girls in your high school that you have more talent in the real world than they ever could have imagined, and then you're going to go on your date with Gravity, and you are going to charm the pants off her. Only, not at the restaurant. That part will happen later.*

"Orion is a warrior," Aurora said.

"That sounds good," I said, crossing my flabby arms.

"He slays beasts and has a huge ego." She pinched her finger and thumb together. "But then he gets killed by a tiny little scorpion."

"Oh."

"In another version he tries to win over this girl, but her dad blinds him."

"Ugh."

I hadn't even thought about Gravity's parents. Having one terrifying dad was enough.

"The story *I* like," Aurora said, "is the one where he's trying to catch these seven sisters, the Pleiades." She pointed to a cluster of stars to the right of Orion's belt. Then she traced a few inches left to a triangle of stars between the two constellations. "But the sisters are protected by the bull, Taurus. Orion believes he's a hero, going after these girls."

"Isn't he?" I asked.

Aurora shrugged. "He probably could have defeated the bull, but then there was the catasterism."

I winced and crossed my legs. "He gets castrated?"

"No. 'Catasterism' means the girls transformed into stars."

Why was everyone transforming into stars and expanding away from me?

"Orion will be chasing those sisters for the rest of eternity," Aurora said with a sigh, as if the idea brought her peace.

We fell silent. The star chart bent in the wind.

I don't know what made me say what I said next—Orion chasing something he could never catch, Aurora's trying to connect to a boyfriend who didn't care about her, the ever-expanding universe . . .

"My mom's an addict," I said.

Aurora looked at me, attentive as the moon. I stared at my shoes.

"She used to wake me up in the middle of the night and we'd play *Dr. Mario* until four, five in the morning. I didn't know why she couldn't sleep. I was just excited because I got to stay up all night playing games."

I scuffed my feet and remembered those late nights snuggling up by her side, flipping multicolored pills onto dancing viruses.

"My parents got divorced when I was eight, and I stayed with my dad," I said. "When I was nine, he flew me out to see her, but . . . she didn't show up to the airport. I waited with the flight attendant for ten hours, staring at strangers' faces, hoping each face would be hers. She never came." I got that burning sensation in my eyes and blinked it away. "When I got home, my dad told me why my mom acted the way she did. He told me horror stories about drugs and alcohol so that I would lead a more disciplined life like he had. And for a while it worked. I always studied, always read, always cleaned up my room. I never drank or smoked pot. I was afraid that whatever addiction had gotten my mom would get me too. So I played video games instead. Ha." I kicked at the gravel on the roof.

"I think that's why he sent me here. He doesn't want me to become like her."

"Do you want to become like her?" Aurora said.

I kept my eyes on my shoes. I was afraid if I looked up, I'd start crying. "My mom's the nicest person I know. In, like, a she's-my-best-buddy sort of way." I cleared my throat. "There was this feeling . . . when I was eight. I loved my mom so much, it hurt. And that's the feeling she left me with. It's never gone away. I've only seen her three times since. My dad is the one who decides when that happens. And even then, yeah, sometimes she's too messed up to show."

The stars wavered in unspilled tears. I felt like my insides were unspooling.

Aurora suddenly stomped on the roof between my legs. "Got it!"

I jumped. "Augh! What?"

She grew bashful. "I was pretending to step on a scorpion for you. Never mind. It was just pretend."

"You're weird," I said. I pinched my eyes and tried to lose that vulnerable feeling. "So." I cleared my throat again. "What does Orion mean for my future?"

Aurora stared at the roof for a beat. Then she threw her head back with a sniff and examined the night sky again, her eyes shining.

"You're going to be here for a very long time, Miles Prower."

I scratched my arm, annoyed. I had poured my heart out

to this girl; the least she could have done was give me a good fortune.

I tossed the empty dandelion stem off the roof. "I preferred the science where stars were being crushed to death."

I walked over to the Silver Lady.

"Do constellations count for points?" I asked.

The Silver Lady gave me a teacherly look. "Constellations aren't science."

"Yeah, I know." I looked at the sky. "Sucks that space is trying to extinguish all those beautiful stars."

"Actually," she said, following my gaze, "it isn't space that does it. Stars are crushed by their own gravity. They're fighting against themselves. Sorry if I wasn't clear."

Huh. Maybe I didn't sympathize with stars then.

I handed the Silver Lady my empty star chart. "We found zero."

I got my scroll stamped and was on my way downstairs when Fezzik "casually" ambled up to the Silver Lady and set his giant frame on the end of a lawn chair. The whole thing tipped forward, and he instinctively grabbed her arm, practically ripping it out of its socket.

Smooth move, Emperor.

Still, I wished him luck. Someone had to get something out of star class.

457,000 POINTS **1 DAY, 4 HOURS UNTIL GRAVITY**

3...2...1...

The next morning I was on fucking *fire*: 3,000 points for running laps; 1,000 for unsarcastically high-fiving G-man; 2,000 for helping Cooking Mama make a kick-ass parfait; 1,000 for squeegeeing the Feed tables; and 3,000 for complimenting everyone's shitty art pieces while I cleaned their paintbrushes.

If my dad wanted me to be nice and do chores at home, all he had to do was establish a point system that awarded a date with a beautiful girl at the end—not in a prostitution way.

In the Feed, Meeki and Aurora discussed something in low voices. Aurora wiped tears from her cheeks. I ignored them and ate my tuna salad while Soup drove a green bean around his lunch tray, pulling tight turns around "mashed potato mountain" and making jumps off "drumstick ramp."

"You gonna come in last place for me today, buddy?" I asked.

"So hard!" he said.

• • •

I stood on a dune overlooking Dry Dry Desert Track. It was shaped like a clamshell (or a kitten's paw print, according to Soup). Despite its adorable shape, racing on it seemed diabolical. From the starting line racers could gun it for a couple hundred feet, until they hit a sharp right turn, four wide wiggles, and finally another straight shot to the finish line.

My heart thumped in my throat. So much rode on this race. I *had* to walk away with the gold.

The sun beat down, making invisible snakes wave off the sand and cooking me in my black shirt. I waved my collar, getting some air onto my chest. At least in *Mario Kart* I never had to worry about sweat dripping into my eyeballs.

Something soft dabbed my forehead. Soup, topless, held out his shirt.

"You can use it as a bandana," he said.

"Yeah, no thanks."

We descended the dune and joined the other Fury Burds by the lumpy blue tarp. "The big Chocobo race!" Fezzik called, spraying Windex on the visors of our crash helmets. Soup grabbed a rag to help. Meeki cracked her knuckles. Aurora had one eye shut and was tracing the track with her finger.

The coach whistled, and the players gathered around the big blue lumpy tarp. He explained that each racer was to complete three laps around the track with minimal corner cutting. Then he yanked the tarp off six go-karts.

"Now *this* is kart racing!" Soup said. "Get it?" He poked

his finger into my side. "Miles? Did you get the *Star Wars* joke I just made?"

"I need you to stop talking immediately."

"Okay."

The karts' paint jobs had been sanded away, leaving the slight silhouette of the Happy Sun Summer Camp logo on the gray metal. That reminded me. The facility was still in beta. I would do whatever it took to win—switch tires, trade karts, even try to convince Soup to ride on the hood of my kart and spit gasoline into my carburetor.

Navi swirled to life around my shoulders. There had to be some way to take advantage of this.

"Players?" G-man clapped his hands. "Before you get out there and shred some rubber, I need to make a quick safety announcement." He placed his hands together as if pleading with us. "This is not *Gran Turismo*, okay? This is not *Mario Kart*. So no bumping into each other, and no throwing banana peels. Ha-ha."

No one laughed.

Behind his back, Scarecrow and I stared each other down. G-man had not said anything about *Twisted Metal*.

"I've put a bit of red tape on each of your speedometers," G-man said. "You are not to go above twenty-five miles per hour, or else you'll be disqualified. Is that understood?"

"Yes!" Soup said.

"I need to hear everyone say it," G-man said.

"Yes," we all said.

Ugh. Why didn't he just have us race sloths instead? Navi wilted and vanished. Maybe there wouldn't be a way to cheat.

"Don't look glum, guys," G-man said. "You get to ride in real go-karts! Not just steer one with a control paddle. This'll be a rush!" He gave us two thumbs-up. "I need to go do expense reports, but have fun!" He clapped again and then jogged back toward Video Horizons.

The coach cleared his throat. "Master Cheefs will get five seconds added to their final time, the Sefiroths will get minus five."

Great. The blue shell of Video Horizons. Now I had to worry about the Sefiroths, too.

"Thirteen racers will compete in three separate races," the coach said. "The gold, silver, and bronze medal winners will be determined by the fastest finish times. Here are your brackets."

He tossed his clipboard onto the ground, and the players crowded around it.

I was in the third bracket:

Dryad
Soup
Sir Arturius
Me
Lion

Thank God Soup was there. At least I wouldn't come in last.

"Dude," Lion said to Tin Man nearby. "I'm gonna be like that kid that ran over his dad after he took his copy of *Halo* away." He snarled out an engine sound as he drove an invisible car over an imaginary body. "B-dump, b-dump. Ha-ha . . . What are *you* lookin' at?"

I quickly looked away.

"Yay! Miles, we're racing together!" Soup said, tugging on my sleeve. "I'm going to name my kart Dr. Vroom. What are you gonna name yours?"

"I don't name karts."

The Gravitator, I thought.

The first kart engine grumbled to life. The low, dirty sound awakened something in me. At first I thought it was the cold metal of fear. But as it spread from my chest and became a tap in my feet, a clench in my fists, mercury sloshing through my head, I realized that it was slightly more than fear. It was determination.

I watched the first race from the sidelines as the karts buzzed around the curves like bees and growled down the straights like . . . jaguars, I guess. I mentally sized myself up against the racers. I wasn't as heavy as Tin Man, who hulked out of his kart and roared down the straight sections, but I definitely wasn't as lightweight as Aurora, who delicately buzzed around the heavier racers during the wiggling turns.

I was a middleweight: Just enough speed. Just enough dexterity. The Mario of *Mario Kart* . . . I hoped.

"You look nervous," Soup said, patting my shoulder. "Want

me to bump into other people with my kart to slow them down for you?"

"Yes," I said. "Yes, I do want you to do that."

He hesitated. "If I do . . . can we hang out when we get back home?"

"Uh."

His eyes were so needy and desperate. Then again, so was I.

"Deal," I said. "If you help me win, we can hang out."

Soup almost exploded with glee and squealed. "*Really*? I live at 2165 West Chesterton in Salt Lake City!"

I tried to hide my shock. That was literally six blocks away from my house.

"Oof, that's really far," I said, not wanting him to have any idea where I lived. "I'll, uh, come to you."

In the second race Aurora, Soup, and Fezzik cheered for Meeki as she cruised around the track. My eyes stayed fixed on Scarecrow, who remained in the lead, until Meeki caught up in the third lap, and at the last moment blindsided him so that they both spun out and came to a dead stop before the finish line. When they walked off the track, Meeki took off her helmet and asked him, "What happened? You crash into the Great Wall of China?"

Scarecrow spit onto the track. "Guess it's true what they say about Asian drivers."

"Go, Meeki!" Fezzik bellowed. "Whirlwind attack!"

The Silver Lady snorted and elbowed him in the side.

Fezzik blushed. "I mean, play nice!" he shouted.

I watched him set his giant hand on the Silver Lady's shoulder. She didn't move it.

Go, Emperor.

The coach whistled and then did some quick math on his clipboard. "After two races the current leaders are Parappa in third with a finish time of six minutes and two seconds and Tin Man in second with five minutes forty-six seconds. And finally, in first place is . . . *Devastator* with five minutes and forty-two seconds."

"I'm sorry!" Devastator said to Tin Man, who looked ready to crumple the kid with his bare hands.

"Bracket three!" the coach called. "You're up."

I clenched my teeth and headed toward the finish line. Five minutes and forty-two seconds. I could beat that. Probably. I walked past Lion, who was tying back his mane; past Soup, who gave me a pat on the butt; past Dryad, who pulled a helmet over her willowy hair; and I sank into the hot plastic bucket seat of my kart.

The Gravitator felt less like a car and more like the skeleton of a car. Scratch that. The carapace of a beetle. I rocked the steering wheel, loosely swiveling the front tires. The hood was pointed east, toward home. If I didn't make that first right turn, if I left the track and cruised across the desert, I might actually make it back to Salt Lake. That is, if I didn't run out of gas or get overtaken by Command's Oldsmobile.

I started the engine, and the kart vibrated to life, making

my man boobs jiggle worse than the boobs in *Dead or Alive: Xtreme Beach Volleyball*. I breathed in the intoxicating smell of gasoline and channeled my jiggling kinetic energy into the engine of my heart.

I put my lips up to the Gravitator's steering wheel. "This track is your bitch," I said. "Use it and then leave it behind."

"You're disgusting."

I turned and saw Dryad in the next kart over. I hadn't realized anyone could hear me.

"Really?" I said. "This from the girl who's dating the greasiest douche bag ever?"

She narrowed her eyes and pulled on her helmet.

The coach stepped to the starting line and raised the starter's pistol into the air.

"Three . . . two . . . one . . ."

He fired.

I stomped on the gas pedal.

The Gravitator's engine *roared*.

I puttered forward.

Dryad shot ahead. Lion's mane followed close behind. Even Sir Arturius sped past me like I was a rolling stone in a rushing river. Only Soup stayed behind the pack, reaching his hand back so he could drag me forward.

I ignored him and punched my kart's steering wheel. "*C'mon!*"

I lagged behind on the straight shot, the speedometer making a slow crawl toward twenty-five. I had to admit it was because I was fat. I was fat, and this proved it. I hadn't asked to be born like this. To have my mom's genes and to be one of the few who understood that Hot Pockets are the perfect food.

We hit the first turn, and I let off the acceleration. The needle bobbed around twenty-five. The other racers were two wiggles ahead. I had to beat Sir Arturius and Dryad by at least five seconds. *Screw this.* The coach was on the opposite side of the track. He was far enough away that he probably wouldn't be able to tell how fast we were going.

I pushed the pedal to the floor. I wiggled around the clam-shell, tires shrieking left then right then left again, and gained enough momentum to sail past Soup, who cheered me on, then Sir Arturius, whose antiquated insults were drowned out by my muffler.

As I approached Lion on the final wiggle, he heard my roaring engine and stomped his own gas pedal. Dryad heard his engine and did the same. We hit the final tight turn, and while Dryad's and Lion's karts skidded to the outside of the track on a thin layer of sand, my weight made the Gravitator's tires grip the asphalt, keeping me tight on the inside. I picked up speed, lunged past Lion, and thanked every Hot Pocket I'd ever eaten as I sped toward the front. The track straightened out again, and I watched myself speed past in the dark reflection of Dryad's visor.

YES.

I flew into the lead for the final stretch of the first lap, then put on the brakes. I passed the finish line at exactly twenty-five miles per hour, the coach's mirrored glasses unnervingly fixed on me. Fifty feet later, I hit the gas again.

The Gravitator hummed. The *Halo* soundtrack boomed through the air. I realized I was singing. *"Bumbumbum BUUUUUM! Bumbumbum BUUUUUUM!"*

I was Captain Falcon. I was Sonic the Hedgehog. I was . . . really fucking fast.

On the second round of wiggles, Dryad motored up into my blind spot. But beyond my extra weight and gripping, I had another advantage. I was pulled by Gravity. Dryad grew cautious around the turns. I ate them up. She put the pedal to the metal for the straight-stretch sections. I practically put my foot through the floor. I was more afraid of missing my date and being stuck in V-hab than I was of becoming roadkill.

I stayed in first for most of the second lap. But on the last stretch my engine coughed like it had been dropped down a disposal.

KKKKRRRRUUUKKK-KK-KK-KK-K.

My speedometer dipped to fifteen.

"*NO!*" I screamed above the horrific grinding. "GRAVITATOR, YOU WILL NOT DIE NOW! THE SECOND WE CROSS THAT FINISH LINE, YOU HAVE MY PERMISSION TO DIE! NOT ONE SECOND BEFORE!"

It listened. The Gravitator actually listened. She swallowed whatever was caught in her engine and bucked forward like a frisky mare.

"Ha-ha!" I patted the steering wheel. "Daddy's gonna buy you an oil cocktail. Anything you want, baby."

I had lost ground. Dryad pulled ahead of me, billowing sand that pinged against my helmet. On the final stretch we both slammed on our brakes. As we passed the finish line, the coach screamed, "Slow down!"

I let off the gas until halfway down the straight shot. Then I floored it again.

Final lap.

Soup had driven so slowly that we actually lapped him. He sped up when I passed and gave me a little wave. I pointed back at Dryad. "Get her!"

Soup drove right at her, forcing her to swerve and nearly lose control of her kart. I laughed maniacally. I didn't want her kart to blow up or anything. Maybe just get a popped tire or something.

I screeched around the first turn and wove with the wiggling curves. On the final wiggle Dryad appeared next to me, as if blossoming out of the desert. I cursed Soup's ineptitude. She swerved and weaved with my kart, perfectly aligning our wheels and inching me toward the inside of the track. Soup tried to accelerate between us to protect me, but Dryad boxed him out. I jerked the steering wheel left, knocking her kart's wheels with mine, but she skidded, recovered, and came right back at me. Our tires separated as we both screeched around the final curve and floored it.

Dryad and I were nose and nose for the last stretch. I

looked ahead to the coach. I needed Dryad to spin out in time for me to slow down to twenty-five miles per hour so as to not be disqualified. But before I could act, Dryad hit me with everything she had. My kart jerked right, but when I tried to recover and hit her back, she swerved left.

The Gravitator's tires slid like butter across the sandy track, rotating me so I was parallel with the fast-approaching finish line.

That was when Soup's kart T-boned me.

They say your life flashes before your eyes. They say you're supposed to be concerned about what you did or didn't do. Loved ones. Hated ones. Joyful moments. Regrets.

But my only thought was, *My face! Gravity!*

Then, *Maybe she thinks road rash is badass.*

My stomach lifted, the horizon flipped, and suddenly my head was vibrating and bucking. Sparks exploded in my vision. Metal screeched in my ears.

Then blackness.

I woke and heard feet running.

And then the horizon righted itself, while my head flopped back and forth. My helmet slid off.

"Miles? Are you okay? Miles! *Miles!*"

A thumb peeled open my eyelids one by one.

"He's conscious," the coach said. "Can you focus on me?"

I tried. Everything was a blur.

"How do you feel?" he asked.

I did a quick check. Head—fine. Neck—little sore. Shoulder—stinging, covered in blood.

The race came back to me.

I'd crashed. I'd lost.

I stumbled out of the kart and wobbled on my feet a bit. The people around me looked like they were underwater.

"Whoa, son," the coach said. "You need to sit back down."

I felt a hand on my arm. I blinked. Dryad.

"Oh my gosh, are you okay?" she said. "That is not what I meant to—"

I pushed her away and walked toward the finish line, where the rest of the players stood watching. The sand felt watery beneath my feet. My shoulder was really starting to burn, but my fury numbed me to it. Things grew clearer as I walked.

I found the skinniest player and shoved him.

"What the hell is your problem?" I asked Scarecrow.

He pressed his chest into mine and stared me down. I clenched my fists and fumed. The players formed a circle of shadows around us.

"Why are you mad at *him*?" Meeki asked me. "He wasn't even racing. Dryad's the one who hit you."

Scarecrow and I ignored her. We only focused on each other.

"I know you planned this," I said. "You had your *woman* come after me."

Scarecrow said nothing.

"You've hated me from the first day for no reason," I said.

He smiled, his nose close to mine.

A hand touched my non-bloodied shoulder. "Son," the coach said, "we need to get you to sick bay."

"Now isn't the time for this," Fezzik said, placing his hand between my and Scarecrow's chests. "We can have a meeting—"

"*No,*" I said, pulling away from the coach's hand and pressing against Fezzik's, so that my chest was touching Scarecrow's. "I want to know why you hate me so bad. I want to know why you sabotaged the race and made me—made me lose *everything.* Go ahead." I opened my arms to the crowd. "Tell everyone."

The players stood around us, listening.

Scarecrow's crooked grin flattened. He looked down and wiped his mouth. "You and I played *DotA* against each other one time."

Defense of the Ancients. A game the Wight Knights and I had been obsessed with for months.

"So?" I said.

"You—" Scarecrow said. "You told me to go fuck my sister."

Everyone gasped. I felt dizzy on my feet.

"That . . . I would never say that."

I would. In the heat of battle, I totally would.

Everyone stared at me with shocked expressions. I avoided Aurora's eyes.

"After it happened," Scarecrow said, "I looked up your gamer tag and found your face online."

I swallowed hard. "It was a moment of passion."

Scarecrow looked me full in the eye. "My sister has Down syndrome."

My face fell. All the Sefiroths and Cheefs and Meeki booed me.

"C'mon, Miles," Fezzik said, touching my good shoulder. "Let's get you to the Fairy Fountain."

He led me toward the facility. I glanced back just in time to see that crooked grin return to Scarecrow's face. That *asshole*.

"Fezzik, look!" I pointed. "He's smiling!"

Fezzik didn't look.

"I'll bet he doesn't even have a sister," I said, still looking back. "I'll bet I just crushed him in *DotA* one time and now he's just trying to get revenge."

"Did you say what he said you did?" Fezzik said.

"I . . ." I didn't answer.

"Don't worry. I'm not going to take away any points. If it happened before Video Horizons, then it's out of my jurisdiction. But I think it's important that you consider how your words affect others, even when you believe you're anonymous."

"Why?" I said. "What's the point if I just lost the race and won't make it out of here in time to get to my date and will just get rejected by every other girl I meet?"

Before he could respond, two scrawny arms wrapped around my waist and squeezed.

"Miles! Miles, Miles, Miles!" Soup said, jumping up and down and making my fat jiggle. "You did it!"

"Careful, Soup," Fezzik said. "He just had an accident."

"Did what?" I said, prying Soup off of me.

"You won!"

"I . . . did?" I turned around. My kart had rolled across

the finish line. And Dryad's . . . was still behind it. She had stopped to see if I was okay. My heart lifted. "Seriously?"

"Yep." Fezzik nodded. "You skidded across."

Soup rolled his hand through the air. "You were like *Psh krnch prk pow! Bang!* Ha-ha! I'm only laughing because you're okay, and I helped you win, so we get to hang out! Hee, hee, hee." He put a hand on my stomach and back and jiggled both. "Do you hate it when I do that?"

"I won?" I said.

Fezzik nodded. "Last I checked, you were gunning for best time."

It was as if some invisible force had pulled my kart across that finish line. The Gravitational pull was strong, and it was helping me win at everything.

My date was destiny.

I immediately headed back toward the coach to get my scroll stamped. Soup skipped alongside me and chanted, "I helped you wi-in! I pushed you acro-oss! Now you have to hang out with me when we get ho-ome!"

I couldn't argue with that. He had helped me win—in a really weird way. And I had promised that I would hang out with him. That didn't mean I had to look excited about it.

"Plus also?" Soup said as if he could sense my hesitation. He mimed sewing.

I quickly slapped his hands down before anyone could see. Then I smiled. I'd almost forgotten. The cross-stitches. They would close my 3,000-point gap.

I patted Soup's head. "I'll let you watch me play video games at your house."

"Yesssssss!"

As we approached the coach, Scarecrow stormed past us. Dryad followed him, saying, "I just wanted to see if he was okay!" She didn't even glance in my direction. Fine by me.

I held my scroll out to the coach. He didn't take it.

"You went above the speed limit," he said.

"Yep," I said, all smiles. "I also almost died." I rolled up my bloody shirtsleeve and showed him my road rash. I sucked through my teeth, even though it didn't hurt that bad. "I'd hate to have to sue this place."

The coach crossed his arms, making his nipples look angrier than usual. "You used that line before."

I stood firm. "I sure did."

It worked this time too.

718,000 POINTS | 1 DAY, 2 HOURS UNTIL GRAVITY

Achievements

"Looks like you could use some rest, adventurer," Fezzik said, back in the Nest.

"Oh, no, I'm fine." I rolled my shoulder, trying not to wince. "I really"—*need points*—"don't want to miss out on therapy."

Fezzik nodded. "I don't want you missing out either. Especially considering it might be your last one. Heh. Just promise to head over to the Fairy Fountain when we're finished."

I gave him a thumbs-up and joined the guild circle.

"No fair!" Soup said. "Why does Aurora get to sit so close to you?"

Aurora and I glanced at each other, found we were only a few inches apart, and then scooted in opposite directions.

Fezzik shut the blinds and turned on the fluorescents, making us all look sunburned and exhausted.

"Exciting Chocobo race today, everyone!" he said. "Especially for you, Miles. Nothing like a few battle scars to bring home, right?"

I rubbed my shoulder and smiled. I'd finally be able to share real scars with a real lady.

"That was the craziest!" Soup said. "Miles was driving, and he went like *rrrrrrrrrnnnnnn—rrrrrrttttttt—*"

"Fury Burds mayor?" Fezzik said. "We're going to talk about some pretty heavy things today. May I have your permission to do that?"

Soup placed his hands together between his knees. "Yes."

"Thank you." Fezzik opened to the guild. "Today I want to start by talking about the desire to be important."

Despite the pain in my shoulder, I was glowing. This could be my last guild therapy. If I participated in every activity, turned in Soup's cross-stitches, and won just one more gold, I was going to make it. I was going to fucking make it. I felt invincible.

There was only one problem. If and when I won the paintball tournament, I'd have about two hours to get back to Salt Lake. It had taken Command more than an hour to drive us to Video Horizons, which means I'd be cutting it close. I wondered if G-man would need to take me straight to Mandrake's or if I'd have enough time to run home to clean up a bit.

"We all want to have a place in the world," Fezzik said. "We want to be acknowledged with good grades, boyfriends, girlfriends, awards, scholarships, and all of the things that make us feel like successful human beings."

No time for a back and crack wax now. But I definitely needed a change of clothes. I'd look like an idiot if I changed back into the *Super Mario* shirt I'd been wearing at the car wash. And these white pants hadn't been flattering *before* spending four days in the desert. Now I looked like a toasted marshmallow that had been dropped in the sand.

"We *feel* important when we game," Fezzik continued. "We feel powerful. The problem is, the more you invest in those other worlds, the more you lose in the world we actually live in. Obviously, for everyone in this circle, the draw to other worlds is strong. It's easy to get swept up in a fantasy landscape with clear challenges, immersive environments, and an attractive avatar who gets updated graphics . . . unlike our real selves. Heh."

"Speak for yourself," Meeki said.

"Heh. Except you, of course, Meeki."

Maybe I could pick up some flowers on the way to the restaurant to draw attention away from the pants. Or maybe I could get a dandelion puffball from Aurora and show Gravity how it mimicked the universe.

"The point is," Fezzik said, "these worlds can make you leave the really important things behind. Health. Cleanliness. Emotional stability. When you've got games on the brain, everything else receives minimal attention. And who could blame you? This world we live in is punishing. You'll never be the best goalie or the best artist or the best student. That's not easy to swallow. Real life seems like it's designed to make you feel helpless. Games, however, are designed to make you feel like the most important thing in the universe. That's what makes it a psychological addiction."

I started when I realized Fezzik was staring at me. "That's why you're here," he said. Then he looked at Aurora. "To learn how to enjoy being good at real life." He looked at Meeki. "To find the power in doing the dishes and getting some exercise and being social." He looked at Soup. "To learn that the most uncomfortable things in life are often the most rewarding." He looked at Zxzord, passed out in his chair. "To learn how to enjoy yourself without harmful stimulation." He slapped his leg. "If you've got those in line, I say play all the video games you want. Just don't tell G-man I said so. Heh-heh."

This talk was unnecessary for me. I was kicking *ass* at real life. In the last few days, I had placed third in a sporting tournament, levitated a Ping-Pong ball, and taken gold in a kart race.

Fezzik rubbed his hands together. "Does anyone want to talk about the hurdles they've experienced when dealing with the real world?"

Aurora raised her hand.

"Aurora. Excellent."

"It seems like real-life hurdles are always moving," she said, playing with her hair. "You want to do something, like paint a wall. But then it's so much harder than you thought it would be. The paint isn't as pretty as it was on the swatch thingy, and the rollers keep sticking, and the ugly old green color keeps showing through, even after three whole coats. And then all of a sudden it's dark outside because you've been painting all day, and you get frustrated and you try to work faster and then you accidentally kick over a paint can and then you have a whole new hurdle, which is convincing your parents to buy you a new carpet."

"Sounds like you're speaking from experience," Fezzik said. "Heh-heh. After a debacle like that, it's no wonder we want to go play a game where the rules are as simple as THERE! DRAGON! KILL! Heh. Excellent, Aurora. Anyone else have frustrating real-world hurdles they've experienced?"

The road rash on my shoulder itched. I tried to scratch it as lightly as possible, but it just made it tickle, so I gave up.

"Miles?" Fezzik said. "You keep going the way you are, you just might be back in the real world tomorrow."

"Nooooooo," Soup said.

"Yes," I said.

Meeki scoffed.

"Bless you," I said.

She looked ready to kill me. "Why is it fair that he gets to leave this soon when he hasn't learned anything?"

I rolled my eyes.

"Care to elaborate, Meeki?" Fezzik said.

"Yeah, *some* of us are trying to grow as people so we can get back and see our friends and families."

"Uh, really?" I said. "Last I checked, you wouldn't even admit you hit your brother."

"Hmm," Meeki said. "Weird that *I'm* the one who won't admit that I hit someone."

That made me shut my mouth. Fortunately, Fezzik seemed distracted by a thought.

"It's true that life isn't fair sometimes," he said. "Most of the time, actually. Some people receive more privileges in life. They're able to pull ahead more quickly than others."

And some people are just naturally more talented, I thought.

"Maybe that's another reason video games are attractive," Fezzik said. "We all start from the same place when we pick up a control paddle. Games are the great equalizer."

Meeki nodded.

Again, Fezzik looked at me.

God, I just wanted out of there.

"Miles, let's say you are, in fact, released tomorrow. What do you think you've learned while you've been here?"

"Plenty of stuff," I said.

"Like what?"

"Um, like, that I'm not terrible at Four Square or kart racing or . . . cross-stitching."

"He's a *real* good cross-stitcher," Soup said. "The best."

I widened my eyes at him to convey that he was saying too much and to please shut up, but Fezzik just nodded. "I'm sure it's nice to find some innate skills in surprising areas, Miles. But I want you to dig even deeper."

"What do you mean?"

"During my training as an addictions counselor, I saw

plenty of people in treatment who set up unrealistic expectations for what would happen once they were released. They were always sorely disappointed. It's like taking on a raid that's seven levels too high but seems so enticing that you can't turn it down."

"Gravity is not seven levels too high for me," I said, hoping that was actually true.

"I'm not saying she is," Fezzik said. "But let's look at a worst-case scenario, shall we?"

I braced myself. I'd been living through worst-case scenarios my entire life.

"What if Gravity isn't interested in dating a gamer?" he asked.

I scratched at some of the sand baked into my pants. "That's fine. I don't think of myself as a gamer."

Meeki snorted. "You're a *player*."

"Very funny," I said. "You need to get girls to be a player."

"I didn't say you were a player who *wins*," she said.

"Okay, okay, heh-heh," Fezzik said. "This isn't about accusing. This is about opening up and understanding ourselves. Go ahead, Miles."

I was so ready to be done with this shit. "'Gamer' is an embarrassing term," I said. "It makes people think of sweaty, chubby, nerdy kids who sit in basements. Don't look at me like that, Meeki. That's not who I'll be to Gravity."

"That's fair," Fezzik said. "But you might be kidding yourself if you believe you're going to leave that lifestyle behind forever. What happens if this date with Gravity isn't everything you want it to be?"

"What do you mean?" I asked.

"What if you don't like her? What if she doesn't like you?"

Why couldn't he just let me win and enjoy it?

"We got along really well," I said.

"Yeah, but you've only seen her one time," he said. "And under pretty romantic conditions, it sounds like—you rescuing her from someone who sprayed her with a hose."

I shifted in my seat. Suddenly I didn't like Fezzik anymore. When had he suddenly become like Casey and my dad?

"That's the honeymoon stage," Fezzik continued. "That doesn't always last. In fact, it never lasts. What happens when the hard part comes along? The part that works like real life and nothing like a video game?"

I regretted bringing up Gravity in our first meeting. If he wasn't going to help me get out of V-hab and was just going to use her against me like this, what was the point?

Fezzik addressed the rest of the group. "If you think about it, video games only ever address the early parts of relationships, right? Rescuing the princess from the castle and whatnot."

What did he know about it? He'd been eating pizzas in a cave.

"This is why I never date princesses," Meeki said.

"Meeki," Fezzik said, "at the risk of sounding like I'm prying, may I ask what your romantic life is like?"

"You may," Meeki said.

"Great."

"And I will say it's none of your business."

"Okay. Heh-heh."

Meeki's shoulders sank a little. "Most people don't have to be embarrassed about who they date."

"What do you mean by that?" Fezzik asked.

"Some people are . . . just more privileged when it comes to their love life."

For the second time I agreed with her. That kid from my high school with the Mustang was with a different girl every time I saw him.

"So true," I said.

Meeki glared at me.

"What?" I said. "I'm agreeing with you."

"Guys," Fezzik said warningly, then waited for us to break eye contact. "No matter what difficulties you have in the dating world, everyone in this circle has made the same mistake. We've poured our attention into video games when it wasn't appreciated elsewhere. But I think we're doing ourselves a disservice by giving all of our love to something that can't reciprocate."

I wasn't doing that anymore. And this was boring. After my performance over the last three days, Fezzik should have excused me to go gargle ice cream in the Feed.

He didn't do that.

"Real relationships are tough," he continued. "Way

tougher than you ever think they're going to be. They require a lot of work from each person. I know I couldn't give the kind of care and commitment needed in a relationship if I were still logging sixty hours a week on games."

I did my best not to laugh. *Does care and commitment include almost ripping the Silver Lady's arm off?*

Aurora raised her hand but then struggled to speak. "I realized . . . that I don't have a relationship with Max that i-isn't on computers. And that makes me really sad."

Fezzik nodded. "It sounds like you were willing to make the effort in the real world. You never shied away from the challenges of the relationship. I can't even imagine how frustrating that was for you."

Aurora gave a slight nod and picked at the scabs on her fingers.

"It sounds like instead of holding him up to your standards," Fezzik said, "you reduced yourself to his."

"Yeah . . ." Aurora sucked through her teeth, and then put her finger in her mouth.

"So," Fezzik said. "What do you think needs to happen?"

"I think . . ." She took her finger out of her mouth and looked at it. "I think he needs to come here."

"Do you think his parents will ever send him?" Fezzik asked.

Aurora shook her head. She squeezed her fingertip. A little orb of blood swelled by her fingernail.

"So what does that mean for you?" Fezzik asked.

"I don't know yet."

"Well," Fezzik said, "you let us know when you find out. You've gained a lot of wisdom since you first walked through that door. I think you're going to leave here a new person." He gave his hearth-fire smile. "And speaking of leaving . . ."

Fezzik turned to me again. Ugh. Why did the Emperor have to be so relentless in real life? I pressed my scuffed-up shoulder, hoping the sting would distract me from his emotional pickaxe.

"Miles, what if you're no good at that next part of the relationship? The part where things get tough? Like they did for Aurora. For everyone."

I thought the last few days had made it pretty obvious that I was ready to do whatever it took to be with Gravity. I didn't need to prove it to Fezzik. So I didn't answer.

"Video games tend to end once the hero gets the girl," he said. "What if things are too hard with Gravity and you want to return to *Arcadia*?"

"I won't"—I thought of my computer desk, stripped of its electronics—"play games except on special occasions."

"Uh-huh, right," Meeki mumbled.

"Okay," I said. "I realize how that sounds. Like I'm addicted. But I'll only play a little on the side. Never as much as I used to. There was just nothing in real life worth returning to. Now there is. . . . And Gravity really liked me, by the way."

Fezzik took a deep breath and softened. "It probably feels like I'm attacking you, Miles. I'm not trying to. Really. I want to see you succeed. I also want to make sure you're equipped to handle things if it doesn't work out the way you've planned it."

I could feel the circle of stares on me. I could feel details of the car wash creeping back in. Details I did not want to think about right then. The fact that Gravity hadn't looked at me much while washing her Schwinn. The fact that she hadn't given me her phone number.

But then I remembered her laugh.

And I remembered I still needed to be earning points.

Fezzik wanted me to open up? I knew just how to do that.

I leaned on my knees and stared at the floor. "I've seen real addiction. My mom had—or, I guess, *has* a major problem with, um, drugs. She abandoned me when I was little. So it's never been easy for me to . . . be a part of real life."

I glanced at Fezzik to see how he was taking this.

"Your problems are all about girls and your mom," Meeki said. "Maybe for you 'V-hab' means vagina habitation."

Soup covered his ears.

"Let him finish, Meeki," Fezzik said.

I glanced at Aurora, then rubbed my face and tried to look as devastated as I had felt in the past. "If I could just date someone, maybe I'd get that confidence back. Then maybe I wouldn't want to play so many games." I took a deep breath. "My mom left me, but maybe Gravity won't. Y'know?"

Fezzik nodded. "That's some good opening up. You've been earning so many points this week, you might find out if that's true tomorrow."

He didn't reach for my scroll. God dammit. I just needed points.

Soup touched my leg. "But you're gonna miss sand castles! We could pretend like we're in Gerudo Desert! Or I can wear your awesome Home Depot hat and pretend like I'm Ash!"

"Nope," I said. "We can't. I will not be here. I will be gone."

"That's *if* we win tomorrow," Meeki said.

I stared her down. "You're not going to sabotage the paint-ball tournament like you did with the fan just to spite me, are you?"

She smiled and shrugged.

"Guys . . . ," Fezzik said.

Zxzord snorted loudly, making us all jump.

Fezzik spent the rest of therapy telling us about anti-escapist games, like *Chore Wars*, which help gamers transition back into the real world.

I watched his lips moving, but I couldn't stop thinking about winning the next day.

I didn't want to think about anything else.

After we returned from the Feed, Fezzik approached me with a stack of cross-stitches, flipping through them like they were some form of currency. From what I could see, every one had a reference to Gravity, except the one on top that said *Miles 'n' Soup*.

Dammit. I should have monitored his work.

"These have been showing up on my bed," Fezzik said.

"Yep," I said, trying to calm my pulse. I had to have those points to make it out the next day.

"They're yours?" he asked.

"Yep," I said.

He winced a little. "I haven't seen you cross-stitching."

"I have!" Soup said from his bunk. "I've seen him. He does it every night after lights-out!"

Fezzik and I gave Soup two very different expressions.

Fezzik sighed. "I see what's happening here." He turned to me. "Do you feel comfortable with this?"

I stared at the face of the friendly giant. If anyone understood rejection and the desperation to go on a date, it would be him.

"I don't know what you're talking about," I said.

He counted the cross-stitches. "This adds up to . . . Wow. Fifteen thousand points."

That I absolutely had to have. I unzipped my adventure pouch and held out my scroll. He didn't take it.

"I need to think about this," Fezzik said.

Shit.

"Um, okay," I said. "Thanks."

You're welcome, Soup mouthed behind him.

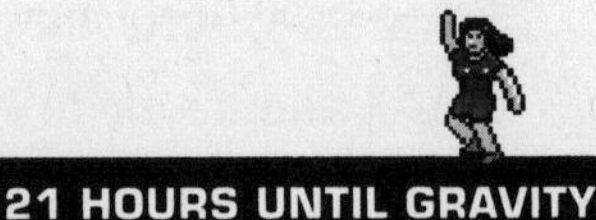

723,000 POINTS 21 HOURS UNTIL GRAVITY

Low Health

"P*sst.*"

I was in the Fairy Fountain, trying to recover from a throbbing head and burning shoulder when *someone* started *psst*-ing at me.

"*Psst.*"

My skin tingled with painkillers. I pretended to sleep.

"*Psst! Miles!*"

I would have strangled Soup if I had thought I could convince one of my other guildmates to cross-stitch for me.

"*Pssssssst!*"

"I'm about to get pretty *psst* myself, Soup," I said, eyes still closed.

"You're funny," he said.

I opened my eyes and squinted at the bright white walls of the sick bay. Zxzord was in the bed next to me, fast asleep. I wanted whatever he was having.

"I brought you a doughnut from the Feed," Soup said. "You can eat it without losing points, 'cause I'm the one who got it."

"Thanks." I took the doughnut and sank back into my pillow. "You're excused."

Soup folded his arms and planted himself in the chair next to my bed. "Wherever you go, I go. That's how sidekicks do."

What good was having Soup around if Fezzik wouldn't even accept his cross-stitches as mine? Although, I supposed he had helped me win the kart race. . . . I closed my eyes, breathed in deeply, and ate the doughnut.

Soup rhythmically kicked the side of my bed. "Miles? What do you miss the most? About back home?"

"Gravity."

"But you barely even *know* her."

"We made a connection. You weren't there, Soup. No one was."

Soup sighed and kept kicking. "I miss my pajamas. My mom made me a Tanooki suit from *Super Mario Bros.* with ears and a raccoon tail."

If he'd had a tail right then, I'd have dragged him back to the Nest by it.

The kicking stopped. Soup was quiet. I opened my eyes. His eyes were wide, and he had both hands over his mouth.

"What?" I said.

"Sorry."

"About what?"

"About talking about my mom."

"It's . . . fine," I said. "I realize other people have moms. It's fine."

Soup looked disappointed in himself. He stopped kicking the bed and just watched his feet swing back and forth beneath his chair. "Do you miss video games?"

"No," I lied.

"But then how come you played them so much? Are you going to stop playing video games forever after you go on your date with Gravity?"

I swallowed the last of the doughnut. "I'll slowly acclimate her to them. I'll play my 3DS in the bathroom at first. Then, when she and I have kids, I'll buy them a console and play it with them. And I'll be like, see? It's for our kids."

"That sounds sad," Soup said.

An owl hooted through the speaker.

"Being in a video game rehab is sad," I said, brushing crumbs from my chest.

"Nuh-uh!" Soup said. "I don't get why you talk about this place like it's a jail. I am *so* much happier here than I am anywhere else. There are friends *everywhere*."

"I'm going to be late for star class," I said, sitting up.

Soup moped. "I wish I could go to star class."

My head was swimming too much to stand.

"Do you need to use me as a crutch?" Soup asked.

"Yeah."

He helped me to my feet. I leaned on his shoulder, and we walked down the dark green hallway.

"You really haven't had any fun since you got here?" he asked.

I thought of throwing the ball at Scarecrow's "hit-me-here" red face. I thought of "magically" making a ball levitate. I thought of my man boobs vibrating while I creamed the others in kart racing.

"I do feel like more of a hero, I guess," I said. "And not in an *Arcadia* way."

"I know you're happy here," Soup said, and poked my cheek. "You get the dopiest smile every time you win. It's really cu— *Whoa*." He stopped walking. "What's *that*?"

There, in the corner of the hallway, was the vent I'd seen on my first night here. But the Dust Fairy was nowhere in sight. The grate was open, just a crack, revealing the green lights, winking one at a time, like they wanted us to follow them into the wall.

I made sure the coast was clear and then slid the grate out of the way while Soup whistled a hollow imitation of the secret music from *The Legend of Zelda*. "Shh," I said. "You're ruining my childhood."

We stared into an impossible space between the walls—almost as if an old hallway had been walled off. A dark passage led to the northeast corner of the building, where more lights pulsed like tiny stars.

"Side quest," Soup whispered.

The word tickled the back of my neck. This was some serious *Stanley Parable* shit.

Soup squealed and clapped his hands together. "What are we waiting for? Let's go!"

"You go first," I said. "I'll keep an eye out."

Soup slid through the grate, his eyes adventure wide. He giggled. "*Spooky.*"

I looked past his silhouette and saw more lights. What the hell was in there?

"*You coming?*" he whispered from the darkness.

Doing in real life what you do in video games can get you into serious trouble. And I don't just mean shooting prostitutes when not playing *Grand Theft Auto*. I was so close to beating V-hab. I needed to keep my nose down, do my classes, and not lose any points for the next twenty hours.

"Go see what's around that corner," I told him. "Then report back to me."

He kept walking, giggling and rubbing his hands together. Once he disappeared around the corner, I quietly replaced the grate, tightened the screws with my thumbnail to keep him out of my hair for the night, and then jogged to the western passage.

Nearly every ounce of me wanted to go on that side quest. I'd been competing for points all week, but nothing had felt nearly so video gamey as watching Soup slide in between the walls. I had to shut off the video game part of my brain and stay focused. I had to earn points in stupid star class.

For Gravity.

A faint "Miles?" echoed down the hallway as I opened the yellow door and ascended the stairs to the roof.

• • •

Something was different.

No eyes were fixed to telescopes. No necks craned toward the stars. The players of star class were gathered around Fezzik and the Silver Lady near the edge of the roof. She had one hand over her mouth. He was down on one knee.

"I've known I wanted to do this since the moment I heard you talk about pulsars," Fezzik said, then laughed too loud, and then wiped his forehead. He reached into his pocket and brought out a small cream-colored box.

The class stood, quieter and more reverent than they ever had for the universe.

"I've been trying to leave the old me behind," Fezzik said, short of breath. "And. Well. You make me feel like a new man. Heh. And so yeah, then I thought, uh, heh, this is where we met. Here. At Video Horizons. Among these kids . . . So. Heh. Why not?"

My heart started to pound as his huge hands fumbled with the tiny box.

Oh God, was this how I looked when I asked out Gravity?

Fezzik managed to get the box open. The diamond was too small to sparkle in the starlight.

"Sue," he said, "would you do me the honor of—"

"Dominic," the Silver Lady interrupted softly. She laid her small hand on his giant shoulder.

All the players held their breath. I felt a physical pain in my chest.

"Can we talk about this in private?" she said.

Fezzik froze. He swallowed loudly and wiped his forehead again. Then he turned and saw us, all of us, the whole class, staring at him, down on one knee. He made a Wookiee sound and awkwardly pushed himself up.

"Please go back to your bunks," the Silver Lady told us. "I'll see you all tomorrow night."

Their difference in size was painfully apparent as Fezzik followed the Silver Lady down the stairs. A part of me wanted to ask her for experience points before they left . . . but it probably wasn't the best time. I also wanted to ask him, *Do you think the Silver Lady could ever love a former gamer?* It probably wasn't the best time for that, either.

The last of the players filed down the stairs. The air smelled of Fezzik's cologne and sweat. Funny that the Emperor of *Arcadia* had tried to give us advice on how to return to the real world. What if I took his advice and stopped playing games just to become like him? Rejected and pathetic?

I was about to descend the stairs, when a voice stopped me.

"I broke three fingers once."

I peered around an air-conditioning unit and found Aurora, sitting on the roof's railing. Her hair was a white blur against the night sky.

"Um," I said. "Okay?"

"I was eleven," she said, eyes on the sky. "I was trying to get superpowers by sticking my hand inside a geode."

I snorted.

She made her hand into a claw like it was still crammed inside the geode. "My hand got stuck. So I got a hammer, and . . ." She raised her other hand in a fist.

"Ouch," I said.

She dropped both hands. "It hurt."

"I'll bet."

"The pain was like a carousel," she said. "Just going round and round. I could barely think. The doctor tried to give me oxycodone"—she shook her hair—"but I refused to take them. I said, 'Aurora, you should know better. Feel the pain so you won't be tempted to stick your hand into any more geodes.'"

"Uh . . . huh," I said. "Why are you telling me this?"

She peered around the air-conditioning unit to make sure no one was at the door. "I hope Fezzik doesn't go back to *Arcadia*, just to make his broken heart feel better."

"What does that have to do with pills?"

She intertwined her fingers in front of her. "I was thinking about what you said about your mom and *Dr. Mario*. I think video games are kind of like medicine."

I leaned against the air-conditioning unit and considered that. Games were the perfect way to get rid of stress. Crappy day at school? Chainsaw an alien in the face. Rejected by another girl? Burn your Sims in an apartment fire. Concerned that you'll be alone for the rest of your life? Stomp some monsters made of marshmallow.

"So just because something helps you forget your pain," I said, "you should stay away from it?"

Aurora kept her fingers twined and bounced them against her knees. "Maybe only when you're trying to recover from something big. Like getting your hand stuck in a geode or breaking up with someone." She crossed her feet, uncrossed them, and then crossed them again. "When your insides are like skinned knees and curdled milk, you gotta learn how to feel better all by your lonesome, without pills or games or anything like that, or else those bad feelings will just keep coming back."

I joined Aurora on the roof's edge. The stars shone on the dunes. Ever since my mom had left, that skinned-knee-and-curdled-milk feeling had rarely left me. Not unless I played video games.

Aurora cleared her throat. "That's why I'm not drinking horchata anymore. Or masturbating. Gotta feel that pain. Gotta get over it all by my lonesome."

My heart fluttered, and I chuckled. "You should tell Meeki that tactic."

Aurora folded her hands between her legs. "I've got enough to worry about for myself right now."

She stared into space. I stared at her.

The air-conditioning unit grumbled to life.

"Like what?" I asked.

Aurora tucked her hair behind her ears, and by the light of the moon, I saw her eyes for the first time. I mean I *really* saw them. She had two pupils in each eye.

I quickly looked away like I'd been caught staring.

"Coloboma," she said. "It's a condition where my pupils never fully formed."

I looked into her eyes again. Sure enough, her pupils were pinched, like the black holes of her eyes were slurping in either side of her irises. They were weird and scary and beautiful at the same time.

"They're pretty, Aurora."

At some point we'd gotten really close to each other on the railing. Our eyes stayed locked until she gave her head a little shake and looked back at the sky.

"We are all made of star stuff," she said. I was halfway through an eye roll when she finished, "But then again so are dog taints."

I laughed so hard I nearly choked on my own spit. Aurora blushed and smiled. I hadn't really seen her smile before.

Before my heart could make a dive, I pushed off the railing and brushed the roof's dust from my pants. "I think I'm over that kind of medicine," I said. "Video games. I'm ready to figure out the real world."

Aurora jumped up too. "Let's get you out of here, then."

I nodded at Orion, forever chasing those sisters. "I thought you said I was going to be here for a long, long time."

Aurora shrugged. "Let's prove me wrong. We can't have this many broken hearts in one place. Yours, mine, Fezzik's. The whole building might collapse. And then the walls will come crumbling down on our heads. And there will be a timer and we'll have to escape before we're crushed to death."

"Sounds fun," I said. I tried to catch her eyes again. "What's breaking your heart, Aurora?"

She just gave a half smile and shook her hair.

"Are you going to break up with Max?" I asked.

She looked at me with those strange eyes of hers but didn't answer.

"Let's get us both out of here, then," I said. "Tomorrow's the paintball tournament. Let's win the shit out of it."

I opened the roof door, breaking the spell of the evening with fluorescent light. We descended the stairs. Aurora twined her fingers in front of her skirt and walked with her eyes fixed on her feet.

A small ticking echoed down the hallway.

"Uh . . ." I touched her shoulder. "I'll, um, catch up with you."

She nodded and returned to the Nest while I jogged to the eastern hallway and found the heating vent.

"*Soup?*" I whispered.

The tiny green lights had all gone out. The space between the walls was silent.

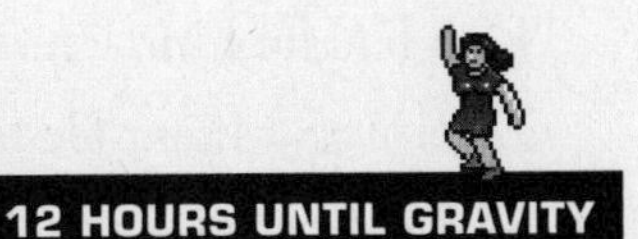

Side Quest

For the first time since being committed to V-hab, I woke before the rooster crowed. No speckled nose peeked over my bed. No nasally voice sang "*Mooooooming.*" I peered down and saw a half-finished cross-stitch that read *Gravity is soooo* sitting on the unruffled sheets of Soup's empty bunk.

I collapsed back onto my pillow. What had I done? I actually felt guilty now. Not just in an "I'm going to lose points" way. I lay there feeling very uncomfortable in my skin until the rooster crowed.

"Where's Soup?" Aurora asked, entering the Nest with her toothbrush.

"Who cares?" Meeki said, still wrapped up in her sheets.

I kept my eyes on the ceiling.

"I'm sure he'll turn up," Fezzik said. He didn't sound worried, just heartbroken. His giant shoulders didn't seem so giant anymore.

I felt bad for him. Until he approached my bed.

"Morning, Miles." He took a deep breath. I could tell I did not want to hear what he was about to say. "I've given it a lot of thought, and I've decided not to give you the points for those cross-stitches."

I jerked upright. "That's not fair."

"No," Fezzik said. "It wouldn't be fair to you if I *did* give you the points. It would be like giving level forty armor to a level five character."

I stared deep into his eyes. "Just because it didn't work out with the Silver Lady, doesn't mean you should take my chance at happiness away."

I could tell that hurt him. But he didn't back down. "I'm trying to do the opposite," he said. "I don't want you making the same desperate mistakes I did."

The speaker crackled above my bed, and G-man's voice came through. "All players to the Hub for an emergency meeting."

Fezzik turned away. My stomach twisted.

I followed the Fury Burds, minus Soup and Zxzord, to the Hub. Part of me was racked with guilt for talking to Fezzik that way, but most of me was trying to figure out how to make up for those missing points. . . . Wax the floors? Do every guild's laundry? Find the missing player I'd lost?

If I made it to my date, I'd make it up to everyone else.

Gray light seeped through the tall, frosted windows, giving the Hub an apocalyptic *Diablo* feeling. I sank into a beanbag chair and braced myself for G-man's announcement. I imagined this numbness was the feeling people got when they realized they'd forgotten to feed their pet for a few days. Or worse, opened an air-conditioning grate, tossed the pet between the walls, and then locked it inside.

G-man climbed onto the stage, clasped his hands together, and stared at us with those shiny, sincere eyes of his. The players sensed something serious was going down and got real quiet real quick.

"We have a Video Horizons first today," G-man said softly.

Oh God. First what? First missing kid? First victim of the thing that dwells between the walls? First splattery death?

G-man bowed his head. Then, lifting it and with increasing volume, he shouted, "Someone found our first *side quest*!"

A gasp ran through the crowd.

"Come on out here, Soup!"

Soup came in through the side door, looking sheepish, exhausted, and yes, even a little heroic. The knots in my stomach unwound as my head began to throb. What had I missed out on?

G-man threw an arm around Soup's shoulders and addressed the players. "We want to instill a sense of adventure in you guys. A sense of exploration. Sometimes the greatest rewards in life are off the beaten path. You have to break the rules a bit"—he raised his hand in caution—"while still respecting the space you're in."

Dorothy raised her hand. "What was the side quest?"

"That secret is reserved for the player who was sharp enough to discover it and daring enough to follow it to its end." *Damn.* "But don't worry. We'll have another side quest set up by next week." *Dammit.* "Although, I am *not* telling you guys to tear this building apart looking for the next one. It should be pretty obvious when you see it."

Dammit all to hell.

"So," he continued, "for the act of curiosity, for impeccable instincts, and for an adventurous spirit, I award you, Soup S. Soupington, *five hundred thousand points.*"

The air was sucked right out of the Hub. Before the Master Cheefs had a chance to boo, Aurora and Fezzik leapt to their feet and burst into applause. I felt the color seep out of me.

But if I felt miserable, it was nothing compared to how Soup looked. If I had been onstage, if instead of wasting my time at pointless star class, where I watched Fezzik make a fool of himself and received zero points for it, I'd actually gone on the side quest and won *500,000 fucking points*, I'd have acted like I was on *The Price Is Right* in the middle of Mardi Gras. I'd have ripped off my shirt and helicoptered it over my head while running around the Hub, screaming like an idiot.

Soup looked like his grandma had just been cut in two by a train.

"And these are *golden* points," G-man said. "Which means you cannot lose them, Soup, no matter what you do."

"You just made that up!" Lion called out.

"Yes, I did," G-man said. He jostled Soup's shoulder. "That officially makes you a third tier, buddy! You'll be out of here in no time."

That was when I understood. G-man wanted Soup out of V-hab. The kid had been point dodging for weeks, and now it was time for him to go home. The side quest had been real, but it was probably only worth 100,000 points at most. I say "only," but that would have made up for the cross-stitches. And a silver medal in today's tournament would have put me over the top.

Dammit.

"You have anything to say, Soup?" G-man said.

All heroism had leaked right out of Soup's pale little face. He searched the audience and found my eyes. "I couldn't have done it without Miles Prower." His face brightened. "Hey! He was the one who made me do it! He showed me where the entrance was and *everything*!" He looked up at G-man. "Can I give Miles my golden points?"

The Master Cheefs booed. The Sefiroths hissed. My heart lifted.

"Shh, none of that," G-man said. "No, Soup. You cannot give points away. Miles needs to earn his own way out."

Soup frowned at me apologetically.

G-man cleared his throat. "We've got our big paintball tournament this afternoon."

"YES!" Lion shouted.

The rest of the Hub whooped and clapped.

"*Normally*," G-man called over the noise, "I wouldn't condone any activity that encourages harming others, but it's what the board wants, so . . . I'd like to encourage the team-building element. That's why I'm going to give the surviving players a bonus twenty thousand points for every one of their guildmates still alive at the end of the final match."

Twenty thousand. I experienced pure elation . . . followed by pure fear. All was not lost. I could make it to Gravity. But only if I won the paintball tournament. And at least one of my guildmates wasn't totally incompetent and stayed alive.

"Okay, everyone," G-man said, "grab some breakfast and get to class."

Soup staggered offstage, arms dangling. He ignored Aurora's congratulations and collapsed into the beanbag next to me.

I patted his little shoulder. "That was a nice thing you did, Soup. Or *tried* to do."

He stuck out his bottom lip. "I guess—" he said in an unnervingly pouty voice. "I guess the thing that makes it better is that I know when we get back home, we get to hang out."

That was so sweet, I could've hanged myself.

"You wanna tell me about the side quest?"

That perked him up. "It was the most *awesome* thing *ever.*"

He told me about it. It wasn't that awesome.

I spent the rest of the morning trying to kill it in my classes while completing every bonus task I could along the way. Soup returned to the Nest to sleep off his adventure. This was good. My brain was freed up to concentrate on guns and shooting people with those guns.

For breakfast I scarfed down the greenest of greens and the fruitiest of fruits to remain spry. *+1,000.* I was still woozy from my crash, so I fought off invisible ninjas in tai chi until I was so exhausted, I thought I might lose the battle against absolutely nothing. *+2,000*. During music I imagined the Silver Lady's bongo playing as a war march. The rhythm made my heart beat *kill* and *kill* and *kill*. The ukuleles only slightly spoiled the effect. *+2,000*.

During lunch my leg was a jackhammer. I'd killed thousands in *Arcadia*. Now I just had to shoot a few real people with paint. I was violently stabbing up asparagus when I felt a sharp pinch on my love handle.

"Gah!"

"For improvement through pain," Aurora said.

"Thanks. Ouch." I rubbed my side. "Do we have to bleed to improve?"

Aurora shrugged and slurped up spaghetti.

"Greetings, adventurers," Fezzik said in a painfully morose voice.

His lunch tray was full of zero-point foods—mashed potatoes and french fries and ice cream. His obvious return to an old addiction made me uncomfortable.

"Today," he said between bites of fried chicken, "I want to talk to you guys about process addiction and intermittent reward. Process addiction is like grinding in *Final Fantasy* when you're already at max level. You just keep entering battle after battle because it feels so . . ." He trailed off and looked at us. "Is any of this getting through to you guys?"

"I don't know what 'inter-mitten' means," Soup said.

Fezzik sighed. He set down his chicken. "What games were you guys playing when Command and Conquer took you?"

Meeki grunted. "I was right freakin' in the middle of *Fire Emblem*."

"*Arcadia*," Aurora said.

"Game of love," I said.

Meeki rolled her eyes.

"*Arcadia*," I said.

"I was picking peaches for my raccoon friend," Soup said. "Conquer ripped the 3DS right out of my hands. It hurt my hands. And my feelings."

"Zxzord was probably in the middle of something else," Meeki said, and chuckled.

Fezzik stared at his food and nodded. "Great games."

We fell into silence. Over at the Sefs' table, I noticed that Dryad sat alone, occasionally touching her cheeks, while over at the Cheefs' table, Dorothy and Scarecrow sat too close and laughed together. I would have almost felt bad for Dryad if she hadn't almost murdered me on the racetrack and smashed my valuable egg.

The Silver Lady came into the Feed, sat next to Dryad, and consolingly patted her back.

Fezzik stood up abruptly. "Excuse me, guys." He left the Feed with his tray.

"He's never talked to us about video games before," Aurora said, watching him go. "Only as references for surviving real life."

"What's wrong with him?" Soup asked.

"He proposed to the Silver Lady last night, and she totally rejected him," Meeki said, eating a mouthful of mashed potatoes. "Dude should have realized he didn't stand a chance."

I agreed with Meeki but refused to acknowledge it.

"So now what?" I asked. "Fezzik's just going to go right back to video games like he told all of us not to do? Isn't he supposed to be our healer?"

Aurora gazed toward the door. "What if giant heartbreak is more painful than a regular-size one?"

No one answered.

"I should go talk to him," Aurora said.

She left the Feed.

"I gotta get to class," I said, and slid my tray toward Soup. "Thanks, buddy."

Fezzik's story was tragic and everything, but there was nothing I could do about it. Besides, Meeki was right. A dude that big should have known he didn't stand a chance.

I jogged to gardening. I had triggers on the fingers. I had bullets on the brain. I had blood in my . . . blood. I asked the Silver Lady if I could water, set the nozzle to jet stream, and scored head shots on the tomatoes, imagining each as a red helmet on a *Halo* map.

The funny thing was, at least for that day, I wanted Fezzik and my dad to be right about violence in video games. I wanted first-person shooters to have turned me into a cold-blooded murderer . . . with paint.

After I knocked a couple of tomatoes loose, their guts splattering across the soil, the Silver Lady quietly took away the nozzle and led me to an area to pull weeds for the rest of class.

Those weeds never knew what hit 'em.

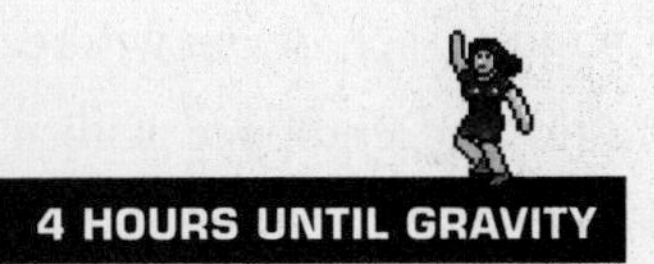

PvP

The sun was a bright blur behind the clouds. The wind blew white off the dunes. Sand whipped our clothes and stung our eyes as the Fury Burds trudged north. Black shapes rose up before us. The giant, melting chess set I'd seen from Video Horizons's roof was actually dozens of black bunkers, towering inflatables that would serve as our battleground.

"The Wasteland," Soup whispered.

All I had to do was be perfect one last time. I might as well have actually been going to war, my heart was hammering so hard.

The three guilds gathered in the shadow of a bunker monolith. The players hummed with excitement. Even Zxzord had dragged his undead ass out of bed at the prospect of shooting someone.

The coach held up a paintball gun and called over the

wind, "Each of you will receive a gun powered by a CO_2 canister and equipped with a hopper—that's this container on top—that has a two-hundred-paintball capacity."

"*Ahem.*" G-man loudly cleared his throat.

"Right," the coach said. "I'm supposed to warn you not to lift up each other's masks—that's your helmet—and shoot each other in the face. Got it?"

"No problem, boss!" Lion said. He licked his lips and rubbed his hands together. Why was G-man giving them these ideas?

While the coach showed us how to load the hopper, I overheard Meeki whisper to Aurora, "*He's got three compressed air guns he's gonna give the Sefiroths since they have the fewest points.*"

"*Is compressed air better?*" I whispered.

Meeki scowled at me.

"Is compressed air better?" Aurora asked for me.

"Those guns can fire twelve paintballs a *second*," Meeki said.

"How?" Aurora asked, seeing my eyes widen.

Meeki curled her middle and index finger around an invisible trigger and rapidly double tapped the air. "It's like being attacked by a swarm of neon bees. You might be able to avoid one, but . . ."

"*Meeki,*" I whispered, "*are you a badass at paintball?*"

She ignored me but told Aurora, "My parents wanted me to let out some aggression, so they let me play every weekend." She looked at her own chest, which seemed to be . . . flatter than before. "Taped my boobs down this morning."

"Round robin," the coach called. "Every guild will fight the other two guilds, and then the two most successful teams will compete in one final battle for the gold. However, you must survive the game in order to earn points. Like G-man said this morning, for every survivor on your team, you'll be granted a bonus twenty thousand. Understood?"

Soup raised his hand. "Do we have to pla—"

I pulled his hand down before he could finish. "Soup, we need as many players as we can get."

"I don't wanna get shot," he said.

"That's easy," I said. "Play perfectly."

The coach handed out masks and protective vests. The Cheefs looked like their bodies had been genetically altered to fill their red armor. The Sefs, in green, looked like a ragtag team of new recruits. The Burds . . . looked like children in purple Halloween costumes.

The coach handed out guns with paintballs to match our armor. I held my gun to my lips. "Make 'em bleed purple."

Fezzik summoned the Burds into a circle. His armpits were two swamps of sweat.

"All right, adventurers," he said, shoulders still deflated. "The big raid. Heh. . . . Here we go." He was doing a terrible job of hiding his heartbreak. "I want you to remember that this isn't about killing each other. It's about self-respect and honoring your guild. It's about helping each other get back into the real world. So . . . get out there, and . . . do a heck of a job."

G-man summoned the guild leaders to discuss rules. Fezzik lumbered away, without having made a single *Final Fantasy* reference. The Fury Burds were left looking less inspired and more depressed.

"Okay, forget that whole speech," I said, leaping up and addressing my guild. "This *is* about killing each other."

For the first time ever, Meeki smiled at my words. Soup hugged himself.

This would be just like pumping up the Wight Knights before a raid, only I wasn't really friends with these people, and if they didn't perform, I'd miss the most important event of my life so far.

"So," I said, "um, when I first got here, I thought you were a bunch of lazy video game geeks." I hadn't actually prepared an inspirational speech, so I had to make it up as I went. "But you want to know what I see now? *Murdering* machines." I sized up my guild. "Zxzord," I said, catching his sunken eyes. "Our undead electric warlock. Clearly, you're the most hard-core among us. How do you feel?"

"Like complete shit."

"Well, then, let's get you out of here and into a proper rehab. Soup . . ." He nestled his little butt into the sand, preparing to be showered with compliments. This was the first time I'd need him to actually perform instead of throwing the game or just obeying my every command. I needed to boost him up with a compliment. "You are . . . the only player in Video Horizons who found a side quest—with my help—and you're superdedicated to your guild. That's why I'm asking you to act as my personal human shield."

"I . . ." He gulped. "It would be an honor."

Now for the person who hated my guts. If Meeki was going to help me win, I would have to find the pathway to her heart. And fast.

"Meeki." She didn't look at me, of course. "I'm sorry I let our egg baby die. It had your grim determination. Well, the Asian half of it did, anyway. Let's win this for the Abomination."

"And Muffin!" Soup said.

"Sure," I said.

Meeki still refused to look at me.

"Also," I said. "Scarecrow is a douche bag. Take revenge on his ass."

"Don't tell me what to do," she said, but then she cocked her gun.

Good enough.

"Finally, Aurora . . ."

The coach blew his whistle. "Guilds to their positions!"

"Um, never mind," I said. "Let's get 'em, guys."

Aurora pinched and twisted the back of my knee.

"GAH!" I rubbed the sore spot. "Right. Pain for healing. Thanks, Aurora."

Fezzik led us to our position, north of the Wasteland. The sand swirled. The sun beat down. The Fury Burds flapped our arms to air out our armpits. We were as ready as we were going to get.

"First up," the coach called. "Burds versus Sefs!"

The coach raised the starter's pistol and fired. The Fury Burds crept into the Wasteland. Bunkers rose up around us like a black stone forest on Mars. I breathed the scalded air.

The Burds dodged and weaved around those alien bunkers, slaying every Sefiroth in sight. Forget their compressed air guns. They had no clue how to use them. I never thought I'd be so grateful for the sizes and shapes of my guildmates. Zxzord lay in the bunker shadows, as skinny as a sliver of darkness. Sir Arturius saw nothing but bunker until purple paint was suddenly dribbling down his visor. Aurora was small and spry . . . and a *terrible* shot. But she missed Parappa only to have the paintball ricochet off the pudgy side of an air bunker and then hit Parappa in the leg.

Then there was Meeki. Meeki the Destroyer. Meeki the painter of deserts. Meeki, the player who waited until Devastator was within two feet before shooting, because she wanted him to "taste it." His sobs echoed across the Wasteland. At that moment there was no doubt in my mind that Meeki had hit her brother with that Wiimote, and I couldn't have been happier about it.

Meanwhile, Soup and I were a two-headed beast, backs together and protected, prowling the alien desertscape. I could feel sweat pooling in my ass crack where he was pressed. For once I didn't shove him away. No one could sneak up on us. They would die if they tried. That was, until a green paintball whizzed three inches from my shoulder and exploded on Soup's throat.

Even though he was sobbing, he managed a grin at having sacrificed himself for me.

The remaining Fury Burds met in the center of the Wasteland and tallied our kills while the sun singed my wounded shoulder.

"Who have *you* killed, fearless leader?" Meeki asked me.

"No one yet," I said, trying to sound like a badass. "But Dryad's still out there. I think she killed Soup, so yeah . . . let's get her."

We all headed in separate directions to hunt Dryad down.

Shield gone, back exposed, I shivered in the desert air. I tried to keep an eye in every direction, but it was impossible. Sweat fogged my visor. I could feel my heart beat in my mask. I was backing up to what I was certain was the wide empty wall of a bunker, when I felt the cold barrel of a gun press into my neck.

Shit.

I turned around slowly.

Dryad put her gun in my face. She did not look victorious. There was a sadness in her eyes.

I slowly raised my hands. "It would be really stupid of you to shoot me," I said.

"Why's that?"

"Because you guys won't win." I took a deep breath and a huge chance. "If you really want to hurt Scarecrow, then you have to let me win."

Dryad narrowed her eyes.

"Think about it," I said. "All of your guildmates are dead.

The Sefs aren't good enough to win in the end. The Fury Burds are. Scarecrow would hate that."

Her eyes remained narrow. I watched her trigger finger tense, and I winced.

"Make him regret it," she said.

I opened my eyes. "I will."

Dryad dropped her gun.

"This is for Muffin," I said. And I shot her in the face . . . plate.

"Next up," the coach called. "Cheefs versus Burds!"

We got our asses handed to us. The Cheefs were everywhere at once—Lion prowling through the bunkers, Scarecrow slipping around corners, Tin Man stomping toward us like a freight train, and Dorothy, the invisible executioner.

Ten minutes after it had begun, the Burds stumbled out of the Wasteland, red-spattered, out of breath, and soaked with sweat. Fezzik had no words of encouragement. He just sat in a shadow and stared off to the horizon.

Thanks a lot, dude.

We peeled off our sweaty armor and used rags to mop off the red paint. It hurt Soup's bruised little throat to talk, so he quietly karate chopped my shoulders. Aurora sat next to me.

"If we win," she said, "what are you going to talk about on your date? Will you tell her you've been in video game rehab?"

I scrubbed the red off of my vest where Scarecrow had shot me. "Maybe I'll tell her I was in a real rehab, so she thinks I'm a badass."

Aurora gave a half grin and glanced at Zxzord, who was rubbing suntan lotion onto his tattoos.

"Or maybe you could just tell her the truth," she said.

"Ha," I said. "How are you going to break up with Max?"

She scratched some red off her mask's visor. "I think maybe I'll do it in *Arcadia*. I'll approach him with my Neon Elf, reveal my true identity, and then break up with him in front of his guild. Let him and everyone else know that the badass he's been adventuring with is actually his girlfriend." She blew paint shavings off her helmet. "But that would require playing more, so I don't know."

"Your true identity, huh?" I said. I stuck out my hand. "I'm Jaxon."

Aurora looked surprised for a second. Then she shook my hand. "Jasmine."

"Huh. Both *J*s."

"Yep," she said.

I noticed she hadn't shaken her hair into her face once that day.

"Let's win this thing," I said, "so I can tell the truth to Gravity and you can break up with Max in style."

Aurora smiled and nodded.

We had barely finished cleaning our armor when the Sefs limped out of the Wasteland, covered in red.

The whistle screeched. "Final round! Fury Burds versus Master Cheefs!"

My stomach filled with butterflies. Butterflies with razor-sharp wings.

"This is it, guys," I said to my guild. "We got this?"

"Got this!" Soup croaked, holding his bruised throat.

"I'll try to convince the wind to favor our paintballs," Aurora said, pouring little mounds of sand in a circle around her.

"Um . . . that would be awesome," I said.

I meant it. That *would* be awesome.

"Zxzord?" I said.

He didn't respond, just lay flat, arms crossed over his face.

"Okay. . . . Um, Meeki?" I said.

Meeki held up her gun. "The Meeki shall inherit the earth."

"Excellent," I said.

"But not for you."

"Still fine," I said. "Everyone, *stay alive*."

I slid on my mask and tried my best not to admit we were probably completely screwed.

The coach blew his whistle.

We stepped into the Wasteland.

A shot rang out.

Again the coach blew his whistle. "Dead Burd!"

Purple paint dribbled down the side of Zxzord's mask. He had shot himself in the head.

"What the *hell* are you doing?" I asked him.

He pulled off his mask and threw it. "I'll be in the bathroom."

"We all know you're faking," I said.

"We're all faking," Zxzord called over his shoulder, and then ambled back toward Video Horizons.

"*Seriously?*" I said. This was the biggest betrayal I'd seen since Leeroy Jenkins.

"Rrg!" Meeki stormed over to the coach. She was arguing that we should get Parappa, the nerdcore kid, on our team because our player committed suicide . . . when red exploded out of the back of her neck.

Again the coach whistled. "Dead Burd!"

"Move, *move*!" I shouted, dragging Soup into the arena by his arm. Aurora ran in the opposite direction.

Soup and I fled deep into the Wasteland and hid behind a long, squat bunker. I peeked over the top and saw the coach point Meeki out of the arena.

Shit. This wasn't fair. We'd lost two players in less than a minute because one of our players was possibly faking heroin withdrawals. I wanted to rage quit the whole game right then. I couldn't.

Sand stung our faces. Gunshots cracked through the dry air. The sand sizzled my ass, and the air smelled like melting bunker plastic. We were in bullet hell.

"*What do we do?*" Soup whispered, terrified.

"I have no idea," I said.

"If we lose," Soup said, "at least we can build sand castles together tomorrow."

"No," I said. "I will not admit defeat."

Another shot. No whistle.

"Okay, here's what we're going to do," I said, before I knew what to say. I searched the Wasteland and pointed to a bunker that towered above the others. "I'm going to boost you up on top of that."

Soup looked worried. "I'm scared of heights."

"Well, then it's a good thing that you're a weaponized *animal* who doesn't know the meaning of heights, isn't it?"

Soup didn't look so sure.

"Come on," I said. "I'll toss you up there like a Pikmin."

He followed me into the shadow of the bunker. I cradled my hands, Soup stepped onto them, and I hefted him up. The bunker wobbled, threatening to tip over. Soup whimpered. But then it stabilized, forming a nice cozy cleft with him tucked inside. He peeked his nose over the edge to look down at me.

"*For every Cheef you kill,*" I whispered, "*I'll spend a whole . . .* afternoon *with you back home.*"

Soup nodded. "I trust you, Miles."

I crept off to find Aurora. A shot rang out behind me, followed by Soup's giddy laughter.

"Miles!" he cried across the Wasteland. "I got one!"

"Well, don't give away your position, idiot," I mumbled to myself. But I was smiling.

The coach whistled. "Dead Cheef!"

Lion walked out of the Wasteland, shoulder splattered in purple, looking like he was about to cry. Three Burds versus three Cheefs. Still terrible odds. Hopefully the remaining Cheefs would follow Soup's voice and not think to look up.

I crept to the west side of the Wasteland, keeping my back to the bunkers, and blinking *maybe* once a minute. Every gust of wind, every ping of sand hitting my visor was a potential end of the world. I passed a droopy bunker with the ghost of the Happy Sun Summer Camp logo on it. It was deflating, softly whistling out air.

I found Aurora crouched beside a wide bunker. Holding a finger to my lips, I gestured her to follow me to the deflated bunker, where I knelt and lifted the vinyl. The bunker's base strained against the ropes that anchored it to the sand, but a small cave formed underneath. Aurora nodded and elbow-crawled inside. I laid it down so she was nothing more than a gun barrel sticking out of a black cave.

"Can you breathe in there?" I asked.

The barrel nodded.

This was it. From here we'd wait them out. The Master Cheefs may have had stealth. They may have had talent. They may have had dexterity. But the Fury Burds had scrawny and skinny kids who could fit under and on top of things.

I headed north.

A shot rang out from the west. No whistle.

"*Come on, Aurora,*" I whispered to the wind. "*Aim.*"

The game stretched on. Scarecrow, Dorothy, and Tin Man couldn't find us, and I, for the life of me, couldn't track any of them. Then they found Soup, who couldn't stop giggling because he'd shot someone. His giggling definitely stopped when the Cheefs surrounded him. Tin Man boosted Dorothy up onto his shoulders, and she shot Soup in the stomach—at the exact same time he shot her.

"I'm sorry, Miles!" Soup sobbed as he exited the Wasteland.

"That'll do, pig," I said quietly. "That'll do."

I mentally leapt around the Wasteland like on a map in a MOBA game. With Aurora hopelessly pinned under the monolith, it was me versus Tin Man and Scarecrow. I had to survive. My love life depended on it.

Gravity. Mandrake's. Tonight.

The thought eased my chattering teeth.

I couldn't fit under any of the bunkers. I'd pop one if I tried to climb on top. I had no choice but to hunt.

I stalked the Wasteland. The Cheefs must've realized we had another trick up our sleeve, that an invisible assassin was taking shots at them, because nothing stirred in the west of the arena save the shifting sand. I headed north.

It goes without saying, but a real fight was a hell of a lot more complicated than video games. I couldn't go inviz or see little red dots on my radar or watch for vision cones coming out of the bad guys' eyeballs. Without a map or X-ray vision or a third-person bird's-eye view, I had to find a new way of tracking my enemy.

Ever since being unplugged, with no headphones filling my ears with explosions and lasers and chipmunks, the world had offered up its subtler sounds—the ticking of Command's Oldsmobile, the buzz of V-hab's fluorescents, the tick of the Nest's bird clock . . .

Tin Man was big. *And* he liked crushing vermin. I closed

my eyes and cupped my ears. The wind howled through the channels of the bunkers. To the east players chatted. To the west a crow cawed. Then, to the south . . .

Krsh, krsh, krsh.

I opened my eyes and crept toward the footsteps. Tin Man tromped through the sand, eyes ablaze. His skin was red. He breathed like an angry bull.

I raised my gun.

"Miles!" a voice screamed. "Behind you!"

I dropped and twisted just as Scarecrow lifted his gun. I shot him twice, purple blossoming from his chest. I felt the splat on the back of my mask from Tin Man's direction a split second before Aurora shot him in the leg.

It was over.

I lay on the hot sand, squinting at the sun, piecing together what had just happened. I wasn't ready to admit what the splat on the back of my mask meant.

"Thanks a lot, *bitch*," Scarecrow said to Aurora, before unloading his gun point-blank into her chest.

She collapsed in the sand. I jumped up to go after him, but Tin Man stepped in front of me. His fists weren't bigger than my head, but they definitely looked that way.

Scarecrow sauntered away. Tin Man slouched after him.

"Dicks!" I called after them. I stood over Aurora. "You okay?"

She groaned and clutched her stomach, red oozing between her fingers.

"*Aurora?*" I dropped to my knees. "Are you really bleeding?"

Aurora pulled off her mask and coughed into her hand, spraying droplets of red. "I'm . . . I'm just . . ." She winced in pain. "A really good . . . *actress*."

I lifted her into my lap and dramatically shook her shoulders. "You're going to make it."

"No—*koff*—I'm not." She blinked her strange eyes, fake-trying to focus on mine. "I have one . . . dying . . . wish."

"What's that?" I asked.

"Tell me . . . the compliments you owe me."

That's right. I'd complimented every Fury Burd except her before the coach had started the game.

"Let's see," I said. "You have fascinating eyes. You make stupid things like dandelions super-interesting. And you don't look too bad while you're dying—or *pretending* to die. You'll probably make a striking old lady."

"I already am a striking old lady."

Aurora died theatrically in my arms. Sand grains fluttered in her eyelashes. A moment later she came back to life and wiped some red off her cheek onto my pants.

"You didn't win," she said.

My brain finally acknowledged the wet plaff against the back of my mask. I was dead. I wouldn't get the points. The numbness released from my rib cage and spread to my arms and legs. *Gravity*. God dammit. God fucking dammit. My eyes grew hot. I sniffed like it was from the dry air.

"No, I didn't win."

"I'm sorry," Aurora said.

"It's okay," I said.

It wasn't.

"You were so close," Aurora said.

I was so close.

I didn't know if I was going to throw up, go blind, or strangle a bunker with my bare hands. I'd lost Gravity. That was it. Because of stupid everything out of my control.

"When I get home, I'll just live at Mandrake's," I said. "She likes that place. She'll have to come in sooner or later. . . . What are you looking at?"

"I'm just counting your eyes," Aurora said.

It wasn't easy looking into those four pupils of hers for long.

The coach whistled, signaling the players back in.

"You need me to drag your dead body out of here?" I asked Aurora.

"I can do it."

We walked out of the Wasteland.

"At least *you* won, right?" I said. "You get to break up with Max now?"

"I guess so." Aurora touched her chest and breathed out some nervousness.

At the sidelines Tin Man was yelling. "That's a lie!"

Meeki shook her head. "Aurora shot him forever ago."

"Where?" the coach asked.

"In the back of the head."

The coach turned Tin Man around. His mask was clean. The coach gave Meeki a look. She walked in a circle around the other Cheefs, roughly grabbing their heads and examining the backs of their masks. She stepped behind Lion.

"They switched!" she said. "I was on the sidelines and saw Lion get hit right here." She rapped on the purple paint blossom on his vest. "So when did he get shot in the head?"

She flipped Lion around. The back of his mask was splattered with purple.

The coach glared at Tin Man, who pointed at Scarecrow. "He told me to do it."

Scarecrow said nothing.

That meant Tin Man had already been out of the game when he'd shot me. . . .

"They cheated?" Aurora said.

"I'm not dead?" I said.

The coach gave a slight nod.

250,000 points. . . . With Aurora still alive, I had *270,000*.

I was over a million.

I'd won.

I had beaten V-hab. And I had done it in four days.

I didn't tear off my shirt. I didn't go cartwheeling around the sand. I just breathed deeply and looked east, toward Mandrake's.

Aurora held out her hand. "Congratulations, Miles."

"What, no pain?" I asked, making my love handle available.

She shook her hair.

I took her hand. I stared deeply into her strange, collapsing eyes before she turned and walked away.

I shook away a feeling.

"Fezzik, what time is it?"

He checked his watch. "Four thirty-nine."

I had to get out of there if I was going to shower before the drive back. I smelled like a sweating corpse. Still, I wanted to show the Fury Burds some respect for helping me win.

Fezzik gave me a half-assed high five.

Meeki refused to lift her hand. "You didn't even kill anyone," she said.

I hugged her with her arms still crossed.

"You can't ruin this for me," I whispered, then released her. "Soup! We did it!"

When I raised my hand to high-five him, he ran and hid in the Wasteland.

I watched him go. He'd be fine. He might be a little lonely for his last week in V-hab, but then he'd go home. I'd go over to his house and we'd spend an afternoon—no, wait, he'd shot two Cheefs—*two* afternoons, doing whatever he wanted. And if I knew Soup, then that would be whatever *I* wanted.

I owed him that much.

"Bye forever, guys!" I said, and awkwardly sprinted across the sand toward Video Horizons.

Congratulation! This story is happy end.

A WINNER IS YOU!

I HAD A MILLION MOTHERFUCKING POINTS!

Gravity was waiting.

Game Over

I was going to see Gravity. Sparkling, charming, no-longer-dripping, wanted-to-date-me Gravity. I walked past the Dust Fairy, mopping and grumbling. I walked past Scarecrow, who for the first time didn't give me that greasy grin. I walked past Zxzord, coming out of the bathroom, looking pale.

I clapped him on the shoulder. "Thanks for nothin', dude!"

V-hab may have been a hellhole, but there really was no better way I could have spent the last few days preparing for my date. Instead of adventuring through *Arcadia* with the Wight Knights (which, if I was being honest, I totally would have done), I'd lost a pound or two, made a couple of friends, and finally opened up about my mom's addiction. Hell, I'd even learned how to play the ukulele, battle invisible ninjas, and make dope sweet-potato hummus. I knew exactly what my and Gravity's second date would look like.

I burst into the Nest like an athlete through the finish line.

G-man was standing by my bunk.

"Come to drive me home?" I asked, holding up my hand. "I don't need the points, but I could use a high five for the road."

He left me hanging. Instead he held up something in a plastic baggie.

My stomach dropped. So did my hand.

"What is that?" I said.

I knew what it was.

"It's an iPod Touch," G-man said. "It's loaded with about a dozen game apps."

The bag dangled between his fingers like he'd discovered a joint in a real rehab. My suitcase sat on the bunk behind him, pockets unzipped. G-man looked at me like he'd just found the iPod in *my* suitcase.

"How did it get in there?" I asked.

He flared his nostrils. "Judging by the smell, I don't want to know."

Oh God. I should have let Command give me a cavity search. That way he'd know my ass held no secrets.

Something written on the half wall caught my eye. "The cake is a lie," I said.

G-man sighed. "I think you'd better come to my office."

"I've been framed."

G-man nodded. "Any way you can prove it?"

"Yes!" I pulled my scroll out of my adventure pouch and unrolled it onto his desk. "Could I have earned this many points if I'd been busy playing games?"

G-man gave a helpless sort of nod. "Even if you played for two minutes after lights-out, it would still be considered cheating."

I pointed at the iPod. "Someone planted it in my suitcase so I wouldn't be able to go home!"

"Who?" G-man asked. "Why?"

"I don't know! Meeki? Dryad? Anyone in the Master Cheefs? And I have no idea why they did it." I took a deep breath, trying to calm my raging heart. Gravity was slipping away. "Who told you it was in there?"

G-man tapped his fingernails on his desk. "I can't disclose that."

I laughed. I was seething. I'd earned a million points in record time, and it didn't matter. The system was corrupt. The game had a bug. The moment I won, instead of an explosion of colors with "VICTORY" written in sparkling golden letters, all that lay before me was a desert.

"Electronics are expressly forbidden at Video Horizons," G-man said. "It's exactly what we're trying to weed out. I hate to say it, Jaxon, but the penalty for breaking those rules is steep."

"How many points?"

"One hundred thousand."

"You're fucking kidding me," I said.

G-man pointed at me. "Language. You want to lose even more?"

A clock hung above G-man's head. 4:58.

I'd performed enough miracles so far. I was not about to quit.

"I got cheated," I said. "I should be able to make it up. Hold a tournament. Today. Right now. Make it any kind of tournament you want. A fight to the death! I don't care! I'll win, and then I can walk out of here, fair and square."

G-man grimaced. "Even if I could do that—and I won't, because it wouldn't be fair to the other players—I'm not sure you're ready to leave Video Horizons. I want to make sure you've really grown here."

"I have!" I said. "Hugely. I've learned tons of new skills. Find me a ukulele. Go look at my cross-stitching! Let's go to the Feed, and I'll make you an amazing tofu scramble!"

G-man gave a pained smile. "And what about socially? Have you made strides in that department?"

"What do you mean?"

"Your dad had some concerns about your lifestyle choices. To send you back after four days, saying you're completely cured . . ."

"You think he won't get his money's worth and will demand a refund."

"No." G-man shook his head. "Absolutely not. My focus is to improve kids' lives. Not turn a profit. But that's not the point here. Some of the stories coming from your guild—"

"Like from who? Meeki? The girl who hit her brother with a Wiimote?"

G-man gave me a look. Why did I have to be such a sarcastic dick in our first meeting?

"I'll sue," I said.

"Excuse me?" he said.

"I was injured. One of the players made my kart crash. My dad's a lawyer. They call him the Mountain."

"Your dad is a retired salesman," he said. "And he signed a waiver stating that Video Horizons is not responsible for any injuries you might incur during your activities here. In fact, I specifically remember him telling me you could do with a few dings and scratches." He rubbed his neck and thought for a moment. "That would be really nice for you, wouldn't it? If I were the bad guy. Some big boss you needed to defeat in the end."

He was the bad guy. He was standing in the way of the princess. He just didn't know it. Because I'd never told him.

"I have a date!" I said. "In . . ." I checked the clock. "Oh God, one hour and fifty-nine minutes. I met her right before I was committed here. At a car wash. It's the best thing that's ever happened to me. I made her laugh. I've never done that before. She was the most beautiful girl I've ever seen, let alone talked to, and—and she said I was the funniest person she'd ever met. If Command and Conquer don't drive me home, like, right now, then I'm not going to make it. This girl is probably the only thing that can make me leave video games behind. Otherwise,

I'm going to go home and just start playing again."

G-man considered me for several moments. "That's an interesting theory," he said. "A girl to solve your problems." He stood, punching his hip to get upright, and supported his weight on the back of his chair. "When I started Video Horizons, I made a promise to myself that every patient who entered this facility would leave changed for the better." Tears welled up in his eyes. "That hasn't happened for you yet, Jaxon. And I think somewhere deep down inside, you know it."

I didn't say the words on the tip of my tongue. I didn't say them because G-man was still the best chance I had of getting out of there.

I stood and left the office without another word. I needed to figure out an escape. *Immediately.* Earning points was out. Walking home was out. G-man wasn't going to help. I paced Video Horizons' halls, searching for an answer. I needed a hearthstone. I needed a homeward bone. I needed a reset button.

And then I found my answer, shyly peeking around the corner of the hallway. Soup. He wasn't running up and latching on to my love handles like he always did. He was keeping his distance, looking as if I wanted to eat him.

Things clicked into place.

Who wanted me to stay at Video Horizons more than anyone else?

Who had mentioned my ugly-ass Home Depot hat even though I'd never taken it out of my suitcase?

Who had painted me inside a Pokéball?

I ran up to Soup, grabbed him by the wrist, and pulled him down the hallway.

"Where are we going?" he asked.

I didn't answer. We scaled the stairs to G-man's office.

I knocked on the door.

"Come in," G-man said.

I placed my hand on the door handle. "I lied," I said to Soup. "You and I live right around the corner from each other. I just didn't want to hang out with you because you're a sniveling little piece of shit."

His face crumpled, and I opened the office door.

G-man was typing something on his phone.

He glanced up. "What's up, fellas?"

"Tell him," I said, shoving Soup's shoulder toward the desk.

Soup looked back at me, confused.

"Tell him you planted the iPod Touch in my suitcase so I'd stay."

G-man set down his phone and intertwined his fingers. "Is that true?" he asked Soup.

Soup looked at me. His eyes glistened. His head sank. He nodded.

G-man narrowed his eyes at Soup. Soup didn't lift his head. I ignored the weird sinking feeling in my chest.

"Sorry I didn't trust you, Miles," G-man said.

"Totally fine." I clapped my hands together. "That means I have a million points again. You have to drive me home now. You promised."

"I don't have to do anything of the sort."

"Wait, what?"

"Not after hearing what you said to Soup outside my door. I'm still deducting the hundred thousand points, but this time it's for ill treatment of one of your fellow players."

I felt the blood rush to my face. "He—he sabotaged my game just so he could spend more time with me."

Soup sniffed and let his head hang.

"What if he did?" G-man said. "Is this how you treat someone who shows you affection? When you strip away all the stories you tell yourself, Miles, you're left with the bare facts of what you did or did not do. I'm keeping you here."

I searched G-man's watery, sincere eyes. "You were never going to let me out anyway."

He shrugged. "We'll never know now, will we?"

It took every bit of energy I had not to put my fist through the wall.

G-man pointed to the door. "Go to guild therapy, or I'm calling Command and Conquer in here."

I nearly tore the door off its hinges. I thundered down the stairs and down the dead fluorescent hall toward the green light of the exit. I kicked the push bar and stepped out into the harsh air of the desert.

I stared past the parking lot, past the dunes. I was trapped in an infinite sandbox, a game that never ended and cheated to keep me in.

What did I do now?

Didilingdingdingdingding. You could stop being such a douche bag, Miles!

Screw you, Navi, I thought. *I won, and it made zero difference. I don't need you anymore.*

I imagined the little fairy sprite's wings drooping. She fluttered across the desert, painting the dunes with fairy dust, and then vanished on the horizon.

The door opened behind me. "You supposed to be in therapy?" Command said.

I didn't turn around.

"You need me to walk you there?" he said. "Or do you think you can find your own way like a big boy?"

Could I make it? If I ran into the desert right then, could I outrun him?

I turned around and went back inside. Command shut the door.

Evil Alignment

Meeki's voice echoed down the Nest's stairwell.

"—inspiration. You're just so amazing and so pretty. But you also make me feel like being pretty doesn't matter. You made me realize that a lot of what I get mad about comes from me believing what people say or—"

I opened the door, and Meeki immediately stopped talking. She glared at me. "Well, that moment's ruined."

The guild circle was set up, but three of the chairs were empty. It was just Meeki, Aurora, and Fezzik. Zxzord was in his bunk.

"Hello, Miles," Fezzik said. He didn't seem surprised to see me. "Have a seat. Meeki, please continue."

She kept glaring at me. "I thought you were gone."

I sat in the circle. "I thought I was too."

"Well, we're happy to have you," Fezzik said. "Do you know where Soup is?"

"With G-man." *The little shit.*

I set my elbows on my knees and pressed my palms into my eyes, trying to quiet my brain. I should have been cruising across the desert toward home.

"Meeki?" Fezzik said. "Go ahead and finish."

"I'll tell her later."

"Fair enough," Fezzik said. "Miles?" I didn't lift my head from my hands. "It's Aurora's farewell guild therapy. Once the new players get here, Command is going to drive her home. Is there anything you'd like to say before she goes?"

I looked up. Aurora's strange eyes glistened with tears. This was the girl who'd predicted I would remain at Video Horizons for a very long time.

"Nah."

"Maybe later," Fezzik said. He slapped his knees, trying to dispel the awkwardness. "Aurora, do you have any last words for the guild?"

"Just . . . be good."

"Lovely and simple," Fezzik said. "Thank you, Aurora. I think I speak for everyone when I say that you've made some incredible growth while you've been here. You've overcome some terrifying obstacles when it comes to how you feel about your appearance, and you've figured out that you deserve better than what your current relationship is offering. We wish you the best on your adventure back in the real world."

He looked at me and Meeki, both unresponsive, and sighed. "Well, let's talk dopamine. I'm sure you guys are experiencing some of that after winning the paintball tournament. Heh-heh."

Nope. All of my dopamine had been slurped right out of my brain by Soup and G-man.

"Video games stimulate the pleasure circuit of the brain," Fezzik continued, "making gamers feel accomplished even though we aren't actually accomplishing anything. Can anyone speak to this?"

"You are without a doubt the most selfish person I've ever met," Meeki said.

I rolled my eyes and sat back. She was talking to me, of course. What else would you expect from a name like "mekillyoulongtime"?

"Care to share your feelings, Meeki?" Fezzik said. "Using non-negative, supportive language?"

Aurora brought her feet up onto her chair and folded into herself.

"He thinks he's better than us," Meeki said. "I wish he had left. We don't need him in the Fury Burds."

"Meeki," Fezzik said, "that isn't what I meant by supportive—"

"Really?" I said. "You don't need me? Even though I earned our guild hundreds of thousands of points? You're welcome, by the way. Oh, *and* I broke Scarecrow's nose for you."

Fezzik gave me a confused look. I didn't care. He could take away every last point I had. It didn't matter anymore.

Meeki locked eyes with me. "Do I *look* like a helpless little girl who needs a big strong man to step in for me? I've won more fights in the last *year* than you will in your entire *life*."

I glanced at her arms, which were, in fact, larger than mine.

"Besides, you didn't break Scarecrow's nose for me. You did that for yourself. You were afraid you were going to lose at Four Square, and hurting him was the perfect excuse to get out of it. If you were disqualified, then losing wouldn't be your fault. And then you could keep pretending you have a snowball's chance in hell with that car wash chick, which, by the way, hate to break it to you, you don't."

I snorted and turned to Fezzik. He hadn't made so much as a Wookiee sound.

"You're obsessed with this princess in another castle BS," Meeki said. "It's ingrained in you. The poor innocent girl is just waiting for you to swoop in and give her everything she's ever wanted. You think Gravity cares about you? You guys exchanged, like, a hundred words, and now you're *obsessed* with her? It's creepy."

I looked at Fezzik again. "Aren't you gonna step in?"

Fezzik breathed in deeply then caught it. "Sometimes an adventurer needs to enter a battle without a protection spell. This could be good for you emotionally, Miles."

I couldn't believe what I was hearing. What did they know about my experience at the car wash? None of them had been there.

Defenseless, without Fezzik as my healer, or Soup as my shield, I refaced Meeki.

"What the fuck is your problem?" I said.

"Miles . . . ," Fezzik warned.

I threw my scroll at his feet. "Take all the points you want." I turned back to Meeki. "I'm just trying to go on a date."

"You don't really care about that girl," Meeki said. "You don't even know her. You just want to be rewarded even though you're lazy and treat everyone like shit." She also threw her scroll at Fezzik's feet. "This has nothing to do with Gravity and everything to do with your malnourished sense of self. You hate women."

"What are you *talking* about? My mom was an *alcoholic*, but I still—"

"What does that have to do with anything?" she said.

"Everything! It—it—" I was so mad, I could barely control my mouth.

"Just because something goes wrong in your life doesn't mean you get to become the wrong in everyone else's," Meeki said. "And nothing has gone *that* wrong for you. Being a straight white guy in middle-class America means your life is set on the easiest setting."

Fezzik cleared his throat. "I think what Meeki is trying to say is that sometimes it's tough for us to recognize our own power, and we exploit the weaknesses of others. It's like . . . if choosing your character's class in *Arcadia* were randomized. Some people would get the warrior class, while others might get stuck with—"

"It's nothing like that," Meeki interrupted. "Miles is a privileged brat who thinks he can do whatever he wants because his life is so hard. 'Oh, boo hoo, my parents got divorced. Oh, I don't get to go on any dates. Oh, someone took my *video games* away.' How do you think it feels being a fat, queer Vietnamese girl? Huh?"

Tears welled in Meeki's eyes. I searched the circle for help. Fezzik had given up. Aurora stayed hidden behind her knees.

I was baffled. "You're talking to me like I'm . . . Scarecrow or something."

"You're right," Meeki said. "I'm sorry. You're nothing like Scarecrow."

"Thank you," I said.

"You're kind of worse. Because you actually believe you're the good guy. But really you just use us to cheat and earn points so you can go on your precious date."

"That's the entire point of this place!" I burst out. "We're all trying to earn points!"

Everything went quiet. Zxzord blinked at us from his bunk. Meeki smiled. "You think I'm the only one who thinks you suck?"

"*Meeki*," Fezzik said.

"Fine. I'm not the only one who wishes you were gone."

I scoffed, but then noticed Fezzik wouldn't meet my eyes. He stared at his giant hands. I peeked through Aurora's folded-up legs and caught her eyes. I had told her so many true things about myself—about airports and loneliness and *Dr. Mario*. But she wasn't stepping in.

"Remember yesterday?" Meeki said. "When Aurora was crying in the Feed?"

"Meeki, don't," Aurora said between her knees.

"That was because of *you*," Meeki said. "You said she was a weirdo."

"No, I didn't!"

"Yeah," Meeki said. "You did. On the roof. She's tried to escape being weird her whole life, but you just come in here and say whatever you want because you think you deserve to get out of here in four days. How's that working out for you, by the way?"

Before I could respond, Aurora stood up. "May I be excused?"

Fezzik nodded, and she hurried out of the Nest.

Meeki's eyes stayed locked on me. "I won't even mention how you treat Soup."

"Soup loves me," I said. I did not sound convincing.

Meeki scoffed. "Soup would love a refrigerator if it could talk to him."

I couldn't argue with that.

"Everything is always about you, Miles," she said. "You take up all the space in guild therapy."

"Is that a fat joke?" I asked.

"No, idiot. With your *voice*. You're disrespectful to everything that happens here. You never listen. And when you talk, it's just so you can earn points."

I stood so quickly, my chair fell over. "What makes you so perfect, huh? Hitting your brother in the head? Ignoring Fezzik and talking about vibrators and Nutella and all the disgusting stuff none of us want to hear about?"

Meeki stood too, and we met in the middle of the circle almost nose to nose.

"Guys," Fezzik said, standing with us.

"See?" Meeki said. "Even after I tell you that you take up all the space, you still don't ask about anyone else. You talk so much that the rest of us barely have time to talk about why we're here. I hit my brother in the head with the Wiimote because he said he could smell my 'girl parts' all over it. But do you give a crap? No, you just care that you go on a stupid date." She shut her trembling jaw and collected herself. "You think *I* ever get to go on any dates? I don't. *Never*."

I fell back into my seat, exasperated, and shook my head. Meeki loomed over me.

"You're the biggest addict of us all. You might leave here, Miles, but you're going to leave here the same privileged asshole as when you were committed."

She sat down and crossed her arms. I was suddenly uncomfortably aware of myself. And not just my man boobs.

Fezzik carefully tried to reignite the warmth in the room. "Arguments like these can be difficult, I think, because we're not properly equipped for them. The more time we spend in a gaming world, the more vulnerable we feel in tough situations, and the more we have to think about things that make us sad, like—"

"I don't get to go on my fucking date!" I yelled.

I was up on my feet again. Fezzik raised his hands like he was ready to restrain me.

"Are you happy?" I said to Meeki. "I should be pulling into Salt Lake right now, but I don't get to fucking go. Because my dad decided that hanging out with him and my stepmom is more important than playing *Arcadia* with my friends. So I have to come here where the classes suck shit, the bullies are worse than they are in school, and some kid is so obsessed with me that he hides an iPod Touch in my suitcase so I lose a hundred thousand points, and instead of going on a date, I get to listen to some *asshole* who won't get off my fucking back because she thinks I'm a douche bag . . . when really I'm just really, really sad and need video games to pass the days until I can move out of my house."

There was a glimmer in Meeki's eye. Almost like she understood. Almost like I'd touched on common ground between Link and Dark Link, where our experiences were the same.

The glimmer quickly faded.

"Boo. Hoo."

I sucked in my breath. "Fezzik," I said, "can I go die in my bunk, please?"

Fezzik opened his mouth to respond, but then nodded instead.

I climbed the bunk ladder and collapsed into bed.

"Why don't we go to the art room?" Fezzik said to Meeki. "Give him some space."

They got up. The lights went out. As the Nest door closed, I heard Fezzik say, "Soup hid something in his suitcase? That doesn't sound like him. . . ."

The door clicked shut. The mockingbird sang for six o'clock. One hour until my date with Gravity. I got out of bed just long enough to smash the clock to pieces.

Continue?

For the first time since being committed to V-hab, I lost track of time. The star stickers glowed a sickly green above my bunk. The air conditioner grumbled.

I lay on my bunk for I don't know how long—staring at nothing, feeling nothing, just imagining lovely, beautiful Gravity, lips painted a sensuous red, sitting alone at Mandrake's.

Then I felt the familiar pat of a giant hand. My head rolled to the side. Fezzik smiled. Or at least tried to.

"What time is it?" I asked.

He looked at the shattered clock. "I think it's a little after seven."

My heart broke. I'd missed it. I had just stood up the loveliest girl I'd ever met.

The star stickers glowed. The universe meant nothing.

"Miles . . ."

"I don't care right now," I said, pulling the sheet over my head.

Fezzik continued anyway. "There are lots of problems with this facility. I personally don't think G-man understands what it's like to struggle with life so much that *Arcadia* becomes your only escape. Being the Emperor got me through some very dark times. . . ." He gave his head a little shake. "Also, games are meant to be voluntary, and gamified therapy seems to bring out the worst in some."

We both pretended he wasn't talking about me.

"But that doesn't mean you and I don't need this place. As fun as video games are, they have given us unrealistic expectations about the world." He went quiet, like he was considering whether or not to tell me something. "I quit games so I could live. But getting turned down by Sue felt like dying." He breathed deeply. "Miles, why would we ever want to pursue something where, with just a little bit of effort, success was guaranteed? There's a reason we play *Arcadia* instead of *LEGO: Batman*. It's the challenge that won't let us take good things for granted."

I pushed the sheet off my head. "A little bit of effort? I worked my *ass* off these last few days."

Fezzik nodded. "That's what I mean by unrealistic expectations. You can't work hard for four days and expect everything to just fall into your lap."

I rolled and faced the wall. "I could if G-man would let me go."

"Maybe," Fezzik said. "But you can't blame him."

Yes, I could.

"I can't say I approve of how you treated your guildmates this week," Fezzik said. "But who knows? Maybe a fair maiden—er, young woman would stop you from going back to *Arcadia*. Maybe she would bring out the best in you."

"She would have," I said, picking at the wall's gray paint.

Fezzik sighed. "And there she is, just sitting at that restaurant, all alone."

I turned back over. "Are you trying to make me feel worse?"

Fezzik smiled. "I don't want you to give up on living in the real world just yet." He held up a cell phone with a *Final Fantasy* case that showed Cloud holding a Buster Sword. "I think you've been knocked down enough. Time for a limit break."

"Fezzik." A hearth fire crackled to life in my chest. "Best *Final Fantasy* reference *yet*."

I sat up and took the phone.

"I already looked up Mandrake's number," he said. "You just have to press call."

The button glowed green on the phone's screen. Gravity was one touch away. I adored Fezzik in that moment. The Emperor of *Arcadia* had swooped into real life and saved me at the last possible second.

"I got ya covered," he said, and blocked me with his giant frame so I couldn't be seen from the Nest door.

I took a deep breath.

I pressed the green button.

It rang.

Contact from beyond the infinite sandbox.

With each ring my heart doubled its speed.

"Mandrake's," a girl's voice said. I could hear the bustle and clink of a busy restaurant in the background.

"Um, hi." My voice shook. "This is a really weird question, but is Serena there? Black hair. Sixteen maybe? Sitting at a table alone?"

"Oh yeah," the hostess said. "I know Serena. She comes in all the time. Let me see if she's here."

The line muffled and went to hold music.

Fezzik looked over his shoulder. "Deep breaths."

I took his advice. It didn't help.

Panic swelled. The exit light buzzed. Fezzik's nostrils whistled. What was I going to say? What would be my excuse? Should I tell her about V-hab? I'd been so anxious to call, I had pressed the button before thinking this through.

As if reading my mind, Fezzik said, "Tell her you were injured in a car crash." He nodded at my shoulder. "It isn't too far from the truth."

I smiled. The music cut. My heart leapt. The phone crackled and fumbled.

"You still there?" the hostess said.

"Yes," I said.

"I don't see her. I don't think she's been in here tonight."

"Oh . . ."

I looked at the phone. Seven fifteen. Fezzik's eyebrows wrinkled.

"You want me to tell her who called if I see her?" the hostess said.

Fezzik heard and shook his head.

"Um, no thanks."

I hung up.

Fezzik took his phone. "She's just running late. Making herself extra pretty for ya."

"Yeah, probably," I said. I hoped.

"I have to go make sure the Burds are set up at the Feed, then I'll come back and we can try again."

"Thanks, Fezzik."

He left the Nest.

I sank back into my pillow. I began to play with the idea "what if?" What if Serena wasn't there when I called back? What if she had stood me up? Had she pretended not to have a phone or a Facebook account in order to get away from me at the car wash? What if she never liked me at all and I really was a pathetic loser that she'd taken temporary pity on, and all of my effort this week had been for a girl who didn't give a damn about me?

Then again, she had laughed. A couple of times. That had been real . . . right?

The green glow of the star stickers grew nauseating. I remembered standing alone at the airport the last time my mom had no-showed on me . . . watching the crowds, hoping each new face would be hers. My insides got that feeling Aurora described as curdled milk and skinned knees.

If I'd been nervous when I'd made that first call, it was nothing compared to when Fezzik returned. Suddenly I was terrified of that phone. It was no longer a matter of what I was going to say to Gravity. It was a matter of whether I'd get to say anything to her ever again.

"Round two," Fezzik said, handing me the phone.

I pressed the green button.

The phone rang.

He gave me a thumbs-up.

"Mandrake's."

"Hi. So sorry. Me again. Did Serena make it there yet?"

"Um, let me check." The hostess sounded annoyed. "It might be a minute. It's really busy."

"Yeah. Sorry. Take your time."

She put me on hold.

Fezzik gave me a kindly smile.

I wanted to think about anything other than what I was doing. The desperation of it. The neediness. And then I remembered. Mine wasn't the only broken heart in the Nest.

I covered the phone. "Were you and the Silver Lady . . . y'know, a couple?"

Fezzik opened his mouth. "It's complicated. Or maybe it isn't. She just doesn't have any room in her life for someone like me." His shoulders deflated, but he still managed that giant smile.

The hold music jumped to another track. My heart jumped with it.

"I know I shouldn't give up on love altogether," Fezzik said. "You don't quit when you get killed in *Dark Souls* for the hundredth—"

The strings music stopped, and I held up a finger.

"You still there?" the hostess asked.

I covered my eyes. "Yeah."

"She's not here. Sorry."

I exhaled. "Thanks."

I looked at the phone. It was 7:48. The screen went black.

"Maybe something came up," Fezzik said, taking his phone.

"No. She was too good for me."

"If you think a girl who stands you up is too good for you, then you're just cranking up your own difficulty setting."

"Maybe," I said.

I sank back into the bed.

"I'll give you some time alone," Fezzik said.

The Nest door closed behind him. All I wanted then was video games. Video games and the Wight Knights. Just give me a computer and an axe and a wave of clockwork chipmunks.

That sounded like the perfect thing.

The only thing.

Heart Piece

I decided to stay in bed until I wasted away to nothing.

But then my stomach started to rumble.

I sat up to go to the Feed and stuff my face with as many zero-point foods as possible. But then I felt nauseous and yet too tired to lie back down. I did anyway.

Nothing was comfortable. Everything sucked. Starvation could not come quickly enough.

Meeki was right. I'd never had a snowball's chance in hell with Gravity. The truth was, I didn't know a damned thing about that girl. I had no idea how she had spent the last four days. Maybe she had mud wrestled. Maybe she had built a homeless shelter. Maybe she had smoked crack and drunk chicken's blood.

It had felt so good talking to her at the car wash, though. I should've realized a girl that pretty and interesting was out of my league. Or maybe Fezzik was right. Maybe she did suck for standing me up. I didn't know.

Every point I'd earned that week had felt like a step closer to her. And it hadn't been. Just because I thought about a girl—constantly, every minute of every day, dreamed of what I would do with her, for her, *to* her—that didn't mean I was leveling up with her, getting further along with her like she was a video game.

But it had kinda felt that way.

I wanted out of my skin. I wanted to quit this character called Jaxon and start a new one. One that was handsomer, stronger, faster, nicer, better at girls. One who didn't give a damn about scoring points.

I rolled onto my side, then back onto my back, and then onto my other side. Maybe I could go steal that iPod Touch from G-man's office to pass the time with video games while I died. I could deal with the iPod's ass smell.

Something floated up in the corner of my vision. I rolled my head to find a cup of horchata and a piece of toast on a napkin. My mouth watered against my will.

I sat up and took them from Aurora. "Thanks." I bit the toast and washed it down with milky sugar. "I thought you'd be out of here by now."

"Command and Conquer are running late," she said, her strange eyes peering up over the bed.

I scooted over. "You wanna join me?"

She let her head rock shoulder to shoulder.

"I only kill clocks," I said. "I promise."

She climbed up the ladder. We sat in silence while I finished the toast and horchata. She and I had had such good conversations on the roof, about moms and boyfriends and video games. Why hadn't she jumped in and saved me from Meeki?

When I finished the toast and horchata, I stuffed the napkin into the cup and dropped it off the bed for the Dust Fairy to take care of.

Aurora dragged her pointer finger along the base sheet. Again. And again. And again.

"What are you doing?" I said.

"Just wondering what thread count these are," she said.

"Did you read the tag?"

She kept dragging her finger. "I'm trying to train my fingertip to figure it out."

"Weird," I said.

She didn't look at me, just ruffled up her nose a little.

Oh, shit. Right. Meeki had said that Aurora had been trying to avoid that word her whole life.

I needed to recover. To prove that Meeki was wrong about me. That she had misunderstood everything I'd said and done. That I *was* a good guy.

"I . . . I mean it, Aurora. That's really weird." I said this like I'd meant it to be ironic the first time. "I don't know when that word became associated with anything bad. I guess it was taken over by popular kids who wanted to make sure that everyone else believed they were normal. But some of my favorite things are weird."

Aurora stopped dragging her finger along the sheet. She rested her chin on her palms and extended her red, raw fingers so they covered her eyes. "Like what?"

"Like . . ." I didn't even have to search my brain this time. "Did you know that H. G. Wells pretty much invented the atomic bomb?"

I told her all about it, with more confidence than I'd had at the car wash.

Aurora vibrated her lips. She was still wearing her eye mask. "Max called me weird a lot. Never in a good way."

"What way does he think of it?"

"I don't know. The way he looks at me sometimes, I'm pretty sure he's imagining the Elephant Man."

"Is that the deformed guy from a long time ago?"

She gave this adorable little nod, lips squished between her hands.

"You're kind of the opposite of deformed, Aurora," I said. "You're actually really pretty."

She uncurled one set of fingers so I could see one of her eyes. "Thank you."

I stared at the uncovered half of Aurora's face. Her beauty had come to me slowly, like an eclipse . . . or the graphics in *Minecraft*—her interesting weirdness, her alien prettiness, the way she noticed the little details of the world, her philosophy on unhealthy relationships and improvement through pain. . . . And hell, she *played video games*. Even with my computer disassembled, I could play at her house.

I'd been so hung up on Serena that I hadn't noticed how awesome Aurora was. She was probably the nicest person I'd ever met.

Serena *was* an asshole.

"Gravity stood me up," I said. "Fezzik let me call the restaurant with his cell phone."

Aurora removed her hand mask altogether. "I guess we're both obsessed with people who suck."

The AC kicked up, and I felt a cool gust against my ankles. I scooted closer to Aurora but tried to make it so slight that she wouldn't even notice it.

I could be better than Max. I wouldn't ignore her and play games all day. I'd talk to her about the universe and flies and anything she wanted. I'd hold her hand and help her forget about her skinny arms and her eyes and her torn-up fingers. I'd help her escape her asshole boyfriend, and she could help me escape my dad's house. I could make her laugh the way I'd made Serena laugh.

I took in the Nest's surroundings. The stars above were fake. Zxzord snored in the bunk below. The demented Felicia Day portrait stared at us from the wall.

"Well, it isn't as romantic as the roof," I said, "but . . ."

I leaned in.

This was it. I'd finally get to kiss someone. Someone beautiful. Someone awesome. Someone who liked me.

Aurora leaned away.

We froze like that.

Her four pupils searched mine. "I am not medicine, Miles Prower."

My stomach sank. "Oh, no . . . I was—"

She quickly climbed down the ladder. My skin ran cold.

"Are you doing this because of Meeki?" I asked.

Aurora was already at the door. "You haven't learned anything, have you?"

"I have!" I said.

"How will you ever love someone when all you can see is yourself?"

And then she left. I hugged my knees and let my head fall between them.

"Smooth, dude."

"Shut up, Zxzord," I said.

Fezzik's voice came down the hallway. "Hey, young lady. Guilding's about to start if you're interested before you head out." He tromped up the stairs and poked his head into the Nest. "C'mon, Miles. Let's go watch other people be humiliated."

I could already imagine Aurora in the Hub, whispering to Meeki about what I'd done. I could already feel Meeki's scowl burning through me.

I kept hugging my knees. "Not really feeling it right now."

"Sorry, adventurer," Fezzik said. "It's mandatory."

"I just . . . I need a minute."

Just because I hadn't kissed Aurora didn't mean I could walk right that moment.

"I'll wait," Fezzik said.

Zxzord stumbled out of his bunk.

Fezzik stepped out of his way. "He lives!"

"He goes to die," Zxzord said, and stumbled down the staircase.

A couple of awkward minutes later, Fezzik and I headed down the hallway, his hand on my shoulder.

"We'll have fun during your last week," he said. "Eat some good food, build some sand castles, talk *Arcadia* when G-man isn't listening . . ."

He was trying to cheer me up. He didn't realize how miserable my remaining time would be. I was trapped in a facility where everyone except him hated me.

The players filed into the Hub. I collapsed into a beanbag chair and sank low. I didn't want to see Meeki or Scarecrow or Dryad or Aurora or Soup or anyone. Maybe Zxzord and I could become bunk buddies.

"Huh," Fezzik said, searching the players. "Where's Soup? He was at the Feed. . . ."

"I dunno," I said.

He got up and left the Hub.

Aurora sat two beanbags over, forcing Meeki to sit next to me. Neither of them looked my way, but Aurora didn't say anything to her. That was nice, I guess. It would've been nicer if she hadn't humiliated me in the first place.

"Okay, everyone!" G-man said from the stage. "We have a new player starting today. Everyone give a warm welcome to . . . Toffette!"

Command led a girl to the stage. My heart did a somersault. I blinked hard, trying to make sense of what I was seeing.

Gravity. Gravity was standing in the Hub.

There was a weird moment when I wondered if I had wanted to see her so much that my subconscious had magicked her across the desert to Video Horizons.

"You look like you just shit your pants," Meeki said to me.

My shock was quickly replaced by the warmest fuzzies I could imagine. Gravity hadn't stood me up. She had been committed to V-hab! She had been kidnapped by Command and Conquer just like I had been.

"*It's her!*" I whispered to Meeki. "You were so wrong! Everything between us at the car wash *was* real. It's Gravity!"

Meeki looked at the stage. A grin crept across her face that made me immediately regret speaking Gravity's name aloud. My face sank.

"Should I tell her you just put the moves on Aurora and totally got rejected?" Meeki asked.

I couldn't hide my horror. I scowled at Aurora, who quickly shook her head.

"It wasn't her," Meeki said. "Zxzord told me." She gave me the biggest grin I'd ever seen her give, and sang, "*Somebody's fu-ucked.*"

Extra Life

Gravity sat in the chair onstage. She looked pissed, refusing to look anywhere but at her nails. God, she was even prettier than I had remembered. I still couldn't believe I was actually looking at her.

But how could I talk to her? She could not, under any circumstances, meet the rest of my guild. They'd try to convince her I was a complete asshole. Also, I needed to change my stupid outfit. I sank even lower into my beanbag chair and willed her not to look in my direction. Right then I needed the Gravitational pull between her and me to drop to zero.

Onstage G-man placed both his hands on Gravity's shoulders, like some kind of mossy-toothed vulture. "We want you to think of Video Horizons as a magical place. . . ."

Meeki continued to smile at me. Aurora avoided my eyes. Dammit. Why hadn't I been just a little nicer? Why had I tried to kiss a girl when I was supposed to have been on a date with someone else?

G-man introduced the three guilds. Fortunately, Gravity wasn't having any of it. Her nails got all of the attention. She glanced up once for a second, but her eyes passed right over me.

"Which guild will lead you to success?" G-man said, and shook the Box of Fate in her face.

Please don't be Burds, please don't be Burds, please don't be Burds.

"I'd rather not," Gravity said, pushing the box away.

"Well, you have to be in a guild," G-man said.

"I really don't," she said.

She was such a badass. Why hadn't I tried that?

"O-kay," G-man said. "I'll pick for you."

He fished around in the box.

Please don't be Burds, please don't be Burds.

"Toffette," G-man said, unfolding the little piece of paper. "You— Sorry. Hold on, players."

Command was signaling G-man from the door. He jogged up onto the stage, and they spoke quietly behind Gravity.

"Hmm." Meeki stroked her chin. "What shitty thing should I tell her about first? How many times you cheated? How you tried to use us all as your personal peons? How you talked about her like she was already your girlfriend? That you tried to kiss Aurora?" Meeki considered Gravity onstage. "Or maybe I should just let her spend some time with you and figure out how shitty you are all by herself."

"Please don't," I whispered.

"I need everyone to quiet down right now," G-man called

from the stage. The adventure was gone from his voice. The Hub fell quiet. "Has anyone seen Soup?"

The players murmured to each other, but no one spoke up.

G-man let the guild paper flutter to the ground. "Okay, we have a player missing."

Meeki noticed the expression on my face.

"This is because of you, isn't it?" she said. "I'll start by telling Gravity about that."

"The police are on their way," G-man said, "but in the interim, we're going to make three search parties. Each guild will head out in a different direction and comb the surrounding area."

Lion raised his hand. "How many points if we find him?"

The Cheefs laughed.

G-man gave them a disappointed look. "This is not the time . . ." He trailed off and studied their faces. "Fine. A hundred thousand."

The Cheefs cheered.

I would have thought they were insensitive, point-hungry lunatics, but earlier that afternoon I would have been ecstatic to earn that many points. Now not only were points meaningless, but it was my fault Soup was missing. It was almost enough for me to stop worrying about what to do about Gravity. Almost.

"Please meet with your guild leaders in the bunks," G-man said. "And bundle up. It's chilly out there."

Lion and Tin Man ran toward the exit like Soup was some rare trophy monster to be hunted.

"Bonus million for finding Atari's *E.T.*!" Lion shouted.

I tried to disappear among the Sefs. I needed to avoid running into Gravity until I was certain she wouldn't see me with anyone in my guild. That was the plan. That was, until I saw Scarecrow heading toward the stage. I froze in the doorway as he slouched up to Gravity and offered his hand.

"Scarecrow," he said. "You should come with the Cheefs. You don't want to hang out with most of these fags, anyway."

Gravity gave a little smile, and I booked it straight back to the stage, stained white pants and all.

"Um, *whoa*," I said, staring at her, wide-eyed.

Gravity's eyes grew wide. "*Whoa*. You're the kid from the car wash!"

"Jaxon," I said.

"I *know*," she said. "Jaxon."

I'd forgotten how big her lips were.

"You know each other?" Scarecrow asked, incredulous.

I would have thought he was a dick, but he was right. There was no good reason I should know a girl this pretty.

Gravity bit her lip and bashfully turned the toe of her laceless shoe on the floor. "He sprayed me with water."

"Heh." I shrugged. "She, um, kept clawing at the furniture."

Gravity laughed. Scarecrow left. It was one of the greatest moments in my life.

Gravity leapt up and slapped my arm. "I thought I stood you up tonight!"

"You did," I said. "But I decided to get back at you by standing you up at the *exact same time*."

She laughed again. I'd almost forgotten how easy things were with her. I got that lovely unwinding feeling I had thought was gone forever.

Gravity covered her face with her hands and then parted them, cradling her cheeks. "This is so embarrassing."

"Um," I said, "you do realize I'm here too, right?"

She dropped her hands, disgusted. "You mean a video game nerd asked me out?"

We both smiled.

"I'd ask what you're in for," she said, "but I already know. Spraying innocent girls at the car wash. They do know that's not a video game, right?"

Something clicked. My *Super Mario Bros.* shirt hadn't been a deterrent. It had been an attractor.

"I thought you were a Luddite," I said. "No car. No phone. Why are you here?"

"Yeah, about that no phone thing . . ."

"You gonna introduce me to your friend?" a voice said behind me.

I turned around and found Meeki with the sweetest smile on her face.

Shit.

"Is this *the* Gravity?" Meeki asked with a fake-shocked expression. "The one you were supposed to go on a date with tonight?"

"Gravity?" Gravity asked.

"Oh, I, uh, didn't want to tell them your real name," I said.

"Aww," she said, nudging my chin. "You talked about me?"

"Uh, yeah," I said, feeling myself blush. I wanted to say something funny, fast. "My name is Miles here, by the way. Miles Prower. Get it? Miles per hour?"

"Clever," Gravity said. She didn't so much as crack a smile.

We had another awkward pause, like the one we'd had at the car wash. Only this time, Meeki was standing there, grinning through every painful second.

"Welcome to V-hab, I guess," I said to Gravity.

I couldn't be cute and clever right then. I was terrified Meeki was going to ask how Gravity and I had met, and then I'd have to explain that it wasn't some dickhead who'd sprayed her at the car wash. It had been me.

"Yo, Toffi." Scarecrow stuck his head back into the Hub. "You coming?"

"You should come with *us*," Meeki said, as sweet as ever. "I can tell you aaaaaaaall about this place."

I couldn't drag my finger across my throat at Meeki without Gravity seeing. So I just stood there. Like an idiot.

Gravity gave me a devastating smirk, then gave the same devastating smirk to Scarecrow, as if she was asking which one of us wanted her along more.

Did I let Meeki reveal every terrible thing about me, or did I send Gravity off with the Master Cheefs, only to be swallowed up into Scarecrow's harem?

"Come with us," I said.

"All right," she said, shrugging.

"Great!" Meeki said.

"Great," I said.

I was going to throw up.

G-man stuck his head back into the Hub. "Players! Let's head out! Now!"

Meeki, Gravity, and I walked to the Nest.

"This is exciting!" Gravity said. "What if the missing kid's *dead*?"

"Then Miles will have a lot of explaining to do," Meeki said.

Gravity laughed. I did not.

We climbed the stairs to the Nest, where Aurora did her best to avoid all three of us.

"Gather around, everyone," Fezzik said. His face was flushed, and he had a very sober look. "It's my fault Soup's missing. I was distracted and only thinking about myself."

"*What a dick*," Meeki whispered just to me.

"Shut up," I said, quietly between my teeth.

"Soup is our little caretaker," Fezzik said. "The Nest wouldn't be the same without him. The pillows wouldn't be as fluffed and the cross-stitch wouldn't be as neat."

Meeki nudged me and whispered, "*Hey, you should show Gravity some of your cross-stitch!*"

"What cross-stitch?" Gravity said.

"Oh, it's a, uh, joke," I said.

"Or what about that watercolor?" Meeki said.

"What watercolor?" Gravity said.

"She's joking."

"Guys?" Fezzik said, and we all shut up. "Let's get out there and find him. He can't have made it far on those little legs of his, but I still think we should hustle."

Fezzik handed out jackets and then shook the lump in the bunks. "Zxzord, *up*."

Zxzord didn't budge.

"*NOW!*" Fezzik bellowed.

Zxzord shot up straight. The undead risen. Fezzik really was a healer.

I needed a hell of a lot more than that to get me out of this situation.

The desert was purple with dusk as Fezzik led us across the dunes, away from Video Horizons. He didn't make any jokes about our party of adventurers heading off into the wilderness—the healer giant, the electric warlock, the Asian warrior, the Elvin oracle, the beautiful time warper . . . and the dude who'd lost our guild's pet.

Sand sucked our shoes; the wind stung our faces. Aurora and Meeki kept their distance, like two satellites. Gravity fell behind and admired Zxzord's tattoos. The sight made me extremely uncomfortable, so I focused on the search.

Soup would be fine. We'd find him. He'd say something annoying like, *Didja miss me?* and jiggle my belly in a way that would let me go right back to hating him.

Why did the stupid kid run away anyway? It wasn't like what I had said was that bad.

And why the hell was Gravity touching Zxzord's arm?

The wind raised the sand, blurring the horizon, making it difficult to make out definite shapes. My mind kept tricking me with little ghost flashes of a Soupy silhouette scrambling up the side of a dune. I'd blink, and he'd be nothing more than sand swirling in the night wind.

Something light and dry brushed my cheek. I whirled, expecting to find Soup. It was Aurora, offering me a dead leaf.

"What is this?" I asked, taking it.

She shrugged and walked away.

We came to a large dune and trekked to the top, huffing and searching in silence. I started to get just a tiny bit worried. How were we supposed to find a little Soup sprite in all that sand? A dune hovel? A tuneless whistle in the distance? Big fat tear drops in the sand? Up to this point, I'd never had to look for the kid. He had always found me. I kept expecting to have him latch on to my leg so I could drag him back to Video Horizons.

"What's *that*?" Gravity asked, flicking the leaf between my fingers.

Thank God she'd left Zxzord behind.

"Oh, um . . ." I looked at the leaf. I had no idea what it was supposed to mean. Rather than explain the weird magicky girl whom I'd tried to kiss just an hour before, I tossed the leaf aside. "It's nothing."

"Hey, Miles!" Meeki yelled. "What if you screamed out an apology? Maybe that would bring him back?"

"What's she talking about?" Gravity said.

"I . . ." I shrugged.

We reached the top of the dune. There was nothing but sand and stars in every direction. Smaller dunes swelled at the bottom of the slope before us, any one of which could have hidden Soup.

"Hmm," Fezzik said. He sized up our guild more than he ever had before the tournaments. "Okay, Burds, it looks like we need to split up. I trust you. I don't think you're going to try to ditch the party. And if you do, you'll probably get hit with an Ice 3 spell and freeze to death."

Even with all of my insulation, I was starting to shiver. I couldn't imagine what Soup's little body was going through.

"I'm calling the peak of this dune the save point," Fezzik said. "If I call, I need you all to return here immediately. Deal?"

"Deal," we all said.

"Not you, Zxzord," Fezzik said. "You come with me."

"No one ever trusts the druggie," Zxzord said.

Gravity giggled.

The guild fanned out as we trekked down the dune, our feet making big impacts in the sand. Gravity stayed with me.

"Funny that we both got committed here," I said.

"Sure is."

"It's almost like the universe—"

"I don't believe in the universe," she said.

"Oh. Ha. Neither do I, actually."

We trod through the sand in silence for a few steps.

"Miles sucks!" Meeki called across the dune.

"Miles doesn't suck!" I shouted back.

Soup wasn't there to defend me. What else could I do?

"Not the charmer with everyone, huh?" Gravity asked.

Oh God. Here it was. How many people had I pissed off in the past week alone? Aurora, Meeki, Soup, G-man, Scarecrow, Dryad, Casey, my dad . . .

"Far from it."

"You sweet on that weird chick with the white hair?" Gravity asked.

"What makes you say that?"

She shrugged. "She gave you a leaf."

In the distance Aurora's hair glowed in the moonlight. "I haven't sprayed her with a hose, if that's what you mean."

Gravity laughed, and I instantly felt a little better. God, I had shot myself in the foot. I'd treated everyone in V-hab like crap, and now it was going to bite me in the ass. She'd see what they saw—a pudgy, desperate gamer who actually had no idea how to interact with humans and was too terrified to admit it.

"I hate to break it to ya," Gravity said, nodding toward Aurora. "I think that chick has a screw loose."

I laughed. "You noticed?"

"Totally. And that Asian chick seems like a total dick. Plus her boobs are weird."

"Ha-ha. Are they?" I said.

"Totally."

I hoped Gravity didn't think my boobs were weird.

This was amazing. Gravity saw exactly what I'd recognized when I'd first gotten there. The Fury Burds sucked. And I was a good guy who was pretty funny every once in a while.

We descended in silence. The back of Gravity's hand brushed the back of mine once or twice. Maybe this would turn out perfectly after all. Gravity and I were locked away together in the middle of the desert, no hope for escape. I might even start point dodging like Soup just to stick around a little longer. Then she and I could be annoyed by him together . . . once we found him, of course.

Before we reached the bottom of the dune, Gravity hooked my arm and whispered, "*Wait.*"

We sat in the soft sand and stayed low as the Burds disappeared behind the smaller dunes. The occasional "Soo-oup" floated in on the wind.

Oh my God. Was Gravity going to kiss me? Her face was so close. I was ready.

"*I've got a crazy idea,*" she whispered.

"What?" I said.

"You know how that giant said no escaping?"

"Uh, yeah."

"Well, what if we *did*?"

I could barely make out her expression in the starlight. I couldn't tell if she was being sarcastic.

"Seriously?"

“Seriously.” She looked toward the road. “They like to make us believe we’re in the middle of nowhere, but we could easily walk back to the highway and hitchhike out of here. Whaddayathink?”

My stomach flipped while my heart swelled.

The good thing about video games with multiple endings is that you can always save in the last hour and go back to replay it differently, to see how things turn out when you make different choices. Not so with real life.

Should I stick with the guild or make a romantic midnight escape?

Gravity was beautiful and laughed at my jokes and played video games and actually wanted to go on a date with me.

Then there was my guild: Meeki, who tore me to shreds. Aurora, who had rejected me. Fezzik, who wouldn’t defend me when I really needed him. Soup, whom I had made run away . . . but only because he’d been acting like a little shit. Zxzord, that asshole, who had told Meeki I’d kissed Aurora *and* who had flirted with Gravity.

“Yeah, let’s get the fuck out of here,” I said.

“*Yessssssssssssss!*” Gravity said, shaking my arm.

Once we were gone, I’d never have to deal with the Fury Burds again. And they’d never have to deal with me.

We crept back up the dune. Once we reached the top, Gravity stopped us again.

“Wait,” she said. “I just got a better idea.”

Falling Through the World

We snuck away under sparkling twilight and ran down the dune back to Video Horizons. We crept past Command, who was pacing the building's perimeter, slipped through the open door, and tiptoed down the dark, green corridor.

I followed Gravity to G-man's office. She opened the desk drawer and rustled through it. "Sweeeeeet." She jangled a set of keys.

"Wait," I said. "Are we—"

"Stealing a car? Yep!"

"O"—I swallowed my terror—"kay!"

She sifted through another drawer. "Aha!" She held up a twenty and then ran down the staircase.

I waited for my heart to catch up. "Cool," I said. "Awesome. This is awesome." I took a deep breath, and then followed. Gravity didn't so much as flinch at Conquer's squeaking shoes echoing down the hallway, as if we couldn't possibly be caught. She made me feel kinda invincible.

We passed the Hub.

We passed the Feed.

We passed the grate where Soup and I had discovered the side quest.

We stepped out into the parking lot with the Oldsmobile that had brought me and Zxzord four days earlier. Beside it was a brown Acura.

"Get in!" Gravity said, unlocking the door and hopping into the driver's seat.

I climbed into the passenger seat and pinched my hands between my knees to keep them from trembling. The stale coffee smell didn't help my anxiety.

"This is so *exciting*," Gravity said, sliding the keys into the ignition.

"Yes," I said, trying to feel as electric as she was. "It is."

"Ugh, cheapo is almost out of gas," she said, reading the meter.

"Well, he probably didn't know we were gonna steal it," I said.

Gravity gave me a cold look, and I tried to pretend like it had been a joke.

"Ha-ha," I said.

"Oop!" Gravity ducked, and pulled me down by my sleeve just as I caught a glimpse of Command stepping into the light of the parking lot. His shadow passed across the speckled dust of the windshield. The parking brake jabbed into my ribs. *I'm cool*, I thought. *I'm cool. I am a . . . cool guy who does cool things like steal cars.*

Gravity peeked over the steering wheel. "Clear!"

She sat up and turned the ignition, and I tried not to panic as the engine struggled to life.

It finally turned over, and something awoke in me.

Adventure . . .

Maybe.

She put the car into gear and lightly accelerated out of the parking lot.

"Where are we going?" I asked, checking the side mirror for any sign of Command.

"We can crash at my aunt's," Gravity said, eyes on the road. "She's the best. She'll let us stay in her guest room for a while."

Guest *room*. Singular. The thought calmed my anxiety.

Once we got onto the open road, Gravity stepped on the gas, rocketing us through the night, and sang in a spot-on Amy Winehouse impression. "*They tried to make us go to V-hab, but we said,* NO, NO, NO."

"Ha-ha," I said.

She swiveled the steering wheel, and we wiggled all over the road. I tried to rub the feeling back into my legs as I glanced out the back window, fully expecting to see swirling red-and-blue lights.

Gravity honked the horn, and I nearly jumped out of my skin.

"Maybe we shouldn't do that," I said. "Ha-ha."

"Do you think this is the car that hit G-man?" she asked.

"What?" I said.

"You don't know?" she said, wide-eyed. "G-man's the dad who got run over by his son after he took his copy of *Halo* away. That's why he started a facility for e-tards."

Headlines flashed through my head. Moments of G-man adjusting his hip or discouraging violence in our activities or getting teary-eyed when talking about trying to improve the lives of players . . .

The images vanished as two cars came down the opposite side of the road. Oh shit. Oh shit, oh shit, oh shit. I knew it. They were cop cars. I almost had a heart attack as they passed us.

"Calm down, dude," Gravity said, noticing my tension. "They're going to look for that missing kid." She swiveled the steering wheel some more. "Do you think this is the car, though? Oh my God, that would be hilarious."

"Ha-ha. Would it?"

She clicked buttons on her door, and both of our windows rolled down. Wind whipped my hair.

What was this life I was beginning? A stolen car. The smell of desert night air. A beautiful girl in the driver's seat. Everything was so alien. At least with Video Horizons, there were rules and guards and my dad knew exactly where I was. Now I truly was falling through the world. Which was great. Right? What did I have waiting for me at home besides a pissed-off dad, an exercise-obsessed stepmom, and an empty computer desk?

This was great.

We sailed through the night down the open highway.

"Farewell, e-tards!" Gravity called out the window.

Good-bye, Zxzord, I thought. *Good-bye, Meeki. Good-bye, G-man. Good-bye, Soup. Good-bye, Silver Lady. Good-bye, Fezzik. Good-bye, Aurora.*

Good riddance.

A fingernail ran up my arm.

"*Wakey-wakey, hands off snakey,*" Gravity sang.

The rushing road started to slow. I rubbed my eyes and squinted at thousands of colorful lights filling the sky. The car stopped and the engine cut.

"Where are we?" I said, yawning.

"Heaven," Gravity said. "Just kidding. We're at a casino." She got out of the car.

I opened my door and stepped into a dusty parking lot. Towering above us was a giant cowgirl creakily kicking her neon boot. We were in the small gambling town Command and Conquer had driven me through on the way to Video Horizons. The night air was dry and cold. The stars were barely visible behind the casino lights. I felt lost.

Gravity looked bored or annoyed or something.

"Hey," I said. "How about that hug?"

"Huh?"

"Oh, uh, at the car wash you said we could hug maybe."

"Um, okay, sure," Gravity said. She threw her arms around my neck and squeezed. There was a brief moment of her softness against my softness, but then she let go and skipped toward the kicking cowgirl. "Come on!"

"Where are we going?" I asked, stumbling after her.

She flapped G-man's twenty back at me. "I'm gonna double this."

"Gambling?" I said.

I wanted to ask if maybe possibly we needed that twenty for gas money. But I also only wanted to be awesome and hilarious on what seemed to be my first date.

"Don't worry," Gravity called back. "I'm real good."

I knew enough about gambling to know being "real good" didn't matter. It didn't work like video games, based on skill level.

"What if you lose it all?"

She spun around and walked backward, giving me that delightful Gravity grin. "I won't."

"Oh, okay. Good." I jogged and caught up to her. "Um, don't you have to be twenty-one to gamble?"

She twirled forward and skipped away from me. "They only ID you if you win a whole bunch of money."

"Isn't that . . . kind of the idea?" I asked.

But she was already through the casino's automatic doors, my voice drowned out by the dings and whoops of a thousand slot machines.

I found Gravity sitting at a blackjack table, feet giddily tapping the little stool. She already had gambling chips in front of her.

I felt queasy. I ignored it. I'd been waiting for this moment for four days. I had beat V-hab and left all of those losers behind. This was going to be awesome.

The card dealer had a shimmery vest. I tried to look casual as I took the stool next to Gravity.

"This is exciting," I said, rubbing my hands together. "I've never actually—"

"Don't sit next to me," she whispered. *"You have a baby face. Might give away the game."*

"Oh, yeah. Okay." I got up and stood behind her.

I had a baby face? Was that a good thing or a bad thing?

Gravity slid a red chip across the green felt into a yellow rectangle. Her hair smelled so good. Her neck looked so pretty. I really wanted to put my hand on her shoulder. But I wasn't sure if that was part of the "game" or not. I really wasn't sure about anything except that I was happy to finally be on my date. It wasn't Mandrake's, but it was still pretty romantic . . . if I ignored the smell of cigarettes and squinted until the nauseating twirly lights were all a blur.

The dealer dealt two cards to each player. Gravity made a little cave with her hand and peeked at her cards. I tried to see but couldn't. She tapped the table. The dealer dealt her a card, faceup. A queen. Gravity looked at me and smiled.

"Yay!" I said, guessing a queen was a good thing. I squeezed her shoulder, then immediately let go.

I have to admit, I was surprised by Gravity's skill. I watched her *quadruple* her money, schooling the blackjack table while sipping three free Long Island iced teas, which the waitress did not ID her for.

"Maybe we should stop now?" I said.

"How about I stop . . . ," Gravity said as she pushed all her chips forward, "*now?*"

She won again.

"Yay," I said.

Yep, I was surprised by Gravity's skill. Almost as surprised as she was when all her chips were gone ten minutes later.

She downed the last of her fourth Long Island, and then I helped her stumble to a chair beneath a giant blue screen with big yellow numbers. Nearby, elderly people fished quarters out of plastic buckets and plunked them into whirling slot machines.

Lights swam across Gravity's eyes. "*Pretty.*"

"Yes," I said. "It is." I nodded approvingly at the hideous carpet, warbled dings, and dehydrated elderly smokers. "So, um . . . why don't you tell me about yourself? Uh, what do you like to do when you're not at video game rehab? Ha."

"Drink," she said.

"I see that," I said. "Anything else?"

She gave an exaggerated shrug. "Sure!"

"O . . . kay."

It was hard keeping a girl entertained on a date. She wasn't laughing at anything I said like she had at the car wash. Was this how she really was? Or was it just the alcohol? I'd never so much as sipped a beer, so I wasn't sure how to tell.

"It's so funny that we both got committed to V-hab," I said. "Not in, like, a universe way or anything."

Gravity didn't respond. Her head rocked slowly back and forth as if she could hear music that I could not. Oh God, what if she was realizing that I was as pathetic as Meeki and everyone at my high school thought I was? The longer Gravity didn't laugh, the more my shoulders tensed.

"Oh, right, um," I said. "Earlier in the Hub you were going to tell me why your parents sent you to Video Horizons."

She rubbed her face, then let her arms flop into her lap. "Remember how I don't have a phone?"

"Yeah!" I said. "I thought you were a Luddite! Ha-ha."

"My parents took it away because I maxed out my mom's credit card playing *Candy Crush*." She threw her arms wide. "Whoopsy!"

"Yeah," I said. "Whoopsy."

My smile faded. My cheeks were sore from holding it so long. Not only was *Candy Crush* Casey's favorite game, but my dad would have *murdered* me if I'd used his credit card without asking. Also, didn't paying to win make gaming completely pointless?

Gravity tugged my collar down so hard, I thought she was going to rip it. "I. Want. Coooooofffffffeeeeeeeeeeee. Will you buy me Starbucks?" She kissed my cheek. "Please?" Kiss. "Please?" Kiss. "Please?"

I touched my cheek and took a moment to let those kisses sink in.

"Uh, I can't. We don't have any money. Remember?"

"Muh." She pushed me away, disappointed.

"Sorry," I said, even though I was thinking, *Weren't you the one who gambled it all away?*

I scanned the casino. My head felt heavy. My stomach was in knots. Maybe I was hungry. I saw a big white banner that read BUFFET $12.99.

"Stay here," I said. "I'm gonna try to score us a buffet."

Gravity rubbed her face. "That's not Starbucks."

"Well, no . . . but they have bottomless coffee."

She stuck out her tongue and let her head flop to the side.

"Don't worry," I said, leaping to my feet. "This is gonna be awesome. I got this."

I strode down an aisle of slot machines, searching for kind faces. This *was* going to be awesome. This would be a story Gravity and I would tell for years to come. The night we went on our first date, and I dashingly got her a buffet with bottomless coffee.

I approached a woman at a lucky-three slot machine. Her plastic bucket was half-full of coins.

"Excuse me," I said, clasping my hands together. "Could I possibly borrow a few quarters from you?"

She took a long drag of her cigarette and considered me. Then, exhaling smoke, she shook her head and pulled the slot machine's handle.

Most of my encounters went something like that.

After approaching nearly every person in the casino before

getting eyed by a security guard, I returned to Gravity, whose head had slumped to the side.

I counted my coins. "I didn't get nearly enough."

"Booooooo," Gravity said into the armrest.

"Ha-ha." I sat next to her.

Why was it so hard for me to have fun right then? Where was charming, sexy, hilarious, relaxed, car wash Jaxon? Man, casino chairs were hard and scratchy. My eyes were watering from all the cigarette smoke. I needed to get us out of there so we could go on a real date. But how? This dungeon was too high-level for me.

"We have no gas and no money," I said. "What are we gonna do?"

"Maybe throw up?"

I helped Gravity outside for some fresh air. She collapsed onto the curb and let her head hang over the gutter. I stepped back, just in case she started puking.

"Seriously," I said. "How are we supposed to get home?"

"You sound like my parents," she said, cheek on the pavement. "They're *tight asses*."

I sat next to her head on the curb and pulled the coins out of my pocket. Four dollars and fifty cents. "This might be enough to get gas back to the city. Where does your aunt live? In the city?"

"She doesn't," she said.

"No, where does she live?"

No response. I cleared some hair that had found its way into her mouth. Was this how my mom had acted when she'd been drunk in front of my dad? Had I just taken Gravity away from exactly where she needed to be?

She rolled onto her back, so she was on the edge of the curb. She closed one eye and traced her finger across the starless sky. "I like people when they're meteorites. It's like they're so pretty leaving their shiny dust across the sky. But then they land in front of you, and they're not glowing anymore. They're just *rocks*, and it's, like, *BLUHH*."

"Are you talking about me?" I asked.

From her horizontal position she grabbed my arm and shook it. "You were so much *fun* at the car wash. What *happened*?"

What had happened? I was on an adventure. A *real* adventure in a casino town, as brightly lit as Midgar, with a beautiful girl and barely any money. Hell, this was as exciting as it got.

And I was hating every second of it.

I jangled the handful of coins. "Maybe this is enough to get us back to V-hab."

"No! *No!*"

Gravity pushed her feet against the concrete, forcing her head into my side.

"Ow!"

I stood up. She just lay there, eyes fluttering to a close.

I squatted in the gutter. "Come on. Let's get you into the car."

The second I touched her arm, she lashed out and pushed me away by the face. I fell backward, and sat hard on my ass.

"If you try to take me back there," she yelled, "I'll tear out your trachea!"

I sat on the asphalt, in shock. She was talking to me like I was . . . like I was Soup or something.

"You'll tear out my *trachea*?" I said. "That's extreme."

"I am . . ." She squeezed her eyes shut and made two tight fists. "*Extreme*."

"Gravity, I'm not leaving a drunk girl at a casino."

She lifted her head and scowled at me with one eye shut. "What the fuck did you just call me?"

"Uh . . ." Oh God, what had I just called her? "I just said, 'Serena, I'm not going to leave—'"

"Why . . . are you . . . trying . . . to control me?" she screamed, banging her fists and feet on the concrete.

This drew a few looks from a couple entering the casino.

"*I—I'm not*," I whispered. "*You're just really drunk*."

"No!" she screamed. "You think I'm gonna be all perfect . . . and then . . . and then fuck you!"

I deflated. This was not how my first date was supposed to go.

"I'm sorry, Serena," I said.

"Bleeehhhhggggg." She made that pukey sound again, and I took another step back. She scrunched her shirt in her fists. "You're giving me a gross feeling in my stomach. That Asian chick was right. You suck. Suck my dick, dude."

I stood up. I turned in a circle, searching the parking lot. It felt like the end of the world.

No. I could save this. I could still be the hero. Through the casino window I saw a glowing green-and-white sign with a double-tailed mermaid.

"How about Starbucks?" I said.

Serena stuck her fist into the air, triumphant. "Yesssssss!"

"Will you be okay here for a minute?"

She gurgled. "Someone's gonna take advantage of me."

"Um . . . okay."

I bent over, threw her arm around my shoulder, and hauled her to her feet. The casino's automatic doors whooshed open in a rush of dings and air-conditioning. I set her in a chair where I could keep an eye on her, then jogged to Starbucks and tried to make sense of their huge menu. I only ever drank energy drinks.

"Um, I'll take a . . . just a coffee, I guess? With milk and sugar?" I looked back at Serena, eyes closed, chin resting on her chest. "Will that make you sick if you're drunk?"

The barista chewed her gum. "Not me."

"Um, okay, yeah, I'll take that. These waters too."

"That'll be five fifty-eight."

"Oh." I shook my coins, hoping more would magically appear. "Just one water, then."

I poured the coins into the barista's open hands, grabbed the coffee and the water, turned around . . . and froze. Three cops stood around Serena.

I quickly ducked behind a support pole. Why were they here? Stolen car? Reckless driving? Underage drinking? Were we about to go to jail? I peered around the pole and watched Serena wipe sweaty hair off her forehead and blink at the cops. They took her arms, trying to get her to stand, but she became a rag doll. They practically had to pick her up and carry her.

I watched the cops lead Serena to the exit. When I'd met her, she had been this beautiful, interesting girl who had actually seemed interested in me. She was still beautiful now, but something had changed. She looked . . . *young*. She looked like a kid. Like me. Where was the girl I'd been dreaming about for four days? Where was the badass at the blackjack table who didn't get ID'd? What had made me care about this girl so intensely so quickly?

When the cops reached the automatic doors, Serena took one glance back toward Starbucks, but only for a moment, like she wanted the cops to take her before I got back.

I winced, waiting for my heart to break.

It didn't.

She didn't want me. She didn't need me. What the hell was I doing?

The coffee steamed in my hand. I tossed it into a trash can, stuck the water bottle into my pocket, and went out a different exit, into the night. The casino lights glimmered on G-man's Acura.

Dammit. Serena had the keys.

Oh well.

I definitely felt that Gravitational pull as I walked out of the parking lot, under the cowgirl's neon boot, and out of the gambling town, down the open road.

I just barely managed to break free.

Flight Path

The casino lights faded behind me. Soon starlight reigned. The dunes were black shadows against the universe. Orion chased the Pleiades across the sky.

"You'll never get 'em, dude," I said.

I walked all night, putting one foot in front of the other down the empty highway. The air was cold. No cars came. All I could hear was wind and crickets and my footsteps. I imagined a beam of light slicing through the sky, shooting out from the horizon where I was pretty sure Video Horizons was nestled. I kept an eye in that direction as I traversed miles of road, passing every sign, curve, and landmark I had memorized in order to *escape* from V-hab.

The walk gave me lots of time to think. To think about triumphantly returning to Video Horizons. To think about swooping in and discovering Soup, half-dead in the sand. To think about giving him mouth-to-mouth in front of all the Fury

Burds, until he spluttered to life. To think about apologizing to Aurora and telling her I realized that Gravity sucked and that she, Aurora, *Jasmine*, was nice and pretty and always seemed to do the right thing. To think about saying, *See? I walked, like, twenty miles back to V-hab just to apologize. And to see you*. To think about her kissing me and fireworks and The End.

I thought about that last part a lot.

The desert didn't stop. The turnoff to Video Horizons was nowhere in sight.

Hours after I had expected to return, the horizon grew chalky, painting the desert in grays. I realized Jasmine probably wouldn't be at Video Horizons when I got back. She had earned a million points and would likely be home by now.

Jasmine was gone.

God, what if I had just waited to try to kiss her? What if I had actually been a nice guy and participated in guild therapy and gotten to know her better and *then* tried to kiss her, so she didn't think I was using her as medicine just to feel better about myself? What if in some alternate ending she had actually wanted to kiss me?

As the sky grew brighter, the dunes grew darker. The horizon became so purple and electric, it could have been right out of *Arcadia*.

Fezzik would still be there, at least. I needed to apologize to him, too. In my opinion that dude was the Emperor of the real world. I had just refused to see it in V-hab because I'd been too focused on myself, and some chick I didn't even know.

It hurt to think of Fezzik returning to *Arcadia*. He had left his cave and ventured to Video Horizons to grow out of himself, or *shrink* out of himself, I guess. As always, the real world was completely unforgiving, and the Silver Lady had rejected him. I needed to get back and tell him that the world was a better place with him out of his cave. The Fury Burds needed our white mage. Er, healer.

Why couldn't I have just said those words to him when he'd brought me his phone to call Mandrake's?

Light broke over the mountains behind me, gilding my path. Maybe it wasn't too late for Jasmine and me. I would try to get her full name from Meeki. I'd contact Jasmine on Facebook and apologize and then ask if maybe she wanted to get together sometime . . . maybe at Mandrake's or something. No pressure.

The morning sky grew white and beaming. The sand twinkled like a golden galaxy. Birds sang, and a speckled lizard scrabbled out of a hole to raise its nose toward the rising sun. Everything was beautiful . . . until it was awful.

The sun rose and roasted me. I sweated through my black shirt and white pants. God, what I wouldn't have given for that stupid Home Depot hat. There was no shade to rest in, so I just kept walking. I took a couple of sips of water, trying to conserve, and then finished the entire bottle. I could have drunk three more. I thought of Soup, who probably hadn't brought any water when he'd run away into the desert.

The sun sizzled the back of my head, and something

dawned on me. Soup probably hadn't planted the iPod Touch in my suitcase. That wouldn't make sense. He'd been with me every possible moment. When would he have had time to sneak it in there? And if he'd wanted me to stay, why would he have tried to give me the points from his side quest? Also, his little butt definitely wasn't big enough to smuggle in an iPod Touch.

Even though he hadn't planted it, he'd still taken credit for the deed so that G-man might give me my points back. Soup had fallen on his sword for me. And I'd called him a little shit for it. Man, I had really screwed that up.

What if he was still lost in the desert somewhere? In this heat, with his size, he could have wasted away to a skeleton by now. I walked a little faster. Someone had finally wanted to be in my life—had begged for my friendship—and I had just pushed him away . . . even by the forehead once. Thanks to Serena, I knew what that felt like now.

I'd been terrible to that kid.

Even though he'd kind of been asking for it sometimes.

Okay, he was asking for it all the time.

Still, I was kind of a dick. Hopefully they'd found him by now.

The sun grew brighter, and the sand and road and rocks and clouds all blended together in a blinding haze. My skin prickled. The asphalt cooked through the soles of my shoes. I took off my shirt and wrapped it around my head. I was hoping to show up to Video Horizons looking somewhat triumphant. Not like Mario's singed and bloated corpse.

But maybe this was what I deserved. I'd been lying to myself all week, thinking of myself as the hero of the story, hearing and seeing only the things I thought would get me what I wanted. Maybe Meeki was right. Maybe I had seen Serena as someone to save. I knew better now. Jasmine wasn't a damsel in distress at the end of the game. She was just on her own adventure. When we met again, she'd see that I recognized that now.

My back started to burn. My shoes were two pools of sweat. My tongue was a dead sponge. Good. I wanted to *feel* the journey, to pay my dues for treating everyone so poorly.

Ten minutes later I changed my mind. I did not want to feel the journey anymore. Why wasn't this desert ending? Where the hell was the giant LEGO? The infinite sandbox had no end.

My head blurred and the sky warped, like I was walking inside a giant hourglass filled with sand. I almost passed out. I covered my eyes just to see darkness for a minute, then trudged on. The road kept going. I still couldn't see a turnoff. I kept walking, then leapt a foot into the air when I almost stepped on a scorpion.

Wait. It was just a sprig of tumbleweed.

I kept walking.

So maybe I wouldn't try to get Jasmine's phone number. I'd show my respect by acknowledging that she had her life together. She was healing and breaking up with Max and being an all-around badass. God, I hoped she did break up with Max. For her sake.

My shadow lengthened on the asphalt before me. It looked disturbingly familiar. Maybe Fezzik was right. Maybe I was Meeki's Dark Link. Treating everyone else like I was better than them. Imagining women as princesses in castles that I needed to rescue. I had smashed Scarecrow's nose and then pretended it had been to protect her honor. Man, she had hit him *so* much harder than I could have. I should have said that in my paintball speech. But no, I'd been too focused on dumb Gravity. Er, Serena.

Ugh. My head was a big sweaty, pulsing lump of confusion.

At least now I could appreciate all that the Burds had done for me. Without them I would've walked into the Wasteland, been shot six times in the balls, and earned exactly zero points. God, I'd give the best paintball speech now.

What was that smell? Was my skin cooking? Could eyeballs turn into raisins? It felt like it. Where the hell was Video Horizons?

A wind kicked up, blowing sand into my eyes and mouth. I would have spit if I didn't need the moisture.

I wouldn't earn any points for finding Video Horizons again. In fact, the opposite would probably happen. G-man would take away my 900,000 for running away. That would be fine by me. I wasn't about points anymore. I was ready to work and be nice. I would earn my million points by cross-stitching something for everyone at Video Horizons.

I'd stitch the sayings that were so important to me, to show I had listened.

> Nobody Puts Princess in a Castle
> Every Warrior Needs an Adventure Party
> People Aren't Medicine
> Everyone's a Grouchy Cow on Their First Day

Yeah, I'd totally make those . . . after Soup taught me how to cross-stitch . . . once Fezzik found him . . .

The turnoff! Thank God, the turnoff. I rubbed my eyes, worried it might vanish in the wavering heat. When it stayed put, I stepped, zombielike, off the road and onto the sand, which squished beneath my feet, and cut diagonally to reach the dirt road sooner. A few minutes later, a sparkly car drove down the highway. A car I could have used to hitchhike. It didn't matter anymore. I was close now.

Who knows? Maybe Jasmine *would* be there when I returned. Maybe she had opted out of going home because she was worried about me. And Soup. Soup and me. Even if she wasn't there, why should I not try to contact her? Because Meeki thought I was an asshole? Psh.

The sun crowned the sky. Something tumbled along the sand and stuck to my shoe. It was a leaf. I picked it up, covering my mouth in shock. Tears came to my eyes. It couldn't be the same leaf Jasmine had given me . . . could it? No. Could it? No, absolutely not. What if it was, though? What if it was a sign? I stuck it behind my ear to give it to her whenever I saw her next. I understood what it represented now . . . Maybe. Hope or something. Who knows.

I kept walking, expecting to see the roof of the facility poke over the dunes with each step. While I was about 90 percent sure that I was walking in the right direction, that I had taken the right turnoff, everything was starting to look the same. I missed Navi. She could flutter over my shoulder and ding and sing *This way! This way!* Stupid real life and its lack of hint systems.

The sun blazed, casting my shadow behind me now. After another eternity of walking, I grew scared that I might have wandered a few degrees in the wrong direction. I reminded myself that I wasn't trying to find a LEGO in an infinite sandbox. I was just trying to find a building in the desert. A well-hidden building, it seemed. I could still do it.

Maybe I'd make it back in time for the sand castle competition. Soup would spray the sand with the hose so it was good and wet for packing into buckets. When he saw me, he'd recognize my dehydrated state and spray me, just like I'd sprayed Serena, and I'd open my mouth and the water would taste like rubber and dirt, and I'd choke when the stream hit the back of my throat, but it would be the best water I'd ever had.

Meeki would be the sand castle's architect. She was good at stuff like that. Zxzord could sleep in the moat. Fezzik could stack the turrets high. And Jasmine . . . probably wouldn't be there. Didn't matter. Even if the Burds were doing a terrible job building, I wouldn't say anything. I'd just pack buckets full of sand and hand them to my guildmates. That is how I'd help the Fury Burds build their castle.

Our castle. Our castle in the desert.

And who knows? Maybe it would fill the freaking sky.

. . .

. . .

. . .

. . .

Seriously, what the fuck, desert? When do you end?

Okay, I understood now. The sand wouldn't allow me to return until I learned all the important life lessons.

Who else had I treated like crap?

Scarecrow . . . was still a dick. I was glad I'd thrown that ball at his face. Him and my stepmom. And Meeki. They all still sucked. Although, Casey did just try to get me to exercise, which I obviously needed. God, my hips hurt.

And okay, maybe I wasn't much better than Scarecrow. I mean, I went after two girls at once, kind of. By accident. And I tried to kiss one of them, even though she had a boyfriend. Dick move. I also said terrible things to a lot of people. If anything, *I* was the one who was still in beta. Definitely not an alpha male. Wait, was it the other way around? Why had no one thrown a ball at my face?

A flat dune rose out among the others. Not a flat dune—a roof! Ha-ha! I knew it! I knew if I learned all the life lessons, Video Horizons would show! Oh God. Yes, yes, yes. I had done it. I had completed my journey across the desert without a flying scarf or anything. YES.

I sprinted—okay, limped toward the parking lot. Maybe the Burds were already building sand castles in the shade on the far side of the building. I couldn't wait for Soup to hug me, just so I could pry him off as if I didn't care.

But first. Water. Yes. Water. I couldn't run, but I powerwalked through the parking lot, toward V-hab's door. If the building vanished in a mirage, I was going to be so pissed.

Oh God. There was a cop car in the parking lot. But even more terrifying was the Xterra beside it, its engine still running. I powerwalked right past the Xterra without looking inside. The driver door popped open. I tried Video Horizons's door. It was locked. Why the hell was it locked? I kept jiggling the handle, not wanting to confront who was behind me.

"Jaxon."

I gave up on the door and turned around. My dad leaned against the Xterra's bumper.

"Well, you got some exercise," he said. "I'll give you that much."

"I have to go inside," I said, jiggling the handle again.

"I was just on my way to find you." He opened the passenger door. "There's water in the cup holder."

I could see it, sparkling and crystal clear in a bottle. I was pretty sure that if I didn't drink something in the next twenty seconds, I was going to collapse into a pile of dust. Also, the Xterra's air-conditioning sounded like pure heaven.

I climbed into the passenger seat, drank half of the water in one go, and then, panting, let my head fall against the headrest. The air-conditioning stung my scalded skin. My dad got into the driver's seat, closed the door, and then stared at me as if wondering how he ended up with a son like me. My eyes were closed, but I knew the look.

"Now that I know you're not dead," he said, "what the hell were you thinking, Jaxon?"

I finished the water. "Do you have anything to eat?"

He fished around behind my seat and handed me a warm protein shake.

Casey had been trying to get me to drink one of these ever since she had moved in. I drank it in one go.

My dad pinched the bridge of his nose.

I leaned my head back and closed my eyes and let my skin drink in the AC. My eyelids were on fire.

"Are you going to answer my question?" my dad said.

"Shh," I said. "Could we just . . . shh for a minute?"

"No, we can't, dammit."

The Mountain was turning into a volcano.

"I gotta go," I said. I pulled on the door handle, but he had locked it. While my fried mind tried to figure out how to open the door, my dad said, "Take your hand off the door handle."

I was so exhausted that my body just sort of obeyed, my arm flopping into my lap.

"What are you doing?" he asked.

"I need to go inside," I said, eyes closed. "Apologize."

"No, what are you doing with your *life*?"

My eyes shot open. "*You're* the one who sent me to V-hab in the middle of nowhere even though I totally had a date with—" My throat was too dry to continue. I closed my eyes again.

"You're right," he said. "I was hoping that if I took away the games, then you would find the tools to pick yourself up and start taking some responsibility. Clearly, I was mistaken."

He put the Xterra in gear and pulled out of the parking lot.

"Wait, *no*. Dad, I have to go back."

"To a facility that lost you? I don't think so."

Video Horizons grew small in the side mirror.

"It isn't their fault. It's my fault."

"That isn't all that's your fault," he said. "You and I are going to the police station, and then we're going home, where you can work off the fines for stealing a car."

Shit. G-man's son hit him with his own car, and then Serena and I stole it. I needed to apologize for that, too.

"Dad." I looked out the back window as Video Horizons vanished behind the dunes. "Rehab is like jail, right? I'll serve time there!"

"I'm not paying for a place that you just run away from. Do you know how expensive that place is?"

"Oh, what? Will Casey not be able to afford another juice cleanse?"

My dad ignored that. I watched the sand pass the window. All of my opportunity for redemption. My last chance to see Jasmine.

"Mom would've listened to me when I said I had a date."

"Your mom didn't drive around for five hours in the middle of the night, trying to find you."

"Psh," I said.

It was all I could say. My dad never did what I wanted. . . .

Because what I wanted was to be an asshole and manipulate people. What if he had let me off the hook and not sent me to Video Horizons? Then I would have gone on a date with a selfish girl, been convinced I still liked her, found out she didn't like me, gone through the heartbreak, and then gone right back to *Arcadia*.

"I'm sorry I called you an asshole, Dad."

He gave me a look, even more skeptical than when I'd told him I had a date.

"You got too much sun, Son," he said.

"I've been an asshole all week. That's why I need to go back. I have a lot of people to apologize to."

My dad looked almost touched. It didn't last. "I didn't want to tell you this," he said. "The director said he won't have you back. He's rethinking the entire treatment process because of you."

"I . . ." My air escaped.

That was probably smart of G-man. Like Fezzik had said, gamified therapy could bring out the worst in kids like me.

"Did they find Soup?" I asked.

"What are you asking?" my dad said. "Did they find . . ."

"Oh, right, sorry. There was a kid missing in the desert. His player name was Soup. Did they find him?"

"They lost *three kids* in one day?"

"We have to go back and find out if he's okay or not."

"No, Jaxon. Simply no."

He didn't slow down. If I just jumped out of the Xterra . . . the road would roll me into a bloody pulp. I let my cheek fall against the warm window.

We drove down the highway, back to Salt Lake. I was going home. To Casey. And rejection texts from girls. And an empty computer desk.

Game complete.

A measly 70 percent complete. If that.

I didn't have any way to contact my guildmates. Hell, other than Jasmine, I didn't even know their real names. I'd never get the chance to thank Fezzik for looking out for me and to wish him luck. I'd never find out if Zxzord was really addicted to heroin or not.

But that wasn't the worst part of leaving the game. I didn't even get any of the NPCs to like me. If V-hab had been *Harvest Moon*, I would have made zero friends in town.

I looked in the side mirror and again mentally said good-bye to everyone at V-hab: Aurora, Fezzik, G-man, Soup. I probably wouldn't see any of them ever again. What had I been thinking, leaving them like I had?

The dunes shrank along the side of the road. I tried to breathe. I was headed home. And it didn't feel like falling through the world. It didn't feel like anything.

Hard Mode

I'm sitting at Mandrake's.

It's smaller than I imagined. Brighter. The light isn't dim and romantic like I thought it would be. None of the silverware matches, there's weird squiggly art on the walls, and all of the waitresses are wearing pants. I watch customers coming through the door. Each time someone walks in, a little bell rings.

It's 7:08.

Is she going to stand me up?

That would suck.

Or would it?

"Would you like more water?" the server asks. The side of her head is shaved, and she has gauges in her ears.

"Um, yes, please." She refills my water while I hold the glass and feel it get colder. My mouth is dry. I'm nervous for some stupid reason. "Uh, she should be here any minute. We said seven, and I came kinda early, so . . ."

"You're fine," the server says. She smiles and leaves.

I tap my feet and drum the table and look around. The hostess is leaning against her podium, texting. I wonder if she's the one I talked to on the night Serena and I stood each other up.

The entrance bell rings. My heart gives a little kick. Speak of the devil.

Serena walks in. I look away, but then think, *That's stupid, there's no reason to look away*, and look back. I wait until she sees me, and then give a little wave. Her eyes slip to the side, as if she didn't notice. Or has never even met me.

I get it. I did abandon her when the cops showed up.

While the hostess seats Serena at a table on the opposite wall, I rearrange my silverware. Once Serena's settled, I steal a glance. She may have ignored me when she came in, but she sat down facing me. She looks pretty tonight—new haircut, blue dress, red lipstick. I remember how she looked the last time I saw her, sprawled-out drunk and sweaty on a casino chair.

I realize I'm staring, and focus on my silverware again.

Is she alone? That would definitely make me feel better if I'm being stood up right now. Actually, it would probably make me feel better either way. Maybe that's an asshole thing to think. It's none of my business if Serena's alone or not.

I decide not to look up anymore, so as to not seem creepy. My fork has dried food on it. That's the problem with dishwashers. They bake the food right in. I start scraping the crusty bits off with my fingernail, when the chair opposite mine scoots out.

"I don't know what I'm doing here," Meeki says, sitting down.

"Oh, hey," I say, lifting my butt to stand, but then, acknowledging she's already sitting, sit back down. "Uh, thanks for coming anyway."

The server pours water into Meeki's glass. "You guys need a minute?"

"Uh, yes please," I say.

Meeki scans the menu as if everything is made of rat tails and insects.

"We're getting separate checks," she says.

I put my napkin on my lap. "I know."

It's strange that I'm about to have dinner with my nemesis, but Meeki was the only player from Video Horizons I could track down online. And that's only because I knew her gamer tag. She started playing *Trivia Crack* right after she was released from V-hab. Mekillyoulongtime has one hell of a score.

I decide not to mention the fact that she's gaming again. That would be hypocritical.

After three straight weeks of daily exercising with Casey and cooking dinner (mostly tofu scramble) and doing the dishes every night, my dad gave me my computer back. The first thing I did was e-mail Fezzik a long apology. He responded a few days later.

The subject read *Greetings from the Desert Temple!*

I've been waiting to read the rest until after this dinner with Meeki, when I'll probably need an elixir.

Meeki slaps her menu shut and lets it fall onto her place mat. She huffs and glares around the restaurant. Behind her the server brings Serena a fancy yellow drink. Serena has stopped pretending I'm not here. Her eyebrows are quirked in my and Meeki's direction.

Part of me wants to wave my hands and mouth, *Not a date.*

"So are you gonna talk, or are you just wasting my time?" Meeki says.

I want to tell her there's no reason to be a dick.

"First of all," I say, "is Soup okay? I called Video Horizons, but G-man would only tell me you guys found him."

Meeki drinks some water and rolls her eyes. "Stupid kid was hiding in the activity chest."

I shake my head. "That kid's an idiot."

"Don't try to find common ground with me," she says.

We fall into silence. Meeki crunches her ice.

Last week I finally decided to go try to unlock the "Don't be a Total Dick" achievement. I remembered the name of the street Soup mentioned, but not the house number. So I combed both sides of West Chesterton, ringing doorbells and awkwardly asking for a kid who was about twelve, loved *Animal Crossing,* and went by Soup.

I knew I'd found the right house when the blinds in the second-floor window suddenly snapped shut.

A man with seventies glasses and a thick mustache answered the door and said, "You must be Miles."

"Actually, it's Jaxon," I said. "Is Soup here?"

The man glanced up the staircase. "Justin's busy right now. Would you like to set up a playdate?"

"Uh, no," I said. "I don't do play . . ."

I trailed off. I had expected a hug. I'd expected tears. I'd expected Soup to make me feel better about myself and how I'd acted.

It took me about eight seconds to realize how stupid that was.

"Yeah," I told Soup's dad. "I'd like to set up a playdate, please."

It's two days from now.

Meeki smirks into her water.

"What?" I say.

"After you ran away, we ritually burned all the cross-stitches Soup made for you. He didn't even cry. Fezzik told him he'd evolved into 'Souperior.'"

Ouch.

"At least he's not obsessed with me anymore," I say, trying not to seem hurt. I can't believe I'm thinking this but . . . I'm nervous to see Soup.

I look at Serena, who has almost finished her drink and is focused on her phone, which her parents must have given back to her. No one has joined her. It makes me feel better knowing I'm not the only person in this restaurant who people want to stay away from.

I know I shouldn't feel better about that.

"Do you keep in touch with anyone?" I ask Meeki.

"Yes."

"Like . . ."

"I'm not giving you Aurora's phone number."

"I know her name is Jasmine," I say. "And I don't want it. I just want to see how she's doing."

Meeki doesn't know I have a dry, crumbled leaf in my pocket.

She swirls her water glass. "She's dating Zxzord."

My stomach flips. "Are you kidding?"

"Maybe."

I laugh in relief. It's uncertain laughter.

Meeki sets her glass down with a thud. "Is this the only reason you brought me down here? To find out how other people are doing?"

"No," I say. "You're right. I'm sorry. How are you?"

"Fine," she says.

I try not to let my anger show. "That's it?"

She considers me for a second. "I'm dating Parappa."

"The nerdcore kid? But . . . he's a—"

Meeki gives me a look that could set the tablecloth on fire. Shoot. What did I say? I only said, like, six words, and suddenly she's pissed. Um, let's see . . . "Nerdcore" is fine because that's just what he does. "Kid" is fine because he's pretty young. Wait. . . . "*He.*" I think back to the look Meeki gave me in the Feed when I said I wanted to throw my spork at "him."

Parappa is a girl?

"That's . . . great," I say. "Congratulations. Uh, she seemed really talented . . . at rapping."

"You know what?" Meeki says, standing, chair screeching. "This was a dumb idea."

"*Wait.*" I reach across the table. "Please don't leave."

Serena is staring at us. I don't care what she thinks. I'm just worried that if no one from V-hab can see I'm changing, getting better, that I'm able to recognize other people for who they are, then I'll have a hard time convincing myself that's true.

"I'm sorry," I say to Meeki. "I didn't know about Parappa. I don't know a lot of things. Please just . . ." I gesture to her chair.

Meeki tilts her head in a really disapproving way that makes this so much harder than it needs to be. That's okay. If I wanted easy, I wouldn't have contacted her.

Meeki's still not sitting down.

"Meeki," I say, "I get it now."

The expression on her face is enough to tell me how she feels about this, but before I can retract, she sits down and hisses at me, "You *don't*. It's not like being a nice guy is a coat of paint that you can just slap on."

"You guys all set over here?" the server asks.

"Actually," I say, "can we have a couple—"

"I'll take the macaroni and cheese," Meeki says.

"Oh." I quickly flip open my menu. "Then I will take the . . . arugula salad."

I've lost ten pounds in four weeks, and I want to keep going. Most people comment on it. Meeki hasn't.

The server leaves with our menus. I gather my thoughts.

"You're right," I say. "I don't get it. Let me try that again." I breathe for a few beats, trying to find the right words. "I *want* to get it. I haven't stopped thinking about Video Horizons since I left. All the people there. I missed out on a big opportunity to learn a lot from you guys, and I've really regretted it."

She is clearly unimpressed.

I try a smile. "I regret not having you teach me how to punch too."

She doesn't smile back, but her tone becomes gentler. Slightly. "That's great for you, Miles, but it's not my job to educate you on how to be a better person."

I nod and think about how Fezzik handled situations like this. Meeki's Protect 3 is up, and I have to get a spell past it somehow.

"That's totally fair," I say. "You are not my teacher." I take another deep breath. "I was thinking about what you said about how being a white guy is like playing the game of life on easy mode."

Meeki crosses her arms. "Uh-huh."

"So . . . ," I say, carefully, "that must mean that being Asian and a girl and gay is like playing the game in nightmare mode?"

"My life is not a nightmare."

"No. You're right. Your life is . . . on a really hard difficulty setting?"

She uncrosses her arms and fiddles with the corner of the tablecloth. "Yup."

"I can't even imagine how tough that is," I say. "I salute you."

Meeki lifts the handle of her fork, drops it, and then lifts it again. "You could actually salute me, you know."

I chuckle. "I'm not doing that."

She shrugs. "Worth a shot."

We fall into silence for a bit. The only way it would be more awkward is if Parappa were with us, rapping. Or if Serena were glancing at us any more than she already is. Now I kinda wish a boy would show up and distract her.

"I'm trying not to screw this up," I say to Meeki. "I'm trying to stay on my toes. I'm trying to be nice. Every moment. It's so much harder than I thought it would be."

"You want a medal?"

I smile. "You want me to salute you?"

She gives a smirk. The tiniest of smirks. But I can practically feel the golden fireworks coming off me.

"Do you . . . ," I say, "want to know anything about me?"

"Not really."

We stare at each other.

"Fine," she says. "How'd you steal G-man's car?"

"Actually, that wasn't my idea," I say. I know I'm totally inviting a scene that could cause my complete embarrassment. But oh, well. "That was— "

I point over Meeki's shoulder.

She looks.

Serena is gone.

"Oh," I say. "Never mind."

I want to tell Meeki all about the car and the twenty-dollar bill and the gambling and the Long Island iced teas, but that stuff is really none of my business.

Our food arrives. We eat dinner, mostly in silence, making fun of Soup every so often, and avoiding the topic of Jasmine altogether. I've been looking forward to this moment for a week, rehearsing in my mind all the different things I would or would not say.

I don't make her laugh once.

ACKNOWLEDGMENTS

I hope you're comfortable. I've got an army to thank.

Thank you, Korey Hunt. It was you, good sir, who first suggested a story set in video game rehab. Thank you for letting me turn our idea into a book after it sat dusty on the shelf all these years.

Thank you, Mark Sorenson, for inspiring Fezzik's gaming metaphors and for reading my stuff aloud so I could fix the awkwardness. Thank you, Andrew Sorenson, for developing a serious gaming habit, neglecting to read this book to check my accuracy, and then playing months of *DoTA* instead, providing me with priceless material.

Thank you to Eric Johnson, Levi Montoya, and Katie Van Sleen for saying truly iconic things that I lifted straight out of our conversations and put into the text. Thank you, Brendan Finch of BirdBrain Science, for keeping me afloat by assigning me articles while I figured out how to publish a book. Thank you, Tesla the Doberman, for letting me tackle you when I found out the book sold. Thank you, Allie Crawford, for letting me borrow your eyes (I hope Aurora did them justice). And big gopping special thanks to Valynne Maetani, who cowrote a book with me that was too funny to be published, and who used her networking web to catch our agent.

John Cusick, thank you for taking me on in a package deal, for giving me invaluable notes on early drafts, and for turning me into a professional writer. I remember the day when your s stopped saying "Hey, pal" and started saying "Hello, sir." That was a good day.

Thank you, Christian Trimmer, for putting up with my sarcasm, and then repaying me tenfold by telling me the book was canceled after I turned it in nine hours late. Thank you for raising the bar on my writing and for turning this story into something true.

Thank you to the rest of the wonderful folks at Simon & Schuster

BFYR, including Justin Chanda, Chrissy Noh, Katy Hershberger, Jenica Nasworthy, and Catherine Laudone. And, of course, a big firework thank-you to Greg Stadnyk, who designed that gorgeous cover, and eBoy, who created the art.

Thank you to my early readers: Shar Petersen, Courtney Alameda, Annette Weed, Tommy Hamby, Christopher Turner, and Brian Green. Thank you, Brooke Kelly, for convincing me I had something worth pursuing; David Lawrence, for teaching me how stars actually work; Alan Grow, for infusing more tension and release into the early chapters; and Alan Mouritsen, for making sure Jaxon wasn't too fixed in the end.

Thank you, Dad, for always providing me with the tools to pursue my dreams, for teaching me tai chi and pottery, and for not being upset when I wanted to read instead. Thank you, Mom, for being so nauseatingly and wonderfully encouraging that I really had no choice but to succeed. No matter whose name is on the dedication, every book is for you.

Thank you, Breana Reichert, for helping me breathe life into Serena, Aurora, and Meeki. I cannot express how much heart and nuance you put into this story and into my life. I love you, honey bear.

Finally, Chris Chambers. The slither in the chimney. The crackle in the hearth. The best writer I know. Thank you for always being merriment in my life, thank you for cemetery strolls, for simple simple, and for coming up with the book title after three six-hour brainstorming sessions. I cannot express how much you did for this book, and I cannot wait for the rest of the world to read your stuff.